Young Adult Fiction
Issues and Trends

Edited by
Sunita Sinha

ATLANTIC
PUBLISHERS & DISTRIBUTORS (P) LTD

Published by
ATLANTIC
PUBLISHERS & DISTRIBUTORS (P) LTD
7/22, Ansari Road, Darya Ganj, New Delhi-110002
Phones : +91-11-40775252, 23273880, 23275880, 23280451
Fax : +91-11-23285873
Web : www.atlanticbooks.com
E-mail : orders@atlanticbooks.com

Branch Office
5, Nallathambi Street, Wallajah Road, Chennai-600002
Phones : +91-44-64611085, 32413319
E-mail : chennai@atlanticbooks.com

Printed in India at Nice Printing Press, A-33/3A, Site-IV,
Industrial Area, Sahibabad, Ghaziabad, U.P.

Preface

> Don't make every fictional teenager into an action hero. Show them as they really are—flaws and all. If YA fiction starts to challenge young adults to think differently about the world around them, it could start to bring a real, important impact to the shaping of a generation.
>
> *The Valley Vanguard* [Vol. 48, No. 23]

The young adult (YA) literature genre has been growing in popularity since the 1970s. A bright spot in an otherwise fluctuating literature market and an integral part of the lives of many teens, YA literature is a powerhouse in the publishing community as well as in schools and homes, reaching out to both non-readers and readers alike. According to Salvner, YA literature is not necessarily a mirror to the world, but rather it is an experience, a form of living. Literature also becomes a way of sharing lives together, to communicate sorrows and joys. Young adult literature also provides a voice for the youth, sometimes sceptical, while at other times upbeat.

Even though today the young adult genre is popular, this genre began quietly in 1951 with Holden Caulfield, a memorable crossover character in *Catcher in the Rye*. Holden was a true-to-life character, one to whom many teens and adults related. Ten years later, Robert Lipsyte and S.E. Hinton made their own impacts as authors of young adult literature, with *The Contender* and *The Outsiders*, respectively. In the early 1970s, with the emergence of *Go Ask Alice*, bookstores began to realize the potential market for young adult literature and stocked the shelves with more young adult books. *Go Ask Alice*, a sexually explicit novel by an anonymous author, was a controversial glimpse into a young teen's tumultuous life. Following the 1970s, the focus on realistic fiction changed. By the 1980s and 1990s, fantasy, horror, and mystery books evolved in the young adult genre. In addition, in the late twentieth century, a considerable shift occurred as authors began to write more books for older teens. In the article, "Ice Cream/I Scream for YA Books," Don Gallo examines the field of young adult literature, comparing it to ice cream—its various flavours and levels of richness. The article proclaims the profundity of the field and the quality of its writers, summarizes historical highlights, defends it against its detractors, and explains the importance of helping students make informed choices by talking about books and having them available in our classrooms. The author also states his personal preferences along with his concern about the increasing length of YA books.

Beyond a typical fiction novel, YA literature is also found in the form of verse novel and the graphic novel structure. The young adult novels in verse have sparked a debate over whether to actually consider them novels or poetry. Since as a genre it is still evolving, the definitions of the verse novel are necessarily elastic. In 2004, Peter Hollindale, writing in the UK journal, *Books for Keeps*, remarked that verse novels were "a fairly recent but fast-growing addition to the repertoire of children's literature". Though he wondered whether the form was to be "a passing fashion", he suggested that it also represented a major step forward in the genres of children's literature, a way of bringing verse back into mainstream storytelling for older readers, opening up a new kind of realism and a new immediacy, as well as marking out some common ground where poetry, fiction and drama can meet.

I would like to focus on a few essential characteristics that the YA novels in verse embody. Firstly, critics agree, young adult verse novels offer an alternative form of poetry to students. Ed Sullivan, in his column for the *School Library Journal*, comments, "Novels in verse can be an appealing, accessible introduction for students turned off by poetry or reluctant to read it. The verse authors write for these books is not like what most students are forced to study in class—it does not require analysis and explication". While the verse novel may have roots in traditional epic poetry, works like Ellen Hopkins' *Crank* are a far cry from the metaphysical poets like John Donne and

Andrew Marvell, whose formality often renders the text inaccessible to students. Next, the novel in verse aims at a merging of genres and techniques not found in other forms. While they sometimes retain some of the straightforward narrative structure found in fictional prose, their form is more often related to novels written in diary entries or letters. Additionally, they also provide a unique ground for exploring and understanding the teenage psyche. In her article "A Fresh Approach to YA Novels", Sherry Shanan observes that "the YA novel-in-poems—a non-traditional story form—is an apt reflection of adolescence, of a time when youth breaks away from authority and social convention". Just as the teens cannot relate easily to the structure of canonical poetry, they often feel that they cannot relate to their themes either. The young adult verse novel, in contrast, deals with themes familiar to teens in well-known settings: sex, depression, death, drugs, family troubles, and academic difficulties.

A graphic novel is another example of a type of formatting within young adult literature. Given the emergent confirmation that graphic novels entice young adult readers, Williams and Peterson suggest that librarians evaluate their graphic novel materials and continue to support the growing structure.

Another popular type of literature that is quite similar to the graphic novel is *manga*. Manga is a Japanese graphic novel or comic book. The interest factor and sales quotient of the manga genre is growing considerably. Manga requires a multimodal set of skills from the reader and offers cultural variety within a curriculum because of plotlines that teens identify with, such as self and sexual identity. It is but natural therefore that the librarians and teachers are amassing this varied and visually stimulating format within young adult literature.

Multi-platform books are also gaining popularity in YA literature. Other than just a printed page, publishers are promoting eBooks, a link to the Internet, a message board, or a videogame that corresponds to the book's characters and plotline. Digitally active teen readers are today more interested in multi-media platforms which provide more avenues of creative involvement in a story.

Various types of genres are available in young adult literature—realistic fiction, teen romance, dystopian society, and mixed genres novels. Begun in the 1970s, the realistic fiction genre relates to the issues of modern teens presenting stories about real and flawed teenaged characters. Teen romance and sexuality are permanent fixtures within the YA genre too as it is a realistic topic—one that pertains to teen in the present day. Dystopian fiction focusing on dystopian societies had been introduced by H.G. Wells and Ray Bradbury who presented grim worlds depicting society's turmoil and eventual downfall. As for now, the focus has shifted on marred and downtrodden societies.

However, the popularity of young adult literature is steeped in controversy, questions, and critiques. The topical issues of puberty, sex, drugs, and bad decision-making are challenged in bookstores and in school board meetings. From Judy Blume's *Forever* to Chris Crutcher's *Athletic Shorts*, characters, topics, and plotlines have been challenged. Profanity in the dialogue and prose pushes boundaries as well; however, authors know they can hook readers by providing a realistic sampling of dialogue in their stories. Teens have no patience for "sugar-coating" or downplaying conversations, let alone downplaying storylines.

The YA novel's primary subtext is usually about identity construction. Young adults are constructing their sense of self and the books they read may be a part of that process. Since young adult literature exerts a powerful influence over its readers at a particularly malleable time in their identity formation, we ought to approach YA literature with the same careful scrutiny, even if it is written about and to young adults, rather than by them.

Young Adult Fiction: Issues and Trends focuses on various issues faced by young people with a unique and understanding perspective. While engendering a healthy understanding of different cultures, and focusing on the importance of equality between all people, this genre encourages young people to read and to connect, helping to shape their young minds for the better. The sixteen scholarly essays in this anthology provide the youth of today with relevant life lessons, which are learnt by characters similar to them.

In her scholarly essay, "In pursuit of Young Adult Fiction", Reena Mitra offers an analytical overview of young adult fiction. Mitra avers, "YA fiction has devotedly engaged itself in addressing the issues and problems of adolescents with a sincerity and reverberation that readers, young adults as well as adults, have not been able to spurn and pass over."

"Spatial Identity and Postfeminist Girlhood in Indian Young Adult Chick Lit" by Anto Thomas Chakramakkil focuses on young adult literature in India and offers a brilliant analysis of Indian chick lit, especially, Vibha Batra's Rinki series. The second part of the essay explores how postfeminism and spatial identity inspire empowered girlhood.

"YA Novels in the College Classroom: A Space to Create Social Justice Warriors" by Padma Baliga and Livia Antony focuses on bringing in questions of social justice into the classroom space by using young adult (YA) novels for this purpose. The authors remark, "In this paper, we shall explore the possibilities of introducing a selection of Indian YA to college students to open up a discussion on social justice."

Shane Peacock has created a boy who bears all the seeds of the character who has mesmerized millions: the relentless eye, the sense of justice, and the complex ego. The boy Sherlock Holmes is a fascinating character who is sure to become a fast favourite with young readers everywhere. "'I Infer, So I Am Free!'—On how Shane Peacock has Subverted Doylean Conception of Inference in Persuading Young Readers in *Eye of the Crow: The Boy Sherlock Holmes, His 1st Case*" by Billy Bin Feng Huang is a well-researched essay. As he remarks, "In this paper, I intend to draw parallelism between Melanie C. Green and Timothy C. Brock's transportation theory and young adult literature, in order to address my first point: the fundamental aim of young adult literature is to persuade young readers. My second point is that while persuading his young audience, Peacock has literally subverted the Doylean conception of inference in *Eye of the Crow: The Boy Holmes, His 1st Case.*"

"Growing out of Location" by Alessandro Monti and Carole Rozzonelli focuses on the theme of domestic alienation in young adult novels. Fictional young adults, either from the subcontinent, India and Pakistan, or from the diasporic lands, the United States and England, live in a disturbing condition of maladjustment the former, due to the burden of the excessive requirements imposed by the family, or in isolating non-hyphenated estrangement and perennial miscegenation of failed shared identities, the latter.

Elena Xeni's paper, "Exploring Traditional and Contemporary Conceptions in Young Adult Literature: The Way from the 'Incapable' to the 'Capable' Young Reader" initiates an exploration of predominant traditional and contemporary social conceptions about the young reader from the adult's point of view. The paper aims at providing an overview of the journey that took a number of centuries and a greater number of adults to construct the role that adults play in the framework of socially constructed conceptions of the young reader and literature for children and adults.

"Environmental Education through Fiction: A Study of Deepak Dalal's Vikram-Aditya Series" by Shobhna Ramaswamy focuses on Dalal's emphasis in his works, on the conservation of forests and wildlife, and his concept of connecting young people with the wilderness.

"Reading *Frankenstein* and *The Strange Case of Dr. Jekyll and Mr. Hyde* in High School: The Oscillating Worlds of 'Beautiful' and 'Ugly'" by Sharmistha Chatterjee Sriwastav examines a wide range of issues that these two novels bring forth to their young readers making them veritable treasure houses of options—options which could make or mar individuals' lives, could give wings to their talents, or toss them to purgatories. It is up to the readers to choose between the two.

"Postmodernism and Indian Adult Literature: A Study of Shiva Trilogy" by Arpa Ghosh concentrates chiefly on Amish Tripathi's Shiva Trilogy to point out certain key features in young adult reading habits. As Ghosh remarks, "While Amish's wonderfully written book has reignited a love for reading in countless school-going and college-going readers and draws attention to such contemporary socio-political issues as the evil of war, misuse of atomic explosives, honour killings, and widow remarriage, thereby holding the attention of young and old (strength, opportunity), his representation of the Shiva myth unfortunately is a far cry from the original myth and may be viewed by purists as distortion, trivialization, and flattening of the same (weakness and threat).

In her essay, "Pedagogical Curiosity in Young Adult Literature" Mehar Fatima interrogates, "Can young adult literature offer suitable way to meet literary standards in our English classrooms, in schools and universities, or is it destined to a marginal function of leisure reading for adolescent learners outside English classrooms?" She critically examines the canons of young adult literature and remarks, "Its purpose is to deal with construction of societies, homes and personal affairs in a democratic world."

Maitree Deb, in her paper, "The Fair and the Foul: Reading the Journey of the Narratives of Agatha Christie's *Murder on the Orient Express* and Satyajit Ray's *Sonar Kella*," tries to examine the course of the narrative structure of the two texts, through the primary trope of physical and psychological journey, which forms a significant part of both the narratives, to explore how two generically opposite and contrasting forces unravel the fair and the foul corners of the human mind.

"Retreat to Primordial 'Id': Reflection on the Marooned Boys' Transposition from R.M. Ballantyne's *The Coral Island* to William Golding's *Lord of the Flies*," by Jyotirmoy Sil studies the scope of the Robinsonade story from Ballantyne's *The Coral Island* set in the Victorian times—an era ruled by the imperialist temperament—to the war-stricken modern context and deviates from the story's orientation confirming/justifying Victorian British priggishness to reveal the unethical bestial kernel or, in the terminology of Sigmund Freud, 'id' active underneath the façade of human civilization.

"Girlhood—Construction of a Female's Childhood in the 21st Century," by Ibha Gupta examines three children's series—*Harry Potter, Artemis Fowl* and *Percy Jackson*, that have been both critically acclaimed and widely popular, to analyze how 'girlhood' is constructed in the 21st century. The paper will illustrate how 'girlhood' portrayed in children's texts can challenge stereotypes such as 'run like a girl' and in the process, empower readers of all genders.

"The Overly Sentimental Musings in *The Perks of Being a Wallflower*," by Saloni Prasad explores in detail, *The Perks of Being a Wallflower*, a contemporary modern coming-of-age novel by Stephan Chbosky, which brilliantly captures the perspective of an introvert, a socially challenged individual who observes life, rather than participating in it.

In her essay, "Robert Cormier: The Forebearer of Young Adult Fiction," Runa, remarks, "The young adult books of the 1970s remain true time capsules of the high school experience and the drama of being misunderstood. Books like Cormier's *The Chocolate War* brought a literary sense to books targeted at teens."

Sapna Kumari in her paper, "Judy Blume: An Undaunted Voice in Young Adult Fiction" examines the portrayal of youth and its predicaments in Blume's works and analyses Blume, "as both an observer and a voice for adolescent girls and boys."

This anthology aims at offering a subtle, illuminating, and accessible exploration of issues and trends in YA fiction which will prove to be very helpful for students and the faculty. This anthology would not have existed but for the efforts of the contributors who patiently wrote and sometimes rewrote their articles at my request. I thank each of the authors for devoting their time and effort to this book. I also wish to thank Dr. K.R. Gupta, Chairman, Atlantic Publishers and Distributors Pvt. Ltd., New Delhi for the confidence evinced in me and for seeing the book through the press.

Sunita Sinha

Contents

Contributors

Reena Mitra, Professor in English, Amity School of Languages, Amity University, Lucknow, Uttar Pradesh.

Anto Thomas Chakramakkil, Associate Professor and Head of the Research Department of English, St. Thomas' College (Autonomous), Thrissur, Kerala.

Padma Baliga did her doctoral studies in the areas of gender studies and Indian children's literature. After teaching for over 20 years, she is now an independent researcher and is currently carrying out her postdoctoral research in Konkani children's literature.

Livia Antony, B.Sc. in Microbiology and an MA in English from St. Joseph's College, Bangalore.

She is currently pursuing independent research and hopes to earn her Ph.D. in Film Studies.

Billy Bin Feng Huang, Ph.D. Candidate, National Chengchi University, Taiwan (R.O.C.).

Alessandro Monti, Retired Full Professor in English, Former Head of the Department of Oriental Studies, University of Turin, Italy. Fellow of Indian Council Relations in 2011 in the Department of Journalism and Mass Communication, Banaras Hindu Universities, Varanasi, Uttar Pradesh.

Carole Rozzonelli, Associate Professor of English, ICT, Communications and Media Law, University of Lyon 2 – Lumière (France).

Elena Xeni, Aristotle University of Thessaloniki, Greece.

Shobhna Ramaswamy, Assistant Professor, Department of English, Kongunadu Arts & Science College, Coimbatore.

Sharmistha Chatterjee (Sriwastav), Associate Professor in English Aliah University, Kolkata, West Bengal.

Arpa Ghosh, Associate Professor, Head, Department of English, Vivekananda College for Women, Kolkata,West Bengal.

Mehar Fatima, Assistant Professor, Department of English, Jamia Millia Islamia, New Delhi.

Maitree Deb, Guest faculty, Muralidhar Girls' College, Salt Lake, Kolkata, West Bengal and Visiting Faculty Techno India University, Salt lake, Kolkata, West Bengal.

Jyotirmoy Sil, Research Scholar, Aliah University, Kolkata.

Ibha Gupta, Research Scholar, Goa University, Goa.

Saloni Prasad (Mrs. Kumar), Professor and Head, Department of English, Commerce College, Patna.

Runa, Assistant Professor, Department of English, Patna Women's College, Patna.

Sapna Kumari, Assistant Professor, Department of English, Patna Women's College, Patna.

1

In Pursuit of Young Adult Fiction

Reena Mitra

It is part of the novel's development and its prevalent preoccupation to explore new and extended boundaries for itself and reconstitute its form and structure. Concepts of what the novel is and what it might be have had such major paradigm shifts in the recent past that one has to make a conscious and conscientious effort to figure out the contours of the serious imaginative and creative repositioning that is in process in the literary fictional world of today. There are sure and unmistakable signs of a characteristic new era of content and style. The novel now, as Malcolm Bradbury puts it, is "in a profitable ferment"[1] from which, hopefully, will emerge a new poetics of fiction.

At the start of the twentieth century great changes in the form and functions of the novel were perceived and by about the 1920s one witnessed the rolling out of what we call modernism today. With the loss of the novelist's faith in reality and chronology, and with his subscription to the relationship between the individual and his social and moral development withdrawn, the novel turned inward to explore consciousness—individual and collective—and in this it conformed to the new pronouncements of philosophy and psychology that had become almost indispensable to our comprehension of experience and actuality. With a host of publications like Wayne Booth's *The Rhetoric of Fiction* (1961), David Lodge's *The Language of Fiction* (1966) and Scholes and Kellogg's *The Nature of Narrative* (1966), the novel increasingly became a deliberate and focused mode of organizing experience, experience of an individual or a group, with the thrust not on the causality of things but on the experience itself which generally distils meaning out of what transpires in life. The contemporary novel foregrounds certain aspects of the text, like states of mind and particular objects which need to be redefined to bring cognizance and meaning to bear upon the life or lives chosen for depiction. The focus is on the experientially real. According to Ronald Sukenick,

> ...the movement of fiction should always be in the direction of what we sense as real.... The novelist accommodates the ongoing flow of experience, smashing anything that impedes his sense of it, even if it happens to be the novel.[2]

It is at this juncture of the growth and development of the English novel in the 1960s and 70s that young adult fiction appeared on the literary horizon with all the authenticity and conviction of lives lived and distress and anguish undergone.

The truth of life or "reality" as Austin Warren refers to it, is effectively registered in our hearts and minds not when we measure it with regard to factual accuracy as it prevails in the actual world of human existence but when we judge it within the world or *Kosmos* as recreated in the literary composition by the author himself, the world structured in terms of the various aspects of the novel—plot, characters, setting, tenor and the comprehensive general design, all collaborating to realize the implicit world view. All great novels furnish a universe epitomizing the experiential and heuristic existence around but each is distinct in what Warren calls its "self-coherent intelligibility".[3]

The whole record of the life of adolescent protagonists as depicted in young adult novels, which started being written in about the 1960s has an amazing air of reality, and the verisimilitude that marks them gives as plausible and intense an impression of life as ever lived by youngsters. The principal characters are intimately portrayed with their past, their proclivities, mental and physical habits and motivations in life from moment to moment with such fidelity that this genre of contemporary fiction is undoubtedly endowed with a kind of conviction that is infectious and permeates the minds of its readers. It has the air of experience lived and felt and the central characters in most cases, conform to the established psychology of adolescents who happen to be the target bracket. There are moments of typical emotional strain resulting from suspense in certain matters and these junctures of uncertainty are characterized by hopeful anticipation or anxiety. There is, on such occasions, a tendency to savour to the full the content of the point in time rendered and, as Joseph Warren Beach puts it, there is "an infinite expansion of the moment".[4]

A lay reader has a legitimate interest in the actions as well as the behaviour of characters in a novel that have an irresistible appeal and are endowed with a degree of authenticity and lifelikeness that helps him identify with the protagonist despite the difference in age that might exist between them. The empathy and connect between the two may be in terms of aspirations as well as circumstances or even with regard to aspects that are not really quantifiable and realizable in terms of the material and the tangible. So, young adult fiction, though sometimes apparently irrational and hypothetical, possesses an abiding concern for a better deal in life that needs to be offered to the younger generation so as to enable it to steer through life with confidence and aplomb.

Young adults are attracted to and are compulsorily drawn into a literary work when they see an idea, an attitude or a chunk of truth passing from their own lives into a creation that is by no means moribund; rather, it is a composition that blazes a trail of hitherto ineffable personal experiences into words which one can readily identify with and bank upon for a true representation of one's own thoughts and feelings. Authors writing about adolescents seem to ferret out their way unerringly to the perfect concoction where life and fiction blend to offer a delineation of a concatenation of significant events that vicariously provides an intellectual satisfaction and the joy of being able to locate meaning in their own lives. And, as Peter Brook, in another context avers, "meaning never belongs to the past. It can be checked in each man's present experience".[5] Young adult authors as well as readers do not fail to draw the elixir provided by such writings which prepare them for the multiplicity of life and its unpredictability.

Till the 1960s young adult fiction comprised the writings of the marginalised consciousness of the adolescents who tried to express themselves and communicate with the world around putting forth their views on issues that concerned them but in the contemporary times, it has assumed a considerable degree of centrality and can in no way, be ignored or overlooked. It is the literature written by adolescents or young adults who savour life as it comes to them, life which is a series of negotiations for love, peace and stability in a world which scourges and lashes them with threats of assault and dissolution. Their narrative method contests the fixed and unchanging nature of reality in life and provides multiple personalized interpretations of experiences that were earlier looked upon as fixed and immutable in nature. The multifarious perspectives presented through an adolescent mind challenges established views about several social practices in life and explores their multiple implications and nuances as affecting young adult life.

The American novelist, Hawthorne, discriminating between "romance" and "novel" with particular reference to the American literary scene, significantly remarked that novels were "presumed to aim at a very minute fidelity, not merely to the possible, but to the probable and ordinary course of man's experience".[6] It is this probability in the lives of young individuals that is highlighted in the fiction for adolescents, who are plagued with numerous and diverse problems which intimidate them with instability and impose on them a life of peril and defenselessness resulting in moral and emotional decrepitude and a constant fear of their own vulnerability.

Youngsters in their adolescent years are, by and large, existentialist in their approach, "existence" being "the fact or manner of existing or living". 'Existentialism' in the *Oxford Reference Dictionary* is defined as "a philosophical theory emphasizing the existence of the individual person as a free and responsible agent determining his or her own development".[7] Young adults, though generally victims of specific conditions prevailing in their lives, are often initiators of change as they rebel against the present infertile conditions to usher in a period of supposedly fruitful and prosperous circumstances. An individual is always confronted with a number of choices and it is the particular choices made that determine the tenor of his life. An adolescent girl or boy needs to exercise an option at every turn of life and it is every notable preference expressed and complied with that weaves the texture of one's individual life. "Existentialism is opposed to all forms of necessitarianism; for existence is constituted by possibilities from among which man may choose and through which he can project himself".[8] Our young generation today does not believe in blindly accepting what Providence has in store for it. With an indefatigable spirit it puts up a brave fight and makes its choices so as to condition the future as it wishes it to be.

Coming now to the distinctive features of young adult literature it would be illuminating to know that the National Council of Teachers of English has defined this genre as

> literature wherein the protagonist is either a teenager or one who approaches problems from a teenage perspective.... Typically, they describe initiation into the adult world, or the surmounting of a contemporary problem forced upon the protagonist(s) by the adult world. Though generally written for a teenager reader, such novels—like all fine literature—address the entire spectrum of life.[9]

It is, however, unfortunate that the entire bulk of young adult literature is often branded as "immature" or a mere "beach read" despite the fact that it has often appealed to some as literature of substance and of unquestionable consequence. The juvenility and inexperience of its adolescent protagonists alone cannot justify their being stamped as "bad" literature. The young children about to step into adulthood may be portrayed as befuddled and disoriented but is not that an undeniable poignant truth with regard to that particular stage in human life? The nostalgic clinging to the evanescent childhood loves and the vulnerability and apprehension of moving into the uncertainties of adulthood are unnerving experiences that are intensified by their simultaneity. This Janus-faced period of life looking back at the naiveté of childhood and ahead at the sagacity and discrimination of adulthood depicts the truth of living life on the cusp. Anyone confronting such a stage in his/her life is an individual in the making and hence at a very crucial stage of development and growth which cannot be shrugged off.

The presence of a child or teenage protagonist in a book does not categorize the work as young adult fiction. The adult and young adult distinction depends primarily, and largely on the author's intentions and his perspective in interpreting issues taken up for analysis. Young adult fiction is not specifically for a particular age-group that is supposed to read mainly "age-appropriate books". *Graceling*, a work of fiction characterized as a young adult novel despite it having some adult scenes in it, is a perfect example of the author's target readership. The age-bracket prescribed for readers of young adult literature is from 12-18 years of age. However, whatever the readership aimed at by the author the ultimate choice is that of the reader.

In the latter half of the twentieth century young adult literature or YA literature as it is commonly referred to, has come up in a largely perceptible manner and is celebrated as a distinct segment of publishing which has carved out its own market despite the rampant absorption of the youth of today in the media and the internet. With the publication of *The Outsider* by S.E. Hinton in 1967 and *The Pigman* by Paul Zindel in 1968, there has been no looking back for literature for young adults which has diversified amazingly in the recent past and now has an unprecedented fare to offer—realistic fiction, historical fiction, problem novels, mysteries, adventure narratives, fantasy and science fiction, non-fiction, biography, poetry, drama, short stories, etc. Evidently then, types of young adult literature are numerous and have branched out into almost every class of literature, specifically fiction.

Academics have identified several salient features of young adult literature. YA authors, they observe, write from the perspective of young individuals. From the point of view of the omniscient narrator to that of the young generation has been a long literary journey. Circumstantial pressures, often compel the characters in YA novels to confront their own problems independently of their parents whose absence does not cripple them in any way. The narration of the stories is rendered at almost break-neck speed with a focus on images of vigour and sturdiness suggesting the energy and spirit of youth.

The purview of YA literature extends to a variety of subjects which are, in the main, reminiscent of contemporary realistic fiction. Included in it are stories of individuals from different racial and cultural groups redolent of the modern concepts of multi-ethnicity and multiculturalism. The monopoly of the whites has been demolished and the characters are no longer all White, middle-class characters. The genre is now one of all-inclusiveness and taboos are few. YA books are essentially buoyant and sanguine with characters displaying remarkable achievements. These characters are confronted with hazards and challenges and in the course of collision attrition is minimal and the moral growth of the characters is astounding. In the novel, the dramatis personae on the stage of life assume the stance of Forster's "round" characters, growing and changing substantially in the course of the novel. The world of young people is convincingly identified and realized and the point of convergence remains a conglomeration of emotions central to their world.

Some developmental and supplementary requisites of adolescents were located by Havinghurst in his publication, *Developmental Tasks and Education*[10] (1972). An understanding of these tasks is a desideratum one cannot relegate to the background in any approach to young adult texts. Young people today have unqualified aspirations of participating in the social life around and wish to acquire a certain self-sufficiency and autonomy, making every effort to shed the colossal way of parental authority. They need to attain sagacity and discrimination in social negotiability and orchestration, a definite orientation in a sex role, preparation for a vocation, precursory readiness for sex, marriage and parenthood, evolution of a personal credo subsequent upon the acquisition of righteous and principled touchstones at the advent of maturity and embarkation on a community life and the undertaking of responsibilities as a conscientious members of one's fraternity. These goals of young adults need to be the reader's frames of reference when trying to construe or comprehend YA novels.

Alternatively, *The Centre for Early Adolescence at the University of North Carolina at Chapel Hill*, under the guidance of its then Director, Joan Lipsitz, released a catalogue of seven developmental needs of young adults[11] which were circulated for observance and compliance. According to this *Centre*, the goals that young adults should strive for are physical exercise, proficiency and accomplishment, self-elucidation, artistic and ingenious expression, healthy social interaction with equals and seniors, consciousness of structure and "clear limits" and significant and meaningful social navigation.

Adolescence and youth experiences, however, are not to be considered taboo for other age groups for essentially all literature is a welcome source of intellectual enlightenment and young adult literature is a bulk of writing that acquaints one with the nuances of living life on the verge of adulthood. Ruth Gainer, in her article, "Against YA" states, "Read whatever you want but you should feed embarrassed when what you're reading was written for children".[12] This implied criticism and the attaching of a stigma to a genre of literature that caters primarily to a raw and inexperienced psyche is not really upright and unbiased for it brushes aside the truth of the naiveté and ingenuousness of the adolescent experience that is irrefutable. A reader of YA literature is by no means a less sophisticated reader. In delving into these texts one is only seeking to acquire an acquaintance with the pubescent and teenage mind. This attempt at empathizing with the adolescent intelligence can rewardingly equip one better to confront life in one's quotidian interactions with people around.

Interestingly enough, a piece of information that has encouraged an enquiry into the genre of YA literature is the statistical fact given by the fiction publisher, Tor Books, with regard to women largely outnumbering men in the submission of drafts of this kind of fiction to publishers, a gender dispensation opposed to that witnessed in, say, fantasy or science fiction. Another YA literature observation comes from the Pew survey which tells us that sixteen to twenty-nine years old are the largest group subscribing to this genre. So, despite the common assumption, YA literature is certainly not age-specific.

Going back to the time when "young adults" actually took root and "teenagers" almost compelled people to take cognizance of their identity and respond to their assertions of selfhood, it needs to be recorded that "Seventeenth Summer" released by Maureen Daly in 1972, is generally accepted to be the first book authored and published professedly for adolescents. It is a novel primarily about the first love of girls. Subsequently, there were sports novels for boys. This marks the beginning of the kind of writing now established as YA fiction.

It was *The Young Adult Library Services Association* that coined the term "young adult" in the 1960s to bring to the fore a mellow and fully developed depiction of the present-day actuality pertaining to adolescents. With the thrust on culture and consequential issues that bear upon the youth, authors in the 1970s started writing with outspokenness and sincerity about subjects related to teens. Judy Blume, Robert Cormier and Lois Duncan are authors of young adult fiction that parents of today recognize well for the high school phase of children depicted by them. Novels like Cormier's *The Chocolate War* introduced a literary dimension to these works written for teens.

However, in course of time, these works evolved into novels focusing on individual problems like divorce, drug abuse, etc. and tended to become hackneyed stories so that the 1980s welcomed more diversified genre fiction addressing the problems and interest of the adolescent world and focusing on issues like rape, suicide, parental death, killing, etc. Teenagers in the 1980s also wanted to read something related to their daily lives and so there was a revival of romance fiction. In the 1990s graver aspects of young adult issues were taken up and topics like the use of drugs, sexuality, alcoholism and teen pregnancy were dealt with. It was in 1997 that J.K. Rowling published the first Harry Potter novel, *Harry Potter and the Philosopher's Stone*. It was a coming-of-age novel that was hailed for its enigmatic quality and the adult reach it offered. Rowling is thus often given credit for resuscitating and revitalizing YA literature. Successive works like *The Hunger Games* trilogy by Suzanne Collins and *The*

Twilight Saga by Stephenie Meyer also provided an impetus to the genre, that has made inroads into other media and categories like mystery fiction, romance novels, etc. and even subdivisions like cyberpunk and techno-thrillers.

Jennifer Lynn Barnes, a young adult author and an erudite scholar of cognitive science observed,

> Just like adolescence is between childhood and adulthood, paranormal or other in between human and supernatural.... Teens are caught between two worlds, childhood and adulthood, and in YA fiction they can navigate those two worlds and sometimes dualities of other worlds.[13]

Another notable feature of YA writing is its continual involvement with transformation. As Lizzie Skurnick puts it, "it shows teen life in full chaos. And that means constant change".[14] Though young adult literature comprises several genres, it essentially employs emotions and sentiments to make readers relate to tales of change and transformation.

David Levithan, while promoting Scholastic's venture for teens, PUSH, in the late 1990s explored young minds to be acquainted with what they really coveted in their literature and he came to the conclusion that

> ...teens wanted things that were real, that they connected with.... It doesn't have to reflect reality directly. They love *The Hunger Games* not because it's real in that it happens but the emotions there are real and it's very relatable.[15]

Writers of young adult fiction do not abstain from dealing with or discussing dark and intimidating issues that teens confront and they do not hesitate to apportion space in their novels to the adolescent problems of identity, sexual abuse, drug/alcohol consumption and suicide. Famous authors like John Green, an American writer, blogger, writer, producer, actor and editor who won the 2006 Printz Award for his debut novel, *Looking for Alaska,* and his sixth novel, *The Fault in Our Stars,* write exhaustively about the plight and predicaments of adolescents so unflinchingly and truthfully that they have won the complete faith of readers. The verisimilitude offered is winsome and subscribers to the novels multiple.

Another exemplary YA author who needs to be mentioned is Meg Cabot, *New York Times* best-selling author of books for adults and teens. Cabot, who has now herself written over forty-five YA books, began by trying to identify literary works she could connect with as a teen. Somehow, she could never accept the fact of girls surrendering before the unavailability of their choices and loves in life. She writes mainly romantic and paranormal fiction and it is unconditional hope that remains her driving force throughout. She has, curiously enough, always been fascinated by science fiction which depicts girls spying on alien planets for she is all for the empowerment of girls. Her works, however, are generally written from the YA point of view.

A major relevance of YA literary works in the lives of adolescents may be that they serve as bridges to the archetypes used in the classics of traditional literature or even a contemporary novel. A Jungian archetype in a character or theme in a YA novel may introduce the perception of a connection and a comparative approach among works of literature. Identifying archetypes may also give clues to students regarding a particular author's style and mode of writing.

Essentially then, young adult literature makes available to the youth of today *personae grata* and subjects that are of interest to them and with whom and what they can relate. Its treatment of the various pertinent issues taken up only ratifies and endorses what is afloat and in no way does it minimize the significance and validity of that which is salubrious and stimulating for teenagers. Also, in fiction, this genre of literature underscores plot and avoids the abstract so that the development of the novel is within the comprehension of the young adult who has still to cultivate the beauty of the conceptual. Last, but not least, is the fact that YA literature/fiction addresses the needs of student readers and thus manages to rivet their attention to whatever of advantage is stated in a language fully comprehensible to the fledgelings and at a cognitive level that corresponds to theirs. The content of the novels generally deals with contemporary issues and with global concerns.

YA writers today explore almost any subject that comes their way for they are well aware of the fact that the target readers are eager for new horizons. Paranormal and dystopian sequences of publication have now been substituted by individual self-contained books. More gay, lesbian and transgender characters now appear in these novels and there is no discrimination between books for girls and those for boys. In fact, we have today what has been christened the "new-adult" fiction (also referred to as NA or post-adolescent fiction), the phrase having been invented by St. Martin's Press in 2009. We confront in them characters in their final teens and early twenties undergoing experiences at the college level.

Swelling in acceptance and response in the 1960s and 1970s and continuing to appeal to the young adults of the day, YA fiction has devotedly engaged itself in addressing the issues and problems of adolescents with a sincerity and reverberation that readers, young adults as well as adults, have not been able to spurn and pass over. Though topics like vulnerability, anxiety, deprivation, aspiration, yearning and desire have already been explored by writers such as Judy Blume, S.E. Hinton and Robert Cormier, they continue to be enquired into by other authors and the response is still overwhelming.

Notes

1. Malcolm Bradbury, Ed. "Introduction". *The Novel Today.* Great Britain: Collins, 1977. 20.
2. *Ibid.*
3. Joseph Warren Beach, "Post-impressionisms : Joyce". *The Twentieth Century Novel : Studies in Technique.* New Delhi: Kalyani Publishers, rpt. 1988. 409.
4. Austen Warren, "The Nature and Mode of Narrative Fiction". *Perspectives on Fiction.* James L. Calderwood and Harold E. Toliver. Eds. New York : Oxford University Press, 1968. 75.
5. Peter Brook, *The Empty Space.* Harmondsworth: Penguin, 1972. 14-15.
6. Cited in Allen, Walter. "Introduction". *Tradition and Dream.* Harmondsworth: Penguin, 1965. 14.
7. Joyce M. Hawkins, Ed. *Oxford Reference Dictionary.* Oxford: Oxford University Press, 1987.

8. Papia Mitra, Ed. *Existentialism : A Reader's Guide*. Kolkata: Shakespeare Society of Eastern India and Avantgarde Press, 2002. 9.
9. "Guideline on Preparing Teachers with Knowledge of Children's and Adolescent Literature". *National Council of Teachers of English Guideline*. Urbana, Illinois, 2004.
10. Robert J. Havinghurst, *Developmental Tasks and Education*. New York: Longman Group United Kingdom, 1972.
11. Joan Lipsitz (Director). "Growing Up" (1980). *The Centre for Early Adolescence at the University of North Carolina at Chapel Hill*.
12. Ruth Gainer, *In Defense of Young Adult Literature—The Odyssey Online*. www.theodysseyonline.com July 4, 2016.
13. Cited in Valerie Bodden, *Young Adults : Essential Literary Genres*. Minnesota: Abdo Publishers, 2017. 9.
14. Cited in Alexis Burling, *Women in Literature*. Minneapolis: Essential Library, Abdo Publishers, 2017. 84.
15. David Levithan, www.quotes. net/citizen – quote/68391

2

Spatial Identity and Postfeminist Girlhood in Indian Young Adult Chick Lit

Anto Thomas Chakramakkil

I

> Traditional and cultural constraints have made the development of a modern 'young adult literature' difficult in India, hence the very applicability of the term is debatable in the Indian context. As a consequence, gender as an issue in books for children in English in India was not considered particularly significant until very recently. However, there are certain notable works that strongly foreground girls, portray them in non-stereotypical terms or raise pertinent gender issues.
>
> (Rangachari, Devika. "Gender as an Issue" n.p.)

Introduction

In traditional Indian children's literature, male perspectives dominate and girls are subjugated to be submissive, obedient, and silent, even when these works are authored by women. However, there are drastic changes to these views in contemporary globalized cultural contexts in India. Children's literature in India is now a burgeoning realm for women writers, and in their writings they often assign the central role to girl characters. When we contextualize this fact against the backdrop of traditional male attitudes in Indian literature, it is polemical because many of these female characters exhibit feminist values. These groups of women writers redefine Indian girlhood as they celebrate as well as imagine their female-messianic roles, simultaneously projecting empowered protagonists that build up positive images of girlhood for the readers and for Indian society as a whole. The late twentieth century concerns of feminist liberation through children's literature have progressively moved towards postfeminist girlhood in the twenty-first century Indian young adult literature.

Disturbing the Universe: Power and Repression in Adolescence Literature by Roberta Seelinger Trites (2000) is a premier critical work that theorizes about Young Adult Literature (YAL). Trites' study begins with an excerpt from T.S. Eliot's poem "Lovesong of J. Alfred Prufrock". The middle-aged man in Eliot's poem procrastinates like Hamlet and contrasts to adolescents who are ever willing to propose love. The excerpts from the poem that Trites' quotes, at its core, asks a germane question of adolescents as well as of the middle-aged:

> And indeed there will be time
> To wonder, "Do I dare?" and "Do I Dare?"
> Time to turn back and descend the stair
> With a bald spot in the middle of my hair—
> (They will say: "How his hair is growing thin!")
> My morning coat, my collar mounting firmly to the chin,
> My necktie rich and modest, but asserted by a simple pin—
> (They will say: "But how his arms and legs are thin!")
> Do I dare
> Disturb the universe? (Eliot qtd., in Trites, 1)

Trites argues that YAL essentially problematizes issues that disturb humanity. There have been, within the last sixteen years, further critical insights into violence, sex, power, resistance, death, and gender-identity in YAL. Consequently, there has been a further boom in the industry of YA books in the West. What is the cultural landscape of teenagers in India? The fast pace of globalization has brought forward the same issues in literature for the young in India too, at least in the English language books, breaking that long silence of Indian literary taste in children's books to retreat into the stereotypes of morals, of retelling of myths, and of being in the comfort zones of family relationships. It was Devika

Rangachari, the Indian English author for children, who made the bold declaration in her presentation at the 33rd IBBY Congress, that Indian Young Adult Literature has "Come of Age". What she meant was that YAL in India has a distinct identity of its own (Rangachari, "Coming of Age"). Recently, critics and scholars in India have begun to take interest in studies of YAL too.

Muse India, an online journal that publishes studies on Indian Literature regularly, in one of the issues (September-October 2015), guest-edited by a famous Indian English children's writer Deepa Agarwal focused on YAL. Devika Rangachari contributed to this one by writing on gender as a problem in YAL. Another prominent article on YAL was that of Panchanan Dalai whose provocative title "Don't Tell My Mother" looked at the issues of reading YAL through analysis based on literary theories. Dalai's article begins with a personal anecdote narrating how the author caught his wife red-handed in the clandestine behavior of reading books meant for teenagers. The wife then confesses that she has been doing it for a number of years even after her marriage and pleads with her husband to not to disclose this secret to her mother. She then reveals the secret that she is an adult who feels like being an eternal teenager. There are many adults who identify themselves with young adults but hesitate to declare the same in public. Vibha Batra has recurrently expressed the truth that in many interviews she identifies herself with the young adults, and she acknowledges that she writes her novels by stepping into the shoes of teenagers. I think all scholars of children's literature have to do so. When the interviewer for the *Deccan Chronicler* asked Vibha the question, "How difficult was it to put you in the shoes of Rinki [the protagonist of her YA Trilogy], and how did you achieve that?" Vibha coolly replied:

> It wasn't difficult at all because I think of myself as a young adult. And as the hubby says, "And act like one at times". In my opinion, life (and of course, being a teenager at some point in your life) is the best research one can get. Being a teenager you can't say no to humour. You can't read children's literature with a long severe face. Suddenly, YA has established itself as a prominent popular genre in India too. (Interview n.p.)

As YAL becomes a prominent sub-genre in children's literature in India, a brief exploration of YAL in general suits the context of this analysis.

Jeffrey S. Kaplan, Associate Professor at the University of Central Florida and a specialist in YA studies, states that YAL covers everything from "contemporary realistic novels to pure flights of fantasy" and has "transformed the landscape of what it means to be a teenager, and more importantly, how teenagers are perceived by themselves and the wider public" (42). Jonathan Stephens, another scholar, comments while he defines the genre, "YA takes its readers to a place where adolescence lives on, a place where that journey toward identity culture is to happen" (40-41). Thus, while some focus upon the age of the intended readers as a significant element, others emphasize the youth experience, its exuberance and eccentricities, as the detrimental principles to define YAL. Whatever be the definition, every specialist in YAL complaints that YAL isn't taken seriously. Observe Cindy Lou Daniel's opinion:

> ...only that contemporary works that have been labeled as YA tend to be ignored by many serious literary critics. Some still believe that YA literature is merely a secondary category of child-like storytelling—didactic in nature—and unworthy of serious literary evaluation, when, in fact, it is really an overlooked and underappreciated literary genre that has only recently begun to attract the critical attention that it deserves. (78)

If YAL is to be taken seriously as books that merit literary excellence and as works capable of generating critical thinking, the initiatives should come forth from children's literature scholars. They should highlight excellence in adolescent literature and promote it by considering its merits for readers and scholars.

Panchanan Dalai's article on YAL, while being innovative, cannot shed the Indian tradition of searching for didactic purposes while reading YAL. He enumerates five great benefits: (1) To educate, (2) To inspire and transform lives, (3) To reveal the young world, (4) To expose societal hegemony, and (5) To enhance literary skills. These are sufficient reasons to promote

YAL; but Dalai's critical article seems to side track YAL and he does not advocate YAL on the grounds that it is purely entertaining and excellent in literary merits. One of the major reasons why Vibha Batra's YA chic lit became the focus of my study is to direct critical attention in Indian universities and colleges on YAL, to bring it into the canon and thus overcome the hesitance in academia about including YAL in university syllabi. In fact, were YAL taught in Indian universities, students would be more at ease with problems in their own lives, as these are similar to those portrayed in YAL. Then the students would have every reason to be motivated to read because a reflection of their own life's activities is seen in the lives of YAL protagonists.

Young Adult Literature in India and Girlhood Identities

There is a definite and embedded link between body image, weight, and sexuality in YAL for girls. Usually, thinner young women are portrayed as powerful and in control, while larger women are depicted as sexually passive and irresponsible. Then, we may say along with Beth Younger who has conducted extensive research on Female Body in Adolescent literature that: "YA literature reflects girls' lives back to them, and this genre contains many representations of young women that illuminate body-image stereotypes" (3). YAL reflects societal stereotypes, and although literary critics often ignore this genre, it remains an important body of work that deserves our critical attention for what it says about body image, the problems of adolescents and about sexuality and gender identity. If traditional YAL stereotypes body image and relates sexuality with thin women, then, Vibha Batra offers a resistance to this cliché. Her protagonist Rinki is quite chubby and doesn't mind being so. Rinki never thinks she is a victim of Bilumia Nervosa. Binge eating and the tendency to be a patient of the eating disorder Anorexia Nervosa is the characteristic temperament of her friend Jugal Varma, a boy nicknamed Google. Rinki is at ease with his behavior because they have many similarities: both are weight-challenged, they have weird hair, they are opinionated, they hate working out, and they are whiny.

Vibha Batra and her pack of gangs in Rinki's story have dared to disturb the universe. Yes, if I were a Tiresias, I would have prophesized that Vibha Batra would soon be addressed as the Judy Blume of India. Judy Blume is cited as one of the forerunners of YAL in USA, and she has constructed a particular view of girlhood through her young adult fiction. In her early works *Are You There God? It's Me, Margaret* (1970), and *Forever* (1975), we notice her frank and graphic portrayals of sexuality. Often these works were dismissed as not worthy literary texts because they were too realistic. Vibha too is frank about sexuality in her trilogy. She has hidden obscenity in expression with symbols and the French art of verlan / *à l'envers*, a linguistic inversion technique often hiding obscenity in expression, as for example, the oft-repeated phrase in the Rinki series, "Too mucking fuch" (*Sweet Sixteen* 49). Thankfully, the censorship authority for books in India lacks in intelligence as well as in reading habits; if not, they perhaps just don't mind Vibha and her companion authors of YAL in India disturbing this part of the universe! The traditional attitude of the world to not to take seriously writings for children and young adults is a boon as well as a blight. It's a boon because all the young adults in body and spirit can have good and interesting reading stuff in future. It's a curse because young adult authors who need support and assistance from the so-called canon makers do not get proper encouragement. But, of course, this universe is created for those who dare to disturb it. My paper attempts to study the escalation in developing Indian perspectives in YAL in Vibha Batra's trilogy and further explores what the repercussions are of daring to disturb this part of the universe while redefining the identities of girlhood in India.

Sweet Sixteen begins with Rinki Tripathi's father breaking the news to Rinki and her mother that his bank has transferred him to Chennai and that they should start packing. Her mother recovers after being upset initially but Rinki is in utter distress because she cannot miss Ankita, her BFF (Best Friend Forever). Her other friends make it worse by comparing Delhi and Chennai. Rinki loves music and makes a playlist reflecting her mood. Finally, they move and are in a new place, with a new language, new neighbourhood, new school and new friends. Rinki who gets admission in a higher secondary school in Chennai has no other option but to choose business studies as her major subject.

She feels bored with business studies and prefers extracurricular activities. Consequently, her grades start dropping and she finds everything but studies awesome. When Rinki comes to school, Robin and Sudha, the classmates who first befriend Rinki, take her around. In the afternoon, they go to the canteen, the place where Romeos' and Juliets' meet. While commenting on different gangs in the school, they point out Priya, the ex-girlfriend of Tejas, a senior student. They also remark that Priya is the president of the Butterfly Club, an exclusive group of girls who need to be "beautiful, rich, and snobbish to be part of that clique" (52). Later, at the Freshers' party she meets Tejas and falls in love with him at first sight. Tejas, whom Rinki fondly calls TJ, soon take her out for week-end parties. Once, Rinki lied to her parents that she is going out for a night-movie with her classmates Robin and Sudha. Rinki's parents are hesitant to allow their daughter to go out at night but finally budge when they are told that the girls are accompanied by their neighbor Sriram. When Sriram takes them out, Rinki changes her plans and persuades Robin and Sudha to go to a discotheque instead in order to have a rendezvous with Tejas. Afterwards, when all the students of the school go on a tour to Ooty, Rinki misses the trip because she has to accompany her parents to Delhi. Although this tour helps Priya befriend Tejas once again, at the end of the novel Rinki re-imagines a lovely time with Tejas, her boy-lover.

In *Seventeen and Done,* Rinki is seventeen and her friendship with Robin and Sudha is stronger. Her dad has been transferred again to Coimbatore and he decides to go alone because he does not want to disturb Rinki's studies. But he does not want Rinki and her mother to be alone in Chennai, so he sends for his aunty, Mausiji. Rinki's mother does not want Mausiji there, nor does Rinki. Robin, Rinki's classmate and intimate friend in Chennai, who has been rather conservative in behaviour has changed and she has started going around with Sriram. Rinki herself has moved from using Facebook to Blackberry Messenger. Rinki also takes online quizzes for teens frequently and she is blogging. She starts a fashion blog called "Chennai Super Chick" and frequently writes on topics such as body weight problems, love-affairs, and hair straightening. Studies still suffer and she has enrolled for tuition in the difficult subject of Accountancy, at her parents' interest. At the tuition class, she frequents her friendships with her male classmates Adit and Google and even starts dating them both, as well as hiding the whole affair from her mother and Mausiji. But soon Rinki quarrels with all her intimate friends in Chennai and block them from her Internet groups. And, then the dreaded board exams come. At the end of this second series, we come to know that Rinki passes her higher secondary examinations and is eligible for college studies.

In the final book in the series, *Eighteen and Wiser*, Rinki wants to visit Ankita, her BFF (Best Friend Forever), in Delhi to celebrate her eighteenth birthday there along with her classmates in Chennai: Robin, Sudha, Google and Adit. But her parents put their feet down. They say that they will not send her unchaperoned; instead, they will accompany the group to Delhi. But then her dad becomes tied up with his work, so Rinki has to celebrate her birthday in Chennai sans Ankita. Finally, she does get to go to Delhi with her parents where Ankita is waiting for her at the airport. The boys follow but the girls cannot make it. At Ankita's it's party time always. The young adults drink alcohol and celebrate, and Rinki witnesses Adit and Ankita falling in love. During the party Rinki is shocked to witness the deep kiss they share, an act that stirs her desire to have had Adit date her, and then Rinki becomes angry with herself and her friends. Once back in Chennai, she takes a part-time job at a fashion magazine. There she is exploited in a weird manner. Her ideas and catchwords are unpaid but she and her young adult friends play their trickster games and take sweet revenge upon the owner of the fashion magazine. Thus, she secures her six thousand rupees safely at home. Then the results come in, college admissions and more. When the college mates go for a tour to Bengaluru, Rinki woos her friends for a trip to Pondicherry. There her friends finally realize that it was just a plot of Rinki to spend the night with her boyfriend Tejas, her lover. She can no longer keep her love for Tejas a secret from her family and friends. Rinki has matured into meaningful love. Thus, as a whole, Vibha's trilogy is a depiction of how Rinki adapts to change, how she handles everything life (and her parents and her teachers and in some cases friends) throws at her.

What is special about Vibha's trilogy isn't just that the main characters are teenagers—Rinki and her gang. What is more significant is that the novels see the world through young adults' eyes. Vibha has stepped into the shoes of teenagers or, as I would say, at heart she is a teenager; her mindset is that of a young adult who has just discovered the secrets of sex, and love, a teen who has just experimented with partying, who has just been weirdly identifying her emotions with music and who has begun enjoying her lot as emotionally addicted to films—someone who has a good playlist of music and a wide collection of films to seek solace for all emotional turbulence and heightened joyful moments, a teenager active online who has made Facebook contacts and Blackberry messages as necessary as life-breath itself. It is Vibha's lack of narrative distancing from young adults that leads to the success of her writing style. We the adult readers can appreciate Vibha only if we have a bit of the teenager left in us. Do we? Yes, definitely, as scholars of children's and young adult literature, we do. In fact, everyone has a teenager hidden inside; it's only that the embers are dying. YAL authors attempt to ignite that fire again. As Veronica Roth, the author of YA trilogy *Divergent* says, "I think everyone's got a little teenager inside of them still and you have to work to help yourself access that teenager" (*Atlantic*). Vibha does precisely this; hence, hers are books meant not only for teenagers but for everyone who has the spirit of the teenager in them. Vibha, then, aids the adult readers to shed the masks of serious adulthood, the hypocrisies we have cherished as our own selves. Reading this YA trilogy we can definitely say that at certain stages of it we are unknowingly tempted to set aside adulthood to try to live like the new generation. Just to share a secret: In fact, I, who often shunned Facebook culture until I seriously read Vibha, suddenly found myself at the computer unthinkingly opening a Facebook account! I argue that, while redefining girlhood, Vibha Batra has defined the characteristics of YAL in Indian English children's literature for girls in certain unique ways quite unknown to critical readers in general. So we need to explore these unique aspects of her writing style, which takes us to the core argument of this article on Indian YA chick lit.

II

> Place is a stage and practice of power; it is also the site of great pleasure
> and possibilities . . . Just as place as a concept is of great significance to
> geography, so too, is it crucial to the study of girlhood.
>
> (Mitchell & Rentschler 1)

YA Chick Lit

Chick lit is a popular subgenre of adult literature for young women that first appeared in England at the last part of the twentieth century with the publication of Helen Fielding's *Bridget Jones' Diary* (1996). Subsequently, there have been many variants of this genre especially in the United States and in other linguistic literary traditions like in France, Poland, Italy, Finland, Hungary, and so on. When we consider the Indian experimentations in chick lit, it is noteworthy that diasporic Indian-American authors attempted writing chick lit first. Kavita Daswani's debut novel *Matrimonial Purposes* (2003) was the forerunner but many other novelists pursued this path. Domestic publication of chick lit soon emerged when Penguin India Books published Swati Kaushal's *Piece of Cake* (2004). This book launch was successful and soon there were many chick lit novels for adult readers in India like Rajashree's *Trust Me* (2006), Advaita Kala's *Almost Single* (2007) and Rupa Gulab's *Girl Alone* (2009).

Chick literature for adolescent readers is a new sub-genre in India and Vibha Batra is the premier author of this type of YAL in the Indian context, and no doubt she is worthy of popular accolades after having successfully published the Rinki trilogy. A discussion of girlhood and identity in Indian YA chick lit is essential especially when YA chick lit, which got established in the early twenty-first century, in general, garners academic disdain even though it builds on a feminist/postfeminist children's literature tradition. The Rinki series addresses classic issues of YA fiction: coming of age, place and identity, sexuality, and material culture. Concurrently, these issues are postfeminist concerns too.

The Rinki series moves beyond the traditional format of fiction writing. Rinki, like every adolescent, establishes her virtual digital identity on Facebook, Blackberry Messenger and Twitter. Every chapter in *Sweet Sixteen* begins with a Facebook status update; each chapter in *Seventeen and Done* has an initial entry on Blackberry Messenger Status; Rinki's Twitter identity as "Rinki Tripathi@Chennai SuperChick" dominates every chapter heading in *Eighteen and Wiser*. These novels break the traditions of fictional narrative by often incorporating e-mails, letters, cell phone calls, diary entries, text messages, instant messaging blurbs, online quizzes, online psychological tests, and website postings in conjunction with traditional fictional narratives. The narrative style reflects current register of language and the frequent usage of slang and obscenity, and employs methods of communication that weren't popular until a few years ago. Because of these out of the ordinary and trendy movements of style readers may mistake Vibha Batra for an innovative writer; but she is conforming to the writing style of chick lit, and there is nothing exceptional about it if we comprehend how chick lit creates a literary tradition of its own.

Young adult chick lit has a pattern, which Campbell (2010) describes concisely: at the center of YA chick lit is a girl who finds herself an outsider at her school because she is newly arrived from somewhere else. The school is dominated by the Queen Bitch and her friends. The protagonist's major epiphany is closely associated with her dangerous hook up with the Queen Bitch's boyfriend, which results in outrageous retaliation from the Queen Bitch. Into this pattern fit common chick lit themes such as eating, shopping and female sexuality, as well as certain characteristic traits like detailed descriptions of clothes, recurrent references to brand names, cell-phones, computers, iPods and other electronic toys generally to narrate the current story apparently to an absent best friend and perceptibly to the reader. Other characteristic components are exclusive private schools, relaxed attitude towards grades and bunking classes, and casual sex. These novels also picture smoking as an indication of sophistication, drinking liquor, subsequent vomiting, parties at which there is no adult surveillance but lots of consumption of alcohol and drugs, very loud music, and dance. The peer group reels in profligate spending. Quite contrary to the social reality of India as a developing country striving towards eradication of poverty, we find these characteristics of Western-developed countries' extravaganza as the dominant traits of Vibha Batra's Rinki series, and thus the novels are meant as reading material for the pleasure of the elite upper middle class, educated, urban youngsters of India whose cultural values and habits are akin to the cultural habits of the Western-sophisticated society. The novelist expresses the newly emerging girl sensibility through a presentation of the living language of twenty-first century, educated, urban, middle-class girls in India.

YA chick lit novels are good examples of coming of age fiction. They help young female readers to make their transition into adulthood by identifying with the protagonist who faces similar situations in life. While the protagonist may seek advice and guidance from peers, she ultimately encounters the reality of life all alone; she learns that she alone is responsible for her own actions. Therefore, Joanna Webb Johnson's study on YA chick lit concludes by emphasizing the significance of chick lit in the coming of age process of contemporary adolescent girls. Speaking of chick lit books for young adults, she says, "They have offered guidance and direction to young women while providing insight into historical and popular culture" (156). YA chick lit is an important source of cultural information for young female readers and it portrays adolescents negotiating the social and sexual standards of the dominant culture. Coming of age is complete with the process of establishing one's identity and finding one's role in life while simultaneously confronting one's emerging sexuality. YA chick lit protagonists attain these stages of maturity and comfort adolescent readers about similar maturation processes in their own lives.

Spatial Identity in YA Chick Lit

Linking place with identity is, especially for young adults, a determinant of meaningful life. Hence, YAL in general and YA chick lit in particular consider space and identity important factors. Although young adults often welcome change and are open to being in a new place, YA chick lit often begins with the phobic discomforts of dislocation from one's favorite geographic boundaries. Place, thus, occupies a key role in YA chick lit. Rinki's first Facebook status update, "If you've ever been uprooted, hauled to a strange place, snatched away from loving friends by heartless parents, paste this as your status message" (*Sweet Sixteen* 1), makes all young adult readers empathize with potential geographic displacements that young adults fear. Young adults associate place with their own identity and dislocation is discomforting because it is a threat to the coherence of their identity. The displacement is often caused by the adult world, for parents and others often are capable, as Ankita, Rinki's BFF, fears, of uprooting a young adult "like an unwanted plant and flung away to a remote, hostile terrain" (8). Therefore, troublesome adults, the potential causes of displacement, are the Other in YA chick literature. These novels project the view that adults do not understand young adults, as there can be no bridge of comprehension between young adults and normal adults.

Place and falling in love are closely associated in young adult chic lit. The way Rinki introduces her romantic lover Tejas is to be noted: "It was there that I first saw him. Tejas" (53). Site does matter when it is the case of love at first sight. Rinki narrates:

> I was huddled with Robin and Sudha in some remote corner, my back to the entrance, when a sudden hush fell over the auditorium. I looked up quizzically and by some magnetic force, my gaze was drawn to him. It was crush, infatuation, adoration, admiration, adulation—everything at first sight. (53)

During the first-year students' Freshers' Party, luck delays a bit in bringing Rinki and Tejas together as the prize-winning couple. Later, when Rinki opts to take part in the school's face-painting competition, Tejas volunteers to be the model for face painting. One of the first questions Tejas asks Rinki connects place and love. He asks, "Chennai. Do you like it?" (77). Perhaps, that question relating to place moves Rinki to the dizzy heights of love and she coolly paints her masterpiece, drawing a peacock on Tejas' face. It is a moment of triumph for the protagonist as she confronts Priya, the Queen Bitch, who is now angry with Rinki for having won Tejas' love. The physical defeat of the Queen Bitch later culminates in the changing room during the fashion show competition when Priya's long mane gets entangled in the blades of the rusted stand-fan and her stresses trapped in the fan have to be cut extremely short. With the love and friendship of Tejas, Rinki's new place is transformed. Initially, Rinki hates her transfer to Chennai. Her Facebook status couldn't afford to give a single positive comment about Chennai. As she develops a deep crush with Tejas, the place undergoes a metamorphosis and she updates her Facebook status: "Delhi – 0 Chennai – 1" (134). Lovers often feel the constraints of place that prevent them from really being in love. When Tejas requests that Rinki spend the weekend with him, she refuses because that Sunday is her mother's birthday and the family spends the time together on such occasions. Then, Rinki thinks, "Why couldn't I be in two places at the same time?" (148). Unfortunately at the end of the year, Rinki misses the students' excursion from school and adding to her tension Tejas and Priya do go on the tour. When the school picnic is set to Ooty, Rinki has to accompany her family to Delhi. Rinki is angry at the bitch queen who rips her lover from her and her emotional tirade highlights her hatred for Priya, "That viper, snake, queen cobra, anaconda, black mamba was trying to wrap herself around my TJ, MY TJ!" (161). Tejas is bewitched by Priya, and Rinki feels lost. But when the story comes full circle, someone turns time back, and Rinki reimagines her love for Tejas: "He was Adam. I was Eve. There was no trouble in paradise. And rotten apple Priya was a tiny speck of dirt under my shoes" (174).

To emphasize the importance of location in YA identity, in the prologue to the second book in the series Rinki begins her Facebook status update by joining the group, "I am from Chennai and that automatically makes me a hundred times cooler than you" (*Seventeen and Done* 1). Ultimately, being young is a physical space or a geographical place; Vibha Batra's term "Youngistan" suits our sense of spatial existence (33). However, parents or adults resemble the Taliban in Afghanistan as Rinki constructs a Parent Comparison Chart of Sudha's and her own parents (33). As a first year college student, in the third book in the series, Rinki bunks the college tour to Bengaluru along with her close friends Robin and Sudha. Rinki has a secret as she persuades her best friends to a trip to Pondicherry while the whole college goes on the tour. Tejas invites her outside from her hotel to spend the night with him and Rinki, wearing her night suit with the dolphin image, makes an adventurous trip to meet him. This is reminiscent of the earlier rendezvous that Rinki and Tejas had in the discotheque at night when Robin and Sudha chaperoned her to Tejas, and Rinki tricked her neighbor Sriram and made her parents believe she was under his guardianship and had gone for the late-night movie. At the end of the series, Rinki declares, "I finally had a real-life, non-imaginary, gorgeous boyfriend" (*Eighteen and Wiser* 192). Space, thus, plays a significant role in YA identity.

Postfeminist Girlhood in YA Chick Lit

Urban-educated Indian teenage girls inhabit a media-dominated environment and sexualized accounts of femininity pervade popular culture. Reading materials furnished to these female young adults are monopolized by postfeminist young women writers that use fiction as tropes of empowerment. Thus, young adult chick lit is congruent with the interests of adult chick lit, which is "historically synchronous with postfeminism" (Bullen 497). YA chick lit is often misunderstood as celebrations of postfeminism with a focus on consumerism, sexuality, gender identity empowerment, and the promotion of teen friendship. Its emphasis on pedagogical function in the process of coming of age of teenage girls is often not represented properly in the critical tradition. Critical research that is multidisciplinary in approach, drawing on feminist girlhood studies, children's literature, education, and cultural studies may alter our demeaning perspective on young adult chick lit. YA chick lit is a popular medium for the enculturation of the young generation, and the interests of the young adult implied audience are sustained by the multimedia format that facilitates media convergence through fiction, bringing young adult chick lit into the realm of media and cultural studies. Even our established children's literature critics in India overlook YA chick lit that operates on the fringes of the mass-mediated literature cultures of postfeminism and consumer capitalism. Vibha Batra's Rinki series is intricately linked to postfeminist girlhood and sexual identity. In other words, postfeminism is the context out of which this pioneering work in teen chick lit emerges. Recurrently, the Rinki series conveys messages of female sexual empowerment. Rinki's narratives and the metaphors and images Vibha Batra uses construct an image of urban, educated, postmodern Indian twenty-first century girlhood and shape the thoughts of liberated girls in India: how they think of themselves and their sexuality and how they evaluate their relationships with others. Thus, the Rinki series has become a pioneering text of Indian YA chick lit, confessing the long-suppressed desires of educated urban girls in my country. By imagining their own selves and sexuality, they empower their own identity. In fact, Vibha Batra plays a significant role in recasting Indian young girls as active agents of their own destiny in our contemporary society. The image of the shy, traditional Indian girl is just a fiction in the urban Indian context where social life is increasingly supporting individual freedom, and contemporary girls have to become responsible for their life choices and decisions. The protagonists of young adult chick lit express their sexual identities in lucid ways when they live in a media saturated society and acquire the lifestyle prone to consumption of brand name products. What sort of sexual identities are the implied teenage readers introduced into in Indian YA chick lit? How is teenage girls' sexual identity narrativized in chick lit? To what extent does the promotion of sexual freedom and choice in chick lit fiction empower/weaken Indian girlhood?

I have argued that the Rinki series is essentially a postfeminist text. What makes a novel postfeminist? Here I resort to the understanding of Rosalind Gill (2007), who notes that perspectives specific to sexual knowledge and sexual practice are fundamental to the postfeminist sensibility. In promoting a postfeminist sensibility, women construct their own sexual self, independent of male desires and expectations of female self by a process of reconfiguration of male gaze. Thereby, women are empowered with their sexual agency as well as in sexual control. These writings, Gill suggests, expose the view that girls are free agents in exploring their own sexual identity. This is exactly what Rinki achieves as a teenage girl who develops her own mature vision of sex and sexual identity at the end of the novel. Postfeminism is the framework which makes possible this socio-cultural landscape possible. Again, Coleman's (2009) study differentiating feminism and postfeminism note the basic difference. According to her, "feminism had never only ever been about individual women's gains and empowerment, that feminism was about the bigger picture, about social relations and systemic injustices (3). On the other hand, postfeminism is essentially on "individual women and free choice" (4). C.M. Orr further clarifies, "Post-feminism assumes that the women's movement took care of oppressive institutions, and that now it is up to individual women to make personal choices that simply reinforce those fundamental social changes" (34). Vibha Batra does not enchant us with a fairytale world of happily-ever-after but there aren't any hints of failure in love too. Thus, the Rinki series is built around Rinki's discourse of choice, freedom and empowerment, leading to her maturation into a mature girl with strong sexual and gender identity.

Conclusion

In our age of globalization, materialism, consumer culture, and media saturation, Vibha Batra's Rinki series offers robust analyses of agency, of resistance, and of subversion in the context of contemporary Indian girlhood. Thus, Indian YA chick lit imagines futures for young women in ways that resist conventional and regressive ideas of femininity, sexuality, identity, and girlhood.

Works Cited

Atlantic. "The 8 Habits of Highly Successful Young-Adult Fiction Authors". 22 October 2013. Accessed on 10 May 2017. <https://www.theatlantic.com/ entertainment/archive/2013/10/he8habitsofhighlysuccessfulyoungadultfiction authors/280722/>

Batra, Vibha. *Sweet Sixteen (Yeah, Right!)*. New Delhi: Penguin Books, 2012.

________. *Seventeen and Done (You Bet!)*. New Delhi: Inked-Penguin, 2013.

________. *Eighteen and Wiser (Not Quite!)*. New Delhi: Inked-Penguin, 2014.

Bullen, Elizabeth, Kim Toffoletti, and Liz Parsons. "Doing what your Big Sister Does: Sex, Postfeminism and the YA Chick Lit Series". *Gender and Education*. 25.4 (2011): 497-511.

Campbell, Patty. *Campbell's Scoop: Reflections on Young Adult Literature*. Lanham & Plymouth: Scarecrow Press, 2010.

Coleman, Jenny. "An Introduction to Feminism in a Postfeminist Age". *Women's Studies Journal*. 23.2 (2009): 3-13.

Dalai, Panchanan. "Don't Tell My Mother". *Muse India*. 72 (Mar-Apr 2017): n.p. http://museindia.com/featurecontent.asp?issid=39&id=2826. Accessed on 02 April 2017.

Daniels, Cindy Lou. "Literary Theory and Young Adult Literature: The Open Frontier in Critical Studies". *Alan Review*. 33.2 (Winter 2006): 78-82.

Gill, Rosalind. "Postfeminist Media Culture: Elements of a Sensibility". *European Journal of Cultural Studies*. 10 (2007): 147-66.

Interview. "I Think of Myself as a Young Adult: Vibha Batra". *Deccan Chronicle*. June 4, 2014. http://www.deccanchronicle.com/140604/lifestyle-booksart/article/i-think-myself-young-adult-vibha-batra. Accessed on October 14, 2015.

Kaplan, Jeffrey S. "Perception and Reality: Examining the Representations of Adolescents in Young Adult Fiction". *Alan Review*. 36.1 (Fall 2008): 42-49.

Mitchell, Claudia and Carrie Rentschler. (Eds). *Girlhood and the Politics of Place*. New York & Oxford: Berghahn Books, 2016.

Orr, C.M. "Charting the Currents of the Third Wave". *Hypatia*. 12.3 (1997): 29-45.

Rangachari, Devika. "Gender as an Issue in YAL". *Muse India*. 72 (Mar-Apr 2017): n.p. http://museindia.com/featurecontent.asp?issid=39&id=2826. Accessed on 6 April 2017.

________. "Coming-of-Age Books That Have Come of Age". *Crossing Boundaries: Translations and Migrations: Proceedings of the 33rd IBBY International Congress,* 23-26 August 2012. http://www.congress2012.ibby.org.uk/transcripts.php. Accessed on 03 March 2015.

Stephens, Jonathan. "Young Adult: A Book by any Other Name...: Defining the Genre". *Alan Review.* 35.1 (Fall 2007): 34-42.

Trites, Roberta Seelinger. *Disturbing the Universe: Power and Repression in Adolescent Literature.* Iowa City: University of Iowa Press, 2000.

Webb Johnson, Joanna. "Chick Lit Jr.: More than Glitz and Glamour for Teens and Tweens". In: Ferriss, Suzanne and Mallory Young (Eds). *Chick Lit: The New Woman's Fiction.* New York & London: Routledge, 2006.

Younger, Beth. *Learning Curves: Body Image and Female Sexuality in Young Adult Literature.* Lanham & Plymouth: Scarecrow Press, 2009.

3

YA Novels in the College Classroom: A Space to Create Social Justice Warriors

Padma Baliga and *Livia Antony*

The move from school to college generally takes young people in India from a fairly homogenous atmosphere to a heterogenous one, where they come across students from different socio-economic and cultural backgrounds, subscribing to various thought processes and ideologies. Students encounter questions of privilege and power, or the lack of them. Patterns of discrimination and bigotry that were present but possibly unseen in their safe, homogenous school set-ups now emerge as a glaring part of systemic inequality. At such a juncture, a language or a literature classroom in college can be fruitfully transformed into a place where teachers not only offer academic instruction but use fiction to create a forum for promotion of critical thinking, self-reflection, empowering conversations, and questioning of social inequality. An impactful way of bringing in questions of social justice into the classroom space is by using Young Adult (YA) novels for this purpose. Getting college students to read literature that connects to the world, they live in is helpful in preparing them for the transition into adulthood. In this paper, we shall explore the possibilities of introducing a selection of Indian YA to college students to open up a discussion on social justice. Due to space constraints, we shall focus on two recent texts, Malik Sajad's (2015) graphic novel, *Munnu: A Boy from Kashmir* and Swati Sengupta's (2013) *Guns on My Red Earth*.

Lee Anne Bell writes that social justice education is necessary in our schools and colleges today "to enable people to develop the critical analytical tools necessary to understand oppression and their own socialization within oppressive systems, and to develop a sense of agency and capacity to interrupt and change oppressive patterns and behaviours in themselves and in the institutions and communities of which they are a part" (2). In this paper, we shall make use of Bell's definition of the term 'oppression': "Oppression signifies a hierarchical relationship in which dominant or privileged groups reap advantage, often in unconscious ways, from the disempowerment of targeted groups... (It) encapsulates the fusion of institutional and systemic discrimination, personal bias, bigotry, and social prejudice in a complex web of relationships and structures that shade most aspects of life in our society" (3). Boys, upper-caste/upper-class students, and urban residents are in a privileged position as against girls, students from marginalized castes and classes, and from rural areas for they benefit from a social and educational system that is biased towards them.

A number of YA novels such as Robert Cormier' *The Chocolate War,* S.E. Hinton's *The Outsiders,* Sherman Alexie's *The Absolutely True Diary of a Part-Time Indian* are built around this theme of being different, being excluded. The Harry Potter series also has Harry feeling excluded and hated on various occasions. While in the later books, it is because of his perceived behaviour, in the first book, it is Harry's status of being poor and an orphan that marks him as an 'outsider'. Antero Garcia writes "the YA genre romanticizes the *other* within books" (60). While in real life, the poor, the physically challenged, the students from unprivileged backgrounds are marginalized and their voices unheard, within the YAL genre, their voices become the dominant voices, and their stories take centerstage.

YA literature has also made use of genres like science fiction and dystopian narratives to engage with real world problems and the need for social change. Roberta Seelinger Trites argues that socially-conscious adolescent literature originated in America in the nineteenth century in the works of Mark Twain and Louisa May Alcott. Both Alcott and Twain, she writes, "relied on adolescents as metaphors for reform; that is, for both of them, the young represented the capacity for change that is necessary for a culture itself to change...their youthful protagonists provided them with a site for the potential to change that is a prerequisite of reform" (xiv). Julia Mickenberg too points out in *Learning from the Left* that in mid-twentieth century, political and social oppositional groups made use of children's literature (considered trivial and unimportant by mainstream writers and critics) to promote a leftist and feminist ideology.

As the children's book publishing industry in India matures, we see the emergence of narratives that are not about fairytale romances or happy school adventures, but deal with darker themes of death, torture, caste, rape and alternate sexualities. *Faces in the Water* by Ranjit Lal tackles the problem of female foeticide by bringing 'alive' the 'ghosts' of the dead girls and taking their brother (and the implied reader) into their lives, their dreams and achievements. *No Guns at My Son's Funeral* and *Weed* by Paro Anand offer us a slightly left-of-centre view of the political crisis in Kashmir as it impacts the children. Payal Dhar's *Burnt Smoke* and Himanjali Sankar's *Talking of Muskaan* deal with protagonists who discover their gay/lesbian identity, and the reactions of friends and family members.

Literature Review

In this paper, we shall draw primarily upon the work of Paulo Freire who wrote about education being a political act, for a teacher who uses a critical pedagogy teaches her students to think and ask questions and seek to make a change. Freire argues that the "banking system" of education fixes people in their oppression (Freire 45). Instead, educators should engage their students in a 'dialogue' to enhance critical thinking and understand oppression (53). The introduction of dialogue in the education system will allow students to perceive the injustice around them, if 'meaningful themes' are introduced into education. Employing content drawn from the self-expression of the oppressed peoples will establish problem-posing education instead of the banking system (80). In addition, the content must relate to a context-driven reality that Freire envisioned as part of a dialogic education that would replace the banking system.

The question of whether reading a carefully curated set of books can impact the cognitive and affective processes of children and adolescents has been studied by several scholars. Kidd and Castano's study of over a thousand participants in a series of experiments indicate that reading literary fiction, in which the writer portrays a character's innermost thoughts and feelings, prompts readers to understand that there are different circumstances, different perspectives, different belief systems, needs and wants. This is a big step in developing empathy in children, and teaching them to be social beings.

Vezzali, Stathi, and Giovannini examined the role of books in improving children's attitudes to those they considered the Other. The 11-13-year-old Italian children they studied read carefully curated books which represented children from different cultures positively. As a result, the attitudes of the children in the study group towards immigrants also changed for the better and they became less likely to believe in immigrant stereotypes.

Bal and Veltkampf's work shows that if a reader is "emotionally transported" into the story, the empathy that is sparked can last for several days after finishing reading. They argue that "there is evidence suggesting that seeing or reading about another person experiencing specific emotions and events activates the same neural structures as if one was experiencing them oneself, consequently influencing empathy" (2).

In their book, *Rethinking Our Classrooms,* Au, Bigelow and Karp declare that if "curriculum and classroom practice" were enabling of critical responses; grounded in the lives of students; participatory; multicultural and pro-justice; while also being visionary and joyful, then "classrooms can be places of hope, where students and teachers gain glimpses of the kind of society we live in and where students learn the academic and critical skills needed to make it a reality" ("Introduction" x-xi).

Munnu: A Boy from Kashmir

Munnu is a graphic novel in the tradition of Marjane Satrapi's *Persepolis* and Art Spiegelman's *Maus,* and like them, makes use of the comic book form to talk about individual history by placing it within the context of national history. The narratives of the nation and the individual intersect and pull at each other as each tries to subsume/resist the other.

Set in Kashmir, famous for its spectacular landscape and its dense militarisation, the novel traces the life of young Munnu who grows up amidst the anti-India insurgency of the 1990s. His lessons in art include "sketching the photos of unrecognisable, disfigured people from the newspapers" (5), people who had been shot at and killed and their bodies mutilated. His schooling is constantly disrupted when teachers and principals sympathetic to the militants' cause are arrested. But through panels that depict teachers using the same methods of torture on their students that the Army imposes on the civilians, Sajad reminds us that everyone, victim, oppressor or bystander, needs to develop a critical self-reflexive perspective or become an agent of systemic injustice. As Freire wrote, "during the initial stage of the struggle, the oppressed, instead of striving for liberation, tend themselves to become oppressors, or 'sub-oppressors.' The very structure of their thought has been conditioned by the contradictions of the concrete, existential situation by which they were shaped. Their ideal is to be men; but for them, to be men is to be oppressors. This is their model of humanity" (45). Sajad's narrative liberates the reader by showing a way out of such horizontal violence.

Munnu makes use of the visual element to remind the reader that the Indian Government's treatment of Kashmir and Kashmiris has resulted in alienating the people of Kashmir from the state of India and from their land as well. The landscape of Kashmir that we see in the panels of the graphic novel is dark and somber, dotted not with chinar trees and snow-capped mountains but with dead bodies and memorials for the dead. The people of Kashmir are represented as hangul deer that are native to Kashmir, while the Indians and foreigners are depicted as human, in defiance of the traditional manner of depicting the enemy as monstrous. While narratives of nationalism depict smiling jubilant Indians rallying around the tricolour, in *Munnu*, the people of Kashmir come together as a community to mourn the dead (34-36, 64-70). Through this, Sajad invites the reader to think about what it is to be 'human' and 'animal', to dwell in ambiguity, and to appreciate the complexity of the Kashmir narrative.

Munnu problematizes words that have become a part of our everyday vocabulary. What do words like ‘home’, ‘belonging’, ‘foreign’ or ‘enemy’ mean when one has been living in a conflict zone for decades? Can Kashmiris feel at home when the streets are filled with the menacing presence of soldiers, sandbags, machine guns and barricades (61, 74-75)? If they cannot venture out freely to meet a friend or buy medicines, can they feel a sense of belonging to the nation that has subsumed their identity and their existence (54-55, 73)? How can their home be a place of refuge if it can be invaded by the Indian Army at any time of the day or night (32-33)? Another book that deals with the 1990s insurgency and its fallout in Kashmir is Basharat Peer’s memoir, *Curfewed Night*. Set in the same time period, it too recounts the author’s experiences as a Kashmiri teenager. In it, Peer writes, “The line of control did not run through 576 kilometres of militarised mountains.... It ran through everything a Kashmiri, an Indian and a Pakistani said, wrote, and did...it ran through families and dinner talk, it ran through whispers of lovers. And it ran through our grief, our anger, our tears, and our silence” (238). A sensitive and thoughtful teacher can use *Munnu* and related texts to encourage students to question media reports of encounters between the government and the citizens; between dominant groups and oppressed groups; and search for a truth that may be more nuanced. Students can also be taught to look inward, to look at the spaces and the people around them with a critical lens.

Guns on My Red Earth

Among India’s most underrepresented peoples are the collection of communities, tribes and districts that make up the ‘Red Corridor’. This consists of districts that have been part of the Naxalite/Maoist movement or in Central Government parlance, “Left-Wing Extremism” (Ramani), and are marked by dire poverty and a large tribal population. Over a long period of time, some of these tribes were absorbed into the caste system of India, especially into the lowest strata (von Fürer-Haimendorf 33). There is a long history of conflict between the tribes and centralised governmental structures that has resulted in the violence that continues in modern-day India. The forms of violence that the Adivasi tribes have endured and continue to endure are manifold, ranging from displacement, sexual assault, physical violence and incarceration. While writers like Arundhati Roy (*Walking with Comrades*) and Rahul Pandita (*Hello Bastar*) argue that the presence of the Naxalites prevents further displacement of the tribals from governmental development projects, there is also the problem of the tribal communities caught in the crossfire between Naxals and the State. The State uses incarceration, torture and 'fake encounters' as tools to counter 'Left-Wing Extremism'; sometimes, innocent tribals and activists are imprisoned as suspected Naxalites. Writers like Mahasweta Devi have represented the sufferings of the tribals extensively and sympathetically in their fiction, but the genre of children's and YA literature has been slow to offer a space for their voices and lives.

Swati Sengupta's *Guns on My Red Earth* attempts to represent the predicament of the tribals of the Red Corridor. It follows the story of a young boy Shanto, raised in Chhotopelia, Lalgarh, in the predominantly tribal belt of Jangalmahal in West Bengal, also a major site of Naxalite activity. Shanto's parents abandoned him as an infant to be raised by his aunt Ashtami and uncle Sukumar, following the strict maxims of the Naxalite movement where, "those who lived and worked in armed Maoist squads were not encouraged to have or keep babies as it hindered their operations" (Sengupta 10). The trope of the abandoned child is common in children's fiction as the reader is more likely to empathise with the situation of the abandoned child. But there is a departure here as the context for Shanto's abandonment is political.

Shanto is asked to help the Maoists by a friend of his called Jhuntu dada even though he is only fourteen years old. He acts as a spy, gathering information about the movement of police forces around Lalgarh. Shanto decides to leave the Maoists after an ambush killed several policemen and civilians, triggering a series of events that climax with him rejecting the violence of the state and the Maoists. Shanto's decision needs to take into account both parties—"And then there was the fear of the

Maoists *and* (emphasis author's own) the police. Neither would spare him" (59). The narrative challenges the Maoist as well as the State forces because of the violence they engage in. The text is written in a realistic manner through Shanto's point of view. His thought process is empathetic to his surroundings and he understands the cause of the oppression from the point of view of both the State and the Naxalites. This empathy augments the moral ambiguity of the text.

Depictions of violence are common across Shanto's narrative. True to the trope of the abandoned child, Shanto's aunt and uncle blame him for their poverty. Shanto is terrified of Sukumar when he is drunk because "He would kick him unsteadily, his kicks and slaps would make Shanto bleed from the nose" (9). Paulo Freire describes this kind of violence as horizontal violence that occurs because the oppressed have internalized the consciousness of the oppressors (22). Shanto's Maoist group ambushes and kills policemen for no apparent reason, exulting in the death of the policemen. Shanto is captured by the police and tortured for any information that he can give them. The graphic description of the torture inflicted on a fourteen-year-old could draw the reader's sympathy towards the countless unnamed tribals who experience this as part of their everyday life.

However, the teaching of this text must include historicization and introduce a deeper understanding of what fictionalisation of a historical struggle implies. There are discrepancies in Sengupta's text. It de-contextualises the male tribal boy as the reader is unable to find markers of tribal identity or even mentions of the history of Lalgarh. Since the Bon Party is mentioned in the text, it is to be assumed that this occurred after the events of Operation Lalgarh (2008-09), aimed at defeating an armed tribal movement. The tribal movement came to be associated with the Maoists over time and its brutal suppression has not been made public. In this regard, it is an omission on the part of the author to overlook the question of Adivasi identity. The Maoists as represented in this book are also at contradiction with Rahul Pandita's history of the movement. He states that the Maoist supreme commander Ganapathi said, "Only when the government forces come to attack us carrying guns do we attack them in self-defence" (48). Thus, the targeting of civilians on the train, which is part of the climax of the text, is inconsistent with what Ganapathi mentions.

Conclusion

Nurturing the spirit of nationalism entails the merging of personal, individual memories with the memories of the larger community, the nation. Using select YA texts, the teacher can initiate a discussion about the ways in which dominant narratives of nationalism create a subset of individual memories centring around British rule, the freedom struggle, and the savouring of independence. Narratives can be undercut through the use of novels that speak from the margin, and subvert the centre. For instance, Arundathi Roy's *The God of Small Things* can be used to have a conversation about the presence of untouchability in Indian society and its insidious entry into all religions. Siddalingaiah's memoir *A Word with You, World,* does not normally classify as YA writing, but it contains a searing and lively description of his childhood and youth as a Dalit. We read of his father being yoked to the plough in place of a bullock, and getting whipped as he ploughed the land (1-2). What does freedom from British rule mean if a group of Indians continue to have the power of life and death over other Indians? What can 'independence' symbolize to the Dalit who is dehumanized and treated as a non-entity? Yet, Siddalingaiah also writes, "The people of our colony were dreamers of dreams" and uses the registers of mischief and laughter to overcome the injustice that marks his world.

Increasingly, we seem to be living in a world marked by prejudice, suspicion of the other, and a slant towards the status quo. Such a society would spell danger for democracy, equality and freedom. Students need to learn within the setting of the classroom to engage in debate, to ponder over issues of injustice and discrimination, and to intervene when necessary. Using young adult texts, students can be encouraged to think of their identity vis-à-vis that of the protagonists, and ask themselves where the differences lie, what causes them and how they can be eradicated. Teachers can tap into their own reading to begin to work towards change by creating a space where young people learn to distinguish nuances, recognize oppression and power play, and act accordingly.

Works Cited

Au, Wayne, Bill Bigelow and Stan Karp. *Rethinking Our Classrooms: Teaching for Equity and Justice.* Rethinking Schools, 2007.

Bal, Matthijs P. and Martijn Veltkamp. "How Does Fiction Reading Influence Empathy? An Experimental Investigation on the Role of Emotional Transportation." *PLoS ONE.* 8(1): e55341, January 30, 2013, pp. 1-12. https://doi.org/10.1371/journal.pone.0055341.

Bell, Lee Anne. "Theoretical Foundations for Social Justice Education." *Teaching for Diversity and Social Justice,* edited by Maurianne Adams, Lee Anne Bell and Pat Griffin, Routledge, 2007, pp. 1-14.

Freire, Paulo. *Pedagogy of the Oppressed.* Translated by Myra Bergman Ramos, Bloomsbury, 2012.

Garcia, Antero. *Critical Foundations in Young Adult Literature: Challenging Genres.* Sense Publishers, 2013.

Kidd, David Comer and Emanuele Castano. "Reading Literary Fiction Improves Theory of Mind." *Science,* 342, 6156, October 18, 2013, pp. 377-80.

Lal, Ranjit. *Faces in the Water.* Puffin, 2010.

Mickenberg, Julia. *Learning from the Left.* Oxford University Press, 2006.

Pandita, Rahul. *Hello Bastar.* Tranquebar Press, 2011.

Peer, Basharat. *Curfewed Night.* Random House India, 2009.

Sajad, Malik. *Munnu: A Boy from Kashmir.* Fourth Estate, 2015.

Sengupta, Swati. *Guns on my Red Earth.* Rupa, 2013.

Siddalingaiah. *A Word with You, World: The Autobiography of a Poet.* Translated by S.R. Ramakrishna, Navayana, 2013.

Trites, Roberta Seelinger. *Twain, Alcott, and the Birth of the Adolescent Reform Novel.* University of Iowa Press, 2007.

Vezzali, L., S. Stathi, and D. Giovannini. "Indirect contact through book reading: Improving adolescents' attitudes and behavioral intentions toward immigrants." *Psychology in the Schools*, 49, 2012, pp. 148-62.

von Fürer-Haimendorf, Christoph. *Tribes of India: The Struggle for Survival*. University of California Press, 1982.

4

'I Infer, So I Am Free!'—On How Shane Peacock has Subverted the Doylean Conception of Inference in Persuading Young Readers in *Eye of the Crow: The Boy Sherlock Holmes, His 1st Case*

Billy Bin Feng Huang

> Emotion is to fiction as truth is to science.... Fictional narrative has its impact primarily through the emotions. When an emotion occurs, we experience it as striking. Sometimes a novel can affect a person's whole identity.
>
> Keith Oatley, "Emotions and the Story Worlds of Fiction," 39.

> Finally there's the solution of the puzzle and this may be why the detective story is so popular in ages of anxiety.... That may well be the attraction of these small literary celebrations of order and reason in our increasingly disordered world.
>
> P.D. James, "The Art of the Detective Novel," 9.

I. Introduction

W. Labov defines a narrative as "one method of recapitulating past experience by matching a verbal sequence of clauses to the sequence of events which (it is inferred) actually occurred" (Language in the Inner City, 359-60). That is, a narrative is a way of verbally reorganizing certain past events, actual or non-actual. And Oatley has argued that even a fictional narrative has a striking power of evoking readers' emotions or even changing their identities. By Melanie C. Green and Timothy C. Brock's theory, it is precisely this power that makes it possible for an author to persuade his or her readers of certain values. Speaking of persuasion, it is one of the paramount objectives of young adult literature. According to Virginia M. Henderson, good young adult literature should provide young readers with the "opportunities and models for learning...[these] positive messages..." ("The Development of Self-Esteem in Children of Color," 20-24); that is, young readers should be persuaded to embrace these positive messages in reading young adult literature. On the other hand, Shane Peacock's *Eye of the Crow: The Boy Sherlock Holmes, His 1st Case*, the first novel of the series, depicts the adventures of young Sherlock Holmes. Above all, it is indeed an exemplary text of young adult fiction; it has won a bunch of awards so far, such as the Violet Downey Award for Best Children's Book in Canada, the Arthur Ellis Award for Best Juvenile Crime Fiction in Canada, etc. Besides, it has secured a spot on the list of the American Library Association's Top Ten Youth Mysteries. In this paper, I intend to draw parallelism between Melanie C. Green and Timothy C. Brock's transportation theory and young adult literature, in order to address my first point: the fundamental aim of young adult literature is to persuade young readers. My second point is that while persuading his young audience, Peacock has literally subverted the Doylean conception of inference in *Eye of the Crow: The Boy Holmes, His 1st Case*.

II. The Transportation-Imagery Model vs. Young Adult Literature: The Persuasion of Young Readers

In their essay "In the Mind's Eye," Green and Brock have constructed their transportation-imagery model of narrative persuasion. According to them, this model consists of five basic postulates: (1) narrative persuasion is limited to story texts, where readers' images are evoked and readers' beliefs are implicated; (2) evoked images enable readers to become absorbed in the narrative world to the extent of leaving behind the real world, at least temporarily; (3) propensity for transportation is affected by readers' attributes (e.g., imagery skills); (4) propensity for transportation is affected by attributes of the text (e.g., artistic craftsmanship); (5) propensity for transportation is affected by the attributes of the context (e.g., aspects of the context that limit the opportunity for imaginative investment and participatory responses) (316-17).

Evidently, Green and Brock's model is built upon a formula: readers tend to create imagery in their minds as they read a narrative; simultaneously, they get transported into the narrative world, in the course of which the narrative will exert their persuasive power over readers. This formula has three variables: the factors of the reader, the factor of the text, and the factor of the context. First of all, Green and Brock's model highlights the significance of readers' creation of mental imagery, "a representation of a particular stimulus that is formed by activation of a sensory system and, thus, is experienced by the organism as having similar qualities to the actual perception of the stimulus" (Dadds, Bovgjerg, Reed, and Cutmore, "Imagery in Classical Human Condition," 90). They believe that it is the cataclysm for narrative transportation as well as narrative persuasion. After his thorough research on reading activities in *Lost in a Book: The Psychology of Reading for Pleasure*, V. Nell concludes that "the reader, using a readymade store of images, at once sees the whole picture—mistily, perhaps, but well enough... vivid imagery is indeed frequently associated with reading involvement" (246). Drawing on Nell's conclusion, Green and Brock validate their theory of linking "the subjective experience of transportation with the formation of mental images" (322). It is these images that cause readers to lose "access to some real word facts in favor of accepting the narrative world the author has created." For instance, "a person transported by a story may not notice others entering or leaving the room" (325). Above all, once the correspondence between readers' mental images and their transportation is confirmed, we can get to perceive how readers get persuaded by the narrative. Here, Green and Brock make it clear that "whether the text is labeled as fact or fiction (as true or not necessarily true), does not limit transportation" (317); namely the actuality of the text, namely whether or not the text is true, is irrelevant to its ability to transport readers. As a matter of fact, a great deal of research dealing with narrative persuasion has echoed their viewpoint. First, J. Bruner differentiates a good story from a well-informed argument, stating that the former "establishes not truth but verisimilitude" (*Actual Minds, Possible Worlds,* 11). J.J. Strange and C.C. Leung assert that stories' verisimilitude has the function of getting indexed into memories. That is, stories can evoke "memories of similar characters and causal circumstances in the minds of the readers" ("How Anecdotal Accounts in News and in Fiction can Influence Judgments of a Social Problem's Urgency, Causes, and Cures," 444). R.C. Schank and R.P. Abelson also agree with them, saying that stories...are the fundamental constituents of human memory, knowledge, and social communication...when it comes to interaction in language, all of our knowledge is contained in stories and mechanisms to construct them and retrieve them" ("Knowledge and Memory," 1-2). Strange further points out that fiction, once working its way into readers' memory, can "vastly extend the life space that constitutes our everyday worlds. Through the vehicle of fiction, we are invited to reconceptualize present, past, and future, and to consider alternatives to our entrenched points of view" ("How Fictional Tales Wag Real-World Beliefs," 282). To put it simply, readers do get persuaded by fictional narratives, though they are indeed conscious of their untruthfulness.[1]

To sum up, Green and Brock's formula of narrative persuasion has factored in three variables, as is previously mentioned. First, Green and Brock argue that readers' "ability to create vivid images and to experience absorption are two conceptually distinct capabilities that may function multiplicatively to facilitate transportation" (327). That is, it is generally agreed that the more imaginative and inclined to get absorbed a reader is, the easily (s)he will get transported into a narrative world. Secondly, they believe it is no doubt that "the artistic craftsmanship of the book or film has some responsibility for enormous differences in reader [viewer] appreciation" and "should directly affect amount of transportation and, hence, persuasive impact" (328). To buttress their argument, they have selected "Murder at the Mall," a "highly involving, imagery-rich," and extraordinarily realistic narrative. It is "a story about a college student, Joan, whose little sister Katie is brutally stabbed to death by a psychiatric patient while they are at the mall." Green and Brock have done their own research, and drawn on other scholars' as well. Then, they conclude that the vivid imagery in the story is responsible for readers' acceptance of the belief that "individuals with violent mental disorders should not be allowed in the community without supervision (if at all!)" (318-19). In other words, the better a text is written, the more transportation it can induce, and the more persuasive it can be. Last but not least, Green and Brock emphasize the factor of readers' participatory responses (p-responses), which are activities such as "thoughts about characters, expressions of preferences about events, or reflections on the broader implications of the story" (Allbritton and Gerrig, "Participatory Responses in Text Understanding," 604). James W. Polichak and Richard J. Gerrig suggest that "readers can be conceptualized as *side-participants* with respect to their experiences of narratives" ("Get Up and Win," 73). By "*side-participants,*" they refer to the readerly roles such as indirect addressees, or even overhearers in a conversation. They conclude that readers, adopting this role, have made the p-responses that help define their emotional experience and shape their "long-term mental representations of a narrative" (92). Gerrig, in his *Experiencing Narrative Worlds,* has further pointed out:

> In particular, I suggested that authors treat readers as side-participants toward whom they direct sincere informatives. What often matters to readers' experiences of narratives is...how they[authors] parcel out information within the text. Much of my focus has been on the cognitive processes readers undertake to construct appropriate representations of this knowledge. (156)

Gerrig has argued that the reader, by assuming the role as a side-participant, can produce the p-response[2] that can facilitate his or her cognitive processes of digesting the information the author has embedded in the narrative. With such a facilitation, "people are able to develop an understanding of the past, an expectation about the future, and a general understanding of how they should act" (Jacobs, "The Narrative Integration," 206). To put it simply, they get persuaded and thus changed.[3]

The above is an overview of Green and Brock's transportation-imagery model of narrative persuasion, whose studies today have been correlated to a number of other areas.[4] Here, as I've stated above, I intend to combine this model and young adult literature.

To be more specific, Green and Brock's transportation-imagery model actually proffers a theoretical framework within which I shall examine the functionality of young adult literature. First, Pam B. Cole, in *Young Adult Literature in the 21st Century,* has listed the major characteristics of young adult literature: the hero(ine) is a teenager, the plot doesn't end in a "storybook" happy ending, and the content is typically a coming-of-age story (49). Cole's definition focuses on the generic attributes of young adult literature; on the other hand, Deborah Kutenplon and Ellen Olmstead have defined classic young adult literature from a pedagogical perspective:

> Books have the potential to socialize young readers and transmit values to them; books have the potential to affect young readers' self-image, attitudes, and emotional and intellectual development.... The best books simultaneously tackle universal adolescent dilemmas while introducing the reader to an individual protagonist in all her/his particularity and conflict, as a person possessing strengths and weaknesses. (Preface, *Young Adult Fiction By African American Writers, 1968-1993,* xi-xiii)

Focusing on the pedagogical function of young adult literature, Kutenplon and Olmstead argue for, or even enhance my previous postulate: young adult literature exerts its influence on young readers by infusing them with positive values and helping to shape their philosophy of life; as the storyline unravels, the teenage protagonist, resolving his or her teenage crisis, sets an example for young readers, even though (s)he also exhibits his or her own weaknesses or strengths, like an average teenager. In addition, Kutenplon and Olmstead's definition has widened the range of this subgenre to the extent of overlapping with serious literature. Indeed, by Kutenplon and Olmstead's definition any literary text fulfilling these pedagogical purposes could fall into the category of young adult literature. Katie Rubakova and Rikki Roccanti have echoed this point of view. In "Connecting The Canon To Current Young Adult Literature," they explore the possibility of labeling some classic texts as young adult literature, and they propose an affirmative viewpoint:

> Although literary critics and educators debate the pros and cons of classic and contemporary texts, we believe these two categories of texts are most powerful when they are connected rather than when pitted against each other. (31-32)

In a way, Rubakova and Roccanti have repudiated certain traditionalists' assumption that young adult literature is characteristic of immature covers and inferior writing, and that "if something is entertaining, it certainly cannot be worthwhile" (Crowe, "Young Adult Literature," 147). And it is this repudiation that enables them to assert that certain classic literary texts should also be subsumed under the classification of young adult literature, now that the latter may share the similar elements with "canonical texts" (34). A notable instance would be Rudyard Kipling's *Captains Courageous,* a *bildungsroman* that describes how Harvey, a spoiled teenager born into a wealthy family, turns out to be a reformed young man by experiencing various tribulations on the ship. Another example is Jack London's *The Call of the Wild.* In this classic novel, Buck, a domesticated shepherd, gets stolen and ends up in the Northern wilderness. In coping with the law of the jungle over there, Buck displays noble power and tremendous wisdom (*Realism and Fantasy,* Zhang, 12, 123).

Starting with the definition of young adult literature, I've argued that the gap between young adult literature and classic literature should be bridged, for plenty of the so-called "canonical texts" not only fit the definition of young adult literature but also serve the function of inculcating young readers. Here, a crucial question has to be asked, "Where does this inculcative power originate from?" Indeed, so far I've been stressing the importance of pedagogical function of young adult literature, regarding it as the hallmark of this subgenre. It is natural to inquire into the origin of its inculcative power. As far as I am concerned, only by answering this question can we understand how young adult literature can relate to Green and Brock's transportation-imagery model of narrative persuasion. First of all, Barbara G. Samuels thinks of realism as an important ingredient of young adult fiction:

> Overwhelmingly,...students liked books with teen protagonists and stories that might be termed realistic fiction.... [They] liked books that seemed real to them or that involved teens with problems that they themselves had or thought those around them had. They selected books because they liked a writer's style, especially the ability to create an exciting, fast-paced story and to make them feel involved in the action through the development of a character. ("Young Adults' Choices," 717)

In Samuels' opinion, teenagers gravitate toward young adult fiction because the author has created a fictional narrative world into which they are drawn. It is noteworthy that this fictional narrative world is built upon Bruner's so-called "verisimilitude," and that its very existence hinges on the author's "artistic craftsmanship," as Green and Brock have put it. Above all, the process of drawing young readers into the author-created narrative world is literally Green and Brock's so-called "transportation." By their model, the vividness of a text plays a determinative role in the efficacy of narrative transportation; likewise, Samuels also stresses the importance of how good young adult fiction should resemble teenagers' world. Thus, it should be clear how Green and Brock's model is applicable in examining young adult fiction. Also, it explains why certain texts in serious literature may be included in the canon of young adult literature: their authors, with their fantastically crafted narratives, have presented a real-life narrative world to which teenagers are attracted! In *A Critical Handbook of Children's Literature*, Rebecca J. Lukens thinks that characters in children's literature may be flat or full, static or dynamic. If they are multifaceted, they should be developed through their appearance, words, thoughts, actions, and other characters' responses to them (59). Lukens apparently adopts the same criteria with serious literature in evaluating characterization in children's literature. In a way, she might as well affirm that the two subgenres do overlap.

In addition, Samuels mentions that young readers are inclined to involve themselves with the protagonist's problem in young adult fiction. Actually, such involvement may be seen as their identification, which is a pivotal concept when it comes to researching young adult literature. Jonathan Cohen defines identification as "a mechanism through which audience reception and interpretation of the text from the inside, as if the events were happening to them" ("Defining Identification," 245). To put it simply, identification occurs when a reader puts himself or herself in a character's shoes. And it commonly takes place when one is reading classic literature. George Eliot once said, "The greatest benefit we owe to the artist, whether painter, poet or novelist is the extension of our sympathies…" (Pinney, *Essays of George Eliot,* 270). Oatley interprets Eliot's statement this way, "…the intention of art, and particularly literary art, is not so much to describe, or inform, or instruct, as to allow meetings of mind" ("Meetings of Minds," 439). By "meetings of mind," Oatley refers to the readerly identification. Now that readers tend to identify the characters of their own choosing whether they are reading young adult literature or serious literature, it is no wonder that the two subgenres may overlap from time to time.

At this point, a closer look into the true nature of the readerly identification should be required. G.F. Kaufman and L.K. Libby point out that the readerly identification happens through an "imaginative process of spontaneously assuming the identity of a character in a narrative and simulating that character's thoughts, emotions, behaviors, goals, and traits as if they were one's own" ("Changing Beliefs," 1). Kaufman and Libby term the readerly identification an act of imagining becoming a character in the narrative and embracing his or her values. To put it simply, it is a serious emulation, or even a process of subjectivization, on the reader's part. By the terminology of transportation theory, we have to note that it must take very strong p-response on readers' part, or that readers must become very active side-participants, before such an identification could be made possible. In fact, J. Webb Johnson believes that adolescent readers' p-response or side-participation may be so strong that it enables them to think of young adult book characters as those they can confide in ("Chick Lit Jr.," 143).[5] That is, the readerly identification is synonymous with Green and Brock's transportation.

Up to now, I have demonstrated the compatibility of Green and Brock's model of narrative transportation with young adult literature, in order to draw a simple conclusion: young readers do get transported into the narrative worlds of young adult literature. Thus, it is self-evident that the inculcative power of young adult literature actually originates from its persuasiveness. To be more specific, transporting young readers into its narrative world, young adult literature serves its pedagogical function by persuading them of a particular values system. For instance, T.W. Bean and K. Moni argue that young adult literature can pedagogically help young readers construct their self-identities, especially "amidst unstable times, mores, and global consumerism" ("Developing Students' Critical Literacy," 642).[6] To sum up, it is like a chain reaction: young adult literature entices young readers into reading it. Then it transports them into its narrative world so that it can get to persuade them.

III. How Shane Peacock has Persuaded Young Readers and Subverted the Doylean Conception of Inference in *Eye of the Crow*

Currently, the research of young adult literature has been considerably diversified, and plenty of its researchers have even branched out into other areas, such as multiculturalism.[7] In this paper, Green and Brock's transportation model of narrative persuasion serves as a reference point at which I examine how young adult literature functions as an inculcator, a transporter, and a persuader. I have mainly addressed two core issues: certain classic texts may also be embedded in the tradition of young adult literature; young adult literature achieves its inculcative purpose by transporting young readers into its narrative world and persuading them. The two core issues have paved the way for my dissection of Shane Peacock's *Eye of the Crow.* As the title suggests, this novel portrays the adventures of young Sherlock Holmes. Now that "the mystery genre generally has appealed to a small but growing group of young readers for decades" (Muse, "Detectives, Dubious Dudes, Spies and Suspense," 33), Peacock's creation of this teen novel must be inspired by Conan Doyle's *Sherlock Holmes* series, which, by Muse, should be popular classic texts within the canon of young adult literature. In his review of *Eye of the Crow,* M. Wayne Cunningham observes that this novel basically targets "dedicated Sherlockians, even young ones." For those young readers who have read Doyle's *Sherlock Holmes* series since childhood, "Peacock's novel is a fascinating depiction of Holmes' coming of age." It would seem that *Eye of the Crow* is as good as a prequel of Doyle's *Sherlock Holmes* series, or that Peacock has built his novel upon Doyle's legacy in the tradition of young adult literature. In some respect, it is true; however, my central argument is that in the course of Peacock's transportation and persuasion of his young readers, he has subverted the Doylean conception of inference in his *Eye of the Crow*. First, classical detectives, whether (s)he is a "thinking machine" who always sits still to reason out the truth, or an "action hero, [*who is*] always at the scene of the crime" (Groves, "Better Holmes and Gardens," 471, *italics mine*), are always characterized by their inferential capabilities. Seemly, Peacock has characterized his boy Sherlock Holmes exactly in this way:

> Sherlock Holmes is an observing machine; has been that way almost since birth. He can size up a man or a woman in an instant. He can tell where someone is from, what another does to make his living. In fact, he is known for it on his little street. If something is missing—a boot or an apron or a crusty doorstep of bread—he can look into faces, examine trousers, find telltale clues, and track down the culprit, large or small. (*Eye of the Crow*, 2)

For instance, one day as the boy Holmes is walking on the street, he comes across a "woman with a bonnet pulled down on her head and a shawl gripped around her shoulders." He instantly makes the following inferences:

> An easy one, thinks the boy. She has recently lost in love, notice the stains around her eyes, the tight anger in her mouth, and the chocolate hidden in her hand. She is within a year of thirty, gaining a little weight, a resident of the Sussex countryside where its unique brown clay has marked the insteps of both her black boots. (3)

A born detective, the boy Holmes undauntedly pursues a case; combining his inferential skills and wisdom, he dissolves every crisis on his adventure (Lin, Foreword, *Eye of the Crow*,

15). In this way, Peacock's boy Holmes seems to resemble Doyle's Holmes. And it is the pedagogical message of *Eye of the Crow*: the courage and wisdom of the young Holmes, as well as his growth and awakening (Lu, Foreword, *Eye of the Crow*, 7). According to Green and Brock, Peacock must give very picturesque descriptions so that his young readers can be transported and persuaded. For instance, in solving the homicide case of the Arab, the boy Holmes must confront Malefactor, head of a group of teenage gangsters in London:

> The first thing to do that night is locate Malefactor. Sherlock doesn't want to try in the light of day—too risky. The police will be watching. But he has to find him. He needs a report on whatever interviews the Irregulars have conducted in Whitechapel. He hides in alleys throughout the rest of the day, but as it wears on, becomes restless. He begins to walk aimlessly, his hat pulled down. It seems like there are Bobbies on every street corner and they all appeared to be looking for him. (156)

Here the boy Holmes has to deal with Malefactor and obviate the police pursuit at the same time. And when he finally meets Malefactor, he gets vital information from him, "There were two screams...a woman's and then a man's.... There was a gentleman of wealth rushing from the area, clutching his face. He entered a private coach: black, red fittings. It left at a gallop" (158). The boy Holmes digests the information and converts it into useful leads, with which he will go on his audacious adventure:

> Malefactor's inquiries have confirmed everything Sherlock has suspected and much more: screams, evidence that the victim saw her attacker, the crows, a rich man fleeing westward in a well-described coach...west towards Mayfair. He knows what he has to do next. He has to stride right into the middle of this battle and begin with his dangerous move. He has to involve his mother. She will be giving lessons in rich Mayfair homes this very week. (159)

The quoted passages portray one of the boy Holmes' adventures, in the course of which he feels the need to resort to his inferential gift. In her review of *Eye of the Crow*,

Marya Jansen-Gruber praises it for being "beautifully crafted and carefully told to keep the reader completely engrossed and engaged." Doubtless, Peacock has ornamented his novel this graphic details and filled it with suspense as well. For Gerrig, readers' suspense works in the same way with vivid imagery; it is also the origin of their p-response or transportation because their suspense is meant "to make readers wait as long as possible without exiting the narrative world in disgust or dismay" (86). Under such circumstances, young readers' imagination will certainly be sent soaring high in reading *Eye of the Crow*; besides, they will definitely end up becoming very active side-participants, and above all, ardent admirers of the boy Holmes. Shelle Rosenfeld has put it to a nicety in her review of *Eye of the Crow*, "...young people familiar with Holmes canon will...like the smart, young detective they find here, and find themselves irresistibly drawn into his thrilling adventure" (44). It is how young readers get persuaded to appreciate the noble, sterling qualities of the boy Holmes', like his bravery, righteousness, resourcefulness, etc. And only by doing so can young readers truly live out the pedagogical message Peacock wishes to convey.

Naturally, this pedagogical message is closely associated with Peacock's characterization of the boy Holmes. As I've previously mentioned, Peacock has seemly characterized the boy Holmes in a similar way as Doyle has characterized his Sherlock Holmes. However, a closer look will reveal that it is a far cry from the truth! And my point here is that as Peacock's characterization of the boy Holmes is completely different from that of Doyle's, for he has literally subverted the Doylean conception of inference at the same time. First, Ross MacDonald thinks, "[*Doyle's*] Holmes, too, is an eccentric: He is a cocaine addict, plays the violin, is insufferably arrogant..." (*The Moving Target*, 70, *italics mine*). Besides, he is characteristic of his "mastery of boxing and fencing, and sitting-room marksmanship that would quicken the heart of an Annie Oakley..." (Estleman, Introduction, *Sherlock Holmes,* x-xi). MacDonald further points out that "in the etiquette-filled minefield of Victorian England...arrogance in the demeanour of an otherwise respectable gentleman would be the height of eccentricity" (70). To sum up, Doyle's Holmes has been characterized as a Victorian bourgeoisie gentleman who, equipped with plenty of fancy, upper-class skills, lives in the urban area. In other words, Doyle's Holmes seems considerably close to Walter Benjamin's so-called "flâneur," a dandy pursuing urban, bourgeoisie fashions (Gilloch, *Walter Benjamin,* 132), or "a poet, who observes daily, urban capitalist life…the dandy… now forced to go on the market" (Mazlish, "The Flâneur," 47). If so, the inferential capability Doyle's Holmes has displayed could be seen as an inherent attribute of a flâneur, as Walter Benjamin says in his well-known *Arcades Project*, "Preformed in the figure of the flâneur is that of a detective…an observer who will not let the unsuspecting malefactor out of his sight". That is, Doyle's Holmes, like a flâneur, appears to internalize the inferential skill set.

Dana Brand, following Benjamin's descriptions of a flâneur, observes, "Like the flâneur, he *[the detective]* removes and distances himself from what he observes in order to achieve his panoramic perspective…" ("From the a Flâneur to the Detective," 237, *italics mine*). As I've stated previously, Doyle's Holmes is fairly close to Benjamin's flâneur. Be that as it may, it doesn't mean that they can be unconditionally equated with each other. In explicating his conception of a flâneur, Benjamin draws on the notion of a detective, which clearly comes from Edgar Alan Poe. On the other hand, authors tend to "impose their own cultural predispositions," especially "in the process of retelling their stories" (Stephens and McCallum, *Retelling Stories*, 4). Diane Simmons argues that a lot of Victorian writers, including Doyle, had such a bourgeoisie, "narcissistic fantasy" which "helped shape the understanding of the imperial role…" (*The Narcissism of Empire,* 2). With such a fantasy in his mind, as Doyle re-cultivates the genre of detective fiction following in Poe's footsteps, it is inevitable that he will create Holmes as a spokesman of the 19th century English bourgeoisie class. Thus, bourgeoisie thinking is often predominant in Holmes' inferences. For example, in "The Adventure of the Norwood Builder," Holmes makes the following inference:

> On looking over the bank-book I found that the low state of the balance was principally due to large checks which

> have been made out during the last year to Mr. Cornelius. I confess that I should be interested to know who this Mr. Cornelius may be with whom a retired builder has had such very large transactions. Is it possible that he has had a hand in the affair? Cornelius might be a broker, but we have found no script to correspond with these large payments. (*Sherlock Holmes,* 795-96)

Evidently, Holmes makes the inference from the perspective of a bourgeoisie gentleman; it almost seems as if Holmes' inference above is hallmarked by the 19th-century British bourgeoisie thinking. In addition, in order to facilitate his inferences, Holmes sometimes has to move around London. Holmes may have an encyclopedic understanding of London and the keys to every Londoner's living room in his hands (Rothfield, *Vital Signs,* 139), but it is not synonymous with Brand's so-called "panoramic perspective." For instance, in "The Adventure of the Empty House," Dr. Watson ventures into an unfamiliar area of London with Holmes:

> Holmes's knowledge of the byways of London was extraordinary, and on this occasion he passed rapidly and with an assured step through a network of mews and stables, the very existence of which I had never known. We emerged at last into a small road, lined with old, gloomy houses, which led us into Manchester Street, and so to Blandford Street. (769)

According to Watson, Holmes doubtless has an intimate knowledge of London; however, it is highly questionable that he sees London from a flâneur's "panoramic perspective," for a flâneur must know the ins and outs of capitalism, serving as "a spy for the capitalists, on assignment in the realm of consumers" (*Arcades Projects*, M6). Therefore, a flâneur's "panoramic perspective" is based on his insight into a capitalist city. Holmes clearly doesn't have such an insight; in his bourgeoisie eyes, the part of London described in the quoted passage above is nothing but a "dark jungle of criminal London" (769).

In conclusion, Doyle's Holmes has an inferential capability that is a saliently rooted in his flâneur-like identity, (though he is not exactly a flâneur). Very often, Holmes' inferences carry the mark of his (or Doyle's) bourgeoisie thinking. Namely, they are constantly made from a bourgeoisie viewpoint, or they may even become a vehicle for Holmes' (or Doyle's) bourgeoisie propaganda. What's more, Holmes is apt to make his inferences on the basis of the leads he gathers from a bourgeoisie perspective.

The above is an analysis of the nature of the Doylean inference. It is part of Holmes' bourgeois identity. Therefore, as readers are fascinated with Doyle's vivid descriptions of Holmes' amazing inferential skills, they are definitely drawn to identify with him (A good example would be that when Holmes was believed to be dead at the end of *The Memoirs of Sherlock Holmes*, "more than twenty thousand *Strand* readers cancelled their subscriptions immediately, and young men and women appeared on the streets in...black armbands and veils" (Estleman, xvi)). By the theorizations about identification postulated above, they become active side-participants sure to embrace Holmes'/ Doyle's bourgeoisie beliefs. It also means that they are inevitably pulled into the narrative London Doyle has created, treating it as the real London (Gerrig, *Experiencing Narrative Worlds,* 206). In consequence, their case scenario perfectly corroborates Green and Brock's model: behind their amazement at Holmes' inferences is their persuasion of Holmes' (or Doyle's) bourgeoisie values. (In some respect, it is precisely the pedagogical message Doyle wishes to deliver through the character of Holmes.)

In contrast, Peacock's boy Holmes makes his inferences in an utterly different manner. First, he can't possibly be viewed as a flâneur, because he is the son of Rose Sherrinford, an only daughter of a well-to-do family, and Wilbur Holmes, a Jew:

> After they [*Wilbur and Rose*] eloped to Scotland, they came home to nothing. Her parents disowned her. His teaching opportunities at the university disappeared as mysteriously as he had once solved scientific problems. And so they moved to Southwark, south of the Thames to the flat over the hatter's shop. She became the wife of an unemployed Jew of foreign origins and took jobs teaching children to sing in upper class houses, and when money became even

> shorter, taking in sewing at home. Wilbur...went farther south to work at a job that paid less...at The Crystal Palace, where he'd seen trained *birds performing in great flocks for massive crowds*. (17, *italics mine*)

This is the impoverished family the boy Holmes is born into. What's worse, he suffers severe racial discriminations, "The boys at school call Sherlock 'Judas,' or 'Old Clothes,' the name for conniving Jewish street vendors." Consequently, he ends up as "a loner" who "doesn't like to talk: it seems he just reads and thinks" (28). Growing up under such adverse circumstances, the boy Holmes regards his innate inferential capability as his own survival skill:

> "My father [*Wilbur*] says that you need to have logic as your first principle in everything you do," begins the boy [*the boy Holmes*], sitting gingerly, aware that his clothes might soil the beautiful French chair. "My weapon against my apparent fate, and Mohammad's, is my brain." (114, *italics mine*)

The boy Holmes utters these remarks in Irene Doyle's upper-class residence. Before that, the police have arrested him for "the possible involvement in a murder" and put him in jail. As he is put under arrest, he realizes, "He can't break down.... He must be like steel...he has to find a solution to this crime" (57). Later on, with Irene's help the boy Holmes manages to escape from jail and flees to Irene's residence. Evidently, when the boy Holmes' life is in grave danger, his inferential capability is the only thing that can keep him alive.

In brief, this is how Peacock has characterized the boy Holmes: a half-bred who lives on the edge of society and needs to depend on his inferential capability to survive the harsh realities. As a matter of fact, by characterizing the boy Holmes this way, Peacock has also created him to be a free individual: as he comes from a low stratum of Victorian society, he is unbound by the rigid social constraints then. This is why he gets to see the British society then in perspective (Lu, 8). "Sherlock cruises around Trafalgar Square, reads the illustrated Police News, sights Charles Dickens, Lewis Carroll, and Disraeli, "the greatest politician in the land".... As well, he's seen the black-faced chimney sweepers, the deformed beggars, and the pickpockets of the streets" (Cunningham). And this is how he gathers clues for his inferences. For instance, the first time he meets Mr. Andrew C. Doyle, the philanthropist, in jail, he makes these inferences:

> *Slight Scottish accent,* thinks the boy, *raised in the Edinburgh area, came to London in his teens, religious, a free-thinker, and a respected philanthropist.* Sherlock sizes him up in an instant. The boy is especially glad of his skill of analysis now. As of today, it will be very important to know others well and imagine what sort of threat they might be.... He can tell many things by the tone of the man's voice...and his clothes. (68-69)

Unlike Doyle's Holmes, who infers from a bourgeoisie viewpoint, the boy Holmes makes these inferences above from a stance of the socially disadvantaged. Not only are they objective, accurate analyses but also they exemplify the boy Holmes' skill set that will help to ensure his own safety. In addition, in order to search for the clues for his inferences, he has to venture into such an area:

> It is like being in a tunnel. The sides of the two-storey buildings lean out over the road, cutting off the setting sun. Filthy children dressed in rags crawl out from nowhere, begging with pleading eyes and outstretched hands. Others have lined up their pathetic shoes on the grim, dirty footpaths, hoping for a sale. They smell as if they've bathed in cesspools. Many cough horribly, and their skin looks green. (32-33)

To answer these questions, "*Where are they* (the crows) *going? Where do they stay at night?*" (31, *italics the author's*), the boy Holmes ventures into an area of London "where four or five families live in single rooms" (33), namely an area whose residents live in a much more miserable condition than he does. On the other hand, he passes through this area after his escape from prison:

> The avenue he is now on is well lit with tall, black iron gas lamps—all the wealthy areas are. He walks north to the end

> of the foot pavement and looks up at the name imprinted on the last building.... He turns left toward the Museum, massive and made of gray stone with Roman pillars, rising on the west side of...Montague. (89-90)

In an attempt to get rid of the police, the boy Holmes is entering "an area where the police would not expect him to be" (89), namely an area populated by the upper-class people. Besides, as his investigation draws to an end, the boy Holmes has to go to Mayfair, one of the affluent areas of London, at the beginning of the "fashionable season," when "the upper class is moving from their country estates into city homes for the summer" (181).

In conclusion, Peacock has characterized the boy Holmes as a mongrel whose inferential capability is not only his pride and joy or his survival skill, but also a way of observing his realities. To be more specific, it is such a creed, "Observe...Deal with the evidence first. Find it" (122), that enables him to ward off an imminent dander. Most of all, "an observing machine" by nature, the boy Holmes often follows his natural instinct for inference to cruise around London, seeing the city as it really is. That is, his inferential capability has made him a free individual who can transcend the unfair social limitations to gain an insight into the cross section of the British society: he can tell various kinds of people apart, ranging from conscientious upper-class members like Irene or Andrew, to "the many forms of darkness and "skullduggery" that seeped through London as eerily as the fog" (Ward), in the course of which he has gradually gained an insight into the true nature of the British society then.

H. Douglas Thompson begins his essay "Masters of Mystery" by stating, "In its simplest form the detective story is a puzzle to be solved, the plot consisting in a logical deduction of the solution from the existing data" (129). Thompson observes a fundamental fact about detective stories, (or at least classical ones): the detective's inference is always the backbone of the story; it is where the dynamic of the story originates from. Framed with the previous theses about the adolescent identification, Thompson's observation literally enables us to argue that teenage readers identify with the boy Holmes whenever he demonstrates his reasoning skills. According to our previous postulate, the instant teenage readers' identification with the boy Holmes occurs, they have become side-participants of *Eye of the Crow*, transported into the narrative world and above all, persuaded of the values Peacock has embedded in the novel. Here, we can actually see these values in perspective: behind his resourcefulness is his quickness to resort to his brilliant inferential skills; in substantiating his inferences, he is brave enough to take action and make keen observations of his surroundings as well as the whole society. Thus, he seems like a truly free individual, who moves up and down in the social hierarchy in the course of his inferences. Of course, all these are part of the pedagogical message Peacock delivers in *Eye of the Crow*.

As a matter of fact, when it comes to the application of inference, Peacock and Doyle also do not see eye to eye with each other. For Doyle, the main purpose of Holmes' inference is to help maintain the order of the British Empire. Michael Cohen, in his *Murder Most Fair,* argues that in plenty of classical detective fiction, such as Doyle's, "society is by nature law-abiding, most people are truth-tellers, and crime is an aberration" (27). "It is the task of the detective to discover what has happened, to sort out the evidence, arrive at a conclusion and pass on the knowledge to judicial process" (Erb, *Murder, Manners, Mystery,* 115). If so, equipped with pure reasoning and inferential skills, the private detective becomes the last line of defence of social order, just as Tony Bennett has observed, "the private eye" of the detective becomes a great helper for "the public eye of power" ("Marxism and Popular Fiction," 216). In other words, human reason and society's law and order are both indexed and clustered together within the parameters of classical detective fiction. A perfect instance would be Doyle's "The Speckled Band." In this story, Holmes first examines the scene of the crime:

> A camp bed, a small wooden shelf full of books, mostly of a technical character, an arm-chair beside the bed, a plain wooden chair against the wall, a round table, and a large iron safe were the principal things which met the eye. Holmes walked slowly round and examined each and all of them with the keenest interest. (414)

Afterwards, Holmes "squatted down in front of the wooden chair, and examined the seat of it with the greatest attention" (414). In view of this "locked room," Sherlock Holmes makes his inference: the killer is the "speckled band" is actually a "swamp adder," "the deadliest snake in India" (420-21), which is kept by Dr. Roylott, a man with "violence of temper approaching mania...intensified by his long residence in tropics" (401). At the end of the story, Holmes beats Dr. Roylott and rescues Helen from the adder originating from an alien culture:

> Beside this table, on the wooden chair, sat Dr. Grimesby Roylott, clad in a long grey dressing-gown, his bare ankles protruding beneath, and his feet thrust into red heelless Turkish slippers. Across his lap lay the short stock with the long lash which we had noticed during the day. His chin was cocked upwards, and his eyes were fixed in a dreadful rigid stare at the corner of the ceiling. (420)

The quoted passage depicts Dr. Roylott's death; with his death the alien threat, of which he is such a paradigm, is neutralized. Jon Thompson states that in Sherlock Holmes stories, Doyle combines "ideologically charged conventions from adventure, detective, and sensational literature" with "strategies of exclusion," which refer to how Sherlock Holmes contains and controls colonial contaminations (*Fiction, Crime, and Empire,* 73). Framed with Green and Brock's model, Thompson's statement literally indicates that as readers finish reading the passage above, they are immediately persuaded that such an Englishman as Roylott, after venturing into the "backward and immortal" colony of the British Empire, "would inevitably endanger the imperial center." As Sherlock Holmes, someone they are sure to identify with, manages to prevent the death of young Helen, he has restored "order after a brief period of savagery and disorder" (Raheja, "Anxieties of Empire in Doyle's Tales of Sherlock Holmes," 419). That is, Holmes' inference in "The Speckled Band" aims at protecting the British Empire from any alien threat, and Doyle's pedagogical message is how unshakable the stability of the British Empire should be under any circumstances.

In contrast, the boy Holmes' inference is applied to an entirely different cause. As mentioned previously, the boy Holmes has been wrongly accused by the police:

> "We have jailed one scoundrel, young sir. But a coin purse is missing. We know that because we found beadwork particular to such an item in the alley. We know you frequent the streets, consort with gangs." "My son does not con..." starts Wilbur, but Sherlock cuts him off. "I know nothing about the purse." "Then you had better come with me," barks Lestrade. (56)

There is no doubt that Lestrade's arrest is ungrounded partly because of the boy Homes' Jewish background and partly because of the police's inaccurate theory:

> We're thieves and work together.... The Arab is bigger and good with a knife, he was simply meant to scare her with it...I [*the boy Holmes*] was young, fast, and street-wise, meant to snatch the treasure and make off with it...the Jew's job. But our robbery went badly. She struggled and the Arab killed her. I fled with the purse. I hid it somewhere in a hurry and I keep going back to the area to get it, but haven't received it yet. That's what they think! (67, *italics mine*)

Under such circumstances, the boy Holmes' inferential capability becomes the only thing that can exonerate him; he must reason out the answers to these questions:

> What sort of place is this for a murder? Is it a place where someone was taken...dragged...or is it a spot where two people agreed to meet? Did the murderer know the woman?.... This wasn't done for money, not for a mere coin purse. But if that is true, why is the purse gone?.... Why did she come here? What sort of woman would be compelled to this place in the night? Who saw her...who smelled her perfume? (122-23)

And above all, what is the crow looking for? And "why would it find it irresistible?" (124). Inferring the answers helps him piece together the truth. At last, he manages to find the killer, a gentleman in Mayfair, who is responsible for his mother's death:

> "The gentleman...the gentleman of the house..." "Yes?" "Gave me tea...made tea himself...and served it to me...a strange brew...it made me..." Her voice fades. Something falls from her hand: the same piece of paper he saw her carrying last night. He sees the address on it this time. The very house he intends to enter tonight. The house where the villain surely lives! (231)

Faced with his mother's tragic death, the boy Holmes still chooses not to take the law into his own hands after tracking him down:

> Inspector Lestrade of Scotland Yard finds a most curious collection of items on his desk the following morning, the day of Mohammad's trial. There is a glittering bracelet, a glass eye splattered with blood, and a stained purse with a letter inside...it is crudely wrapped in a newspaper... [*There*] is a detailed explanation of what happened on the night of the Whitechapel murder. It answers every question anyone could possibly have, tells of the sacrifice of brave Rose Sherrinford Holmes, and identifies the murderer and where he can be found. (244, *italics mine*)

That is, even if he cries out loud, "JUSTICE!" (232) on seeing his own mother's death in person, he still decides to turn over to the authorities all the evidence he's come by at the risk of his life. On the surface, it may appear like an act of complying with the justice system; however, a closer look will prove this shallow observation erroneous. First, as Lu points out, *Eye of the Crow* depicts how the boy Holmes, after experiencing a false accusation and seeing the British society as it truly is, takes on the challenge of a life-long, persistent pursuit of justice (8). In this respect, *Eye of the Crow* is a *bildungsroman* with an emphasis on why the boy Holmes "became devoted to the cause of justice" (Jansen-Gruber); namely, the boy Holmes applies his inferential capability to the pursuit of genuine justice, the higher moral codes. He turns the murderer over to the police not because he is shackled by the British law, but because he's made a conscientious moral choice: it's not up to him to decide on the life and death of another man, no matter how guilty he is. This is where the boy Holmes' inferences apply.

If the boy Holmes employs his inferential capability to pursue true justice or higher morality, then we can see once again how he is a free individual: he freely moves within and outside the British law. He doesn't stubbornly cling to the belief that the British justice system is impeccable or trustworthy, especially when it fails him. His escape from prison indeed constitutes a contravention of the British law, and only by escaping the massive manhunt of the British police can he use his reasoning skills to acquit himself of the false charge. Here, he is clearly an individual distrusting and above all, violating the law. On the other hand, upon inferring the truth, he doesn't presume to be above the law but lets the British justice system do its work. Apparently, the boy Holmes' inferential capability has made him a free individual who is unrestricted by the rigid letter of the law but only answers to his own conscience and regards the true morality as his guidelines. At this point, the pedagogical message Peacock attempts to convey is self-evident: true justice will eventually be served, and no one has the right to take the law into his or her own hands. Furthermore, the identification theorizations and Green and Brock's model can come in handy: identifying with the boy Holmes, an expert in making inferences, adolescent will be transported into the narrative world and persuaded of the pedagogical message.

IV. The Recapitulation

There are two rationales for my research: (1) In her "Detective Stories and the Primal Scene," Geraldine Pederson-Krag argues that detective stories are characterized by their readers' tendency to identify with the characters, which surely brings them unlimited gratification (15); that is, the significance of readerly identification shouldn't be overlooked. Joel Black states that in classical detective stories, like Edgar Alan Poe's "The Purloined Letter," "the sleuth's attention and the reader's interest are directed to a document that plays a crucial role in the narrative" ("(De)feats of Detection," 79); namely, a classical detective story must mainly thematicize how the ultimate truth is reasoned out. Combining both their viewpoints, we may conclude that in classical detective stories, the detective's inference should be put in a centralized position and may be treated as the primary factor when it comes to the readerly identification (2). By Green and Brock's transportation-imagery model, narrative imagery should be viewed "as the engine of enduring narrative impact" (Green, Brock, and Strange, "Insights and Research Implications," 352). That is, the author's vivid descriptions will invoke the readers' identification. With their identification, readers readily play the role as the side-participant, who will be transported into the narrative world and persuaded of the values the author has incorporated into the story. This is how the pedagogical purpose of adolescent literature gets fulfilled.

With the two rationales, I've examined how Peacock has subverted the Doylean conception of inference in persuading his readers in *Eye of the Crow*. And my findings can be summarized in the following table:

	Doyle	**Peacock**
the nature of inference	1. the attribute of a flâneur-like, upper class gentleman	1. a survival skill of a half-bred living on the edge of society
	2. a carrier of the author's ingrained bourgeoisie thinking	2. enables the detective to be a free individual who sees a cross section of the British society then
the application of inference	The detective must apply his inferential capability to the cause of maintaining the British Empire's social order and stability. That is, the detective's reasoning skills should be a defense line for the British Empire's interest.	The detective should use his inferential capability not to follow the law blindly but to pursue genuine justice or higher moral codes. That is, the detective's reasoning skills may offer a chance for the true justice to be served.
the outcomes	Sherlock Holmes is characterized as a spokesman of the bourgeoisie class or the protector of the British Empire's interest. Doyle wants to persuade his readers of bourgeoisie thinking and British imperialism.	The boy Holmes is portrayed as a free individual. Through the agency of his inferences, he is free to transcend the social classes, see the society in perspective, and seek the true justice. Peacock wants to persuade his readers of the values of bravery, wisdom, perceptiveness, free thinking, and righteousness.

The table above is the synopsis of this research. With it, we can go on to examine the repercussions of Peacock's subversion on three causally interconnected levels. On the characterizational level, Peacock's boy Holmes is portrayed as a tough teenager of action, to the extent of resembling "a hard-boiled detective" (Wang, Foreword, *Eye of the Crow*, 12), that is, a detective much closer to real life. On the level of canonic development, *Eye of the Crow,* with such a characterization of the boy Holmes, has taken the Sherlockean legacy to a brand new direction, as Ward has pointed out, *Eye of the Crow* is "a re-creation [*which*] can shed new light, illuminating hidden and untold elements of the original storyworld" (*italics mine*).

On the level of the narrative transportation and persuasion, most of all, *Eye of the Crow* could be a stronger text than the traditional Holmes stories, as adolescent readers tend to identify "both with similar characters and ones who resembled the ideal persons they wanted to become," namely the characters with a lot of qualities they wish they could have been (Kokesh and Sternadori, "The Good, The Bad, and The Ugly," 152). Most critics agree that Peacock has created both a vividly depicted narrative world in *Eye of the Crow*. And the boy Holmes is so well characterized that he is a character "enriching the book" and a lot easier to identify with (Fiscus, 134). In such a case, young readers will certainly be more motivated to identify with the boy Holmes, in which case they will be transported deeper in the narrative world of *Eye of the Crow*. Hence, the persuasiveness of the novel will be greatly increased, and its pedagogical purpose could be better served. This observation helps to explain why *Eye of the Crow* has won so many awards, and why four more novels have already been spawned in this series (Alethea K. Helbig and Agnes Regan Perkins think "Mystery-detective and thrillers are among the best for sheer reading pleasure" (Preface, *Dictionary,* xx). To some extent, the viewpoint above simply has proven them wrong!)

V. Conclusion

In "Critiquing *Calypso*," Catherine Butler states, "Reading, like writing, is both a critical and a creative act, which always a dialogic relation between what the reader brings to the text…and what the text offers to the reader" (273). Butler's main emphasis is the mutuality of the reading, and it can help to perceive Green and Brock's transportation-imagery model: readers offer their p-response to the text, and the author in turn transports them into the narrative world he has vividly created in the text and eventually persuades them. In this paper, I have parallelized this model with the concept of identification, a keyword when it comes to discussing the pedagogical value of young adult literature. Though plenty of critics are still inclined to think of young adult literature as "precariously low from the lowest rung of the literary ladder" (Johnson, 141), it doesn't mean that young adult literature is literarily valueless. First, young adult literature and serious literature do overlap from time to time, for both of them may be vehicles for delivering pedagogical messages. And the key factor is young readers' identification. My point is that their identification involves very strong p-response, so it will simultaneously trigger the transportation-persuasion process. Within this theoretical framework, I've examined how Peacock has subverted the Doylean conception of inference in *Eye of the Crow*. For Doyle, a gentleman detective should be equipped with the inferential skills, so they should be tainted with bourgeoisie thinking; besides, they should be used for protecting the British Empire. As a consequence, Sherlock Holmes is characterized as a bourgeoisie upholder of the British Empire. Once Doyle has won his readers' identification with Sherlock Holmes, he has also transported his readers into the narrative world of the Sherlockean stories and persuaded them of the British Imperialism. In contrast, for Peacock, the boy Holmes must depend on his inferential skills for survival; they enable him to be free to transcend class barriers and see the British society in perspective. Moreover, the boy Holmes applies his inferential capability to the pursuit of true justice. As a result, the boy Holmes is portrayed as a free individual. After invoking young readers' identification with the boy Holmes, he has transported them into the narrative world of *Eye of the Crow* and persuaded them to emulate the boy Holmes. This is also why *Eye of the Crow* could be such an award-winning novel; it is a highly persuasive text, whose pedagogical purpose is so effectively served.

Notes

1. Quite a bit research has been conducted with regard to the persuasiveness of fiction. For instance, both John R. Searle and M.L. Pratt have seen how humans are susceptible to fiction. The former observes, "It is after all an odd, peculiar, and amazing fact about human language that it allows the possibility of fiction at all. Yet we all have no difficulty in recognizing and understanding works of fiction." The latter gives a personal experience, "Without the slightest hint of infidelity, I can recount an anecdote I heard from someone else whose name I can't remember to an audience I don't know about events I didn't witness that happened somewhere I've never been." Both of them believe that our susceptibility to fiction can increase its power to persuade readers. See John R. Searl, "The Logical Status of Fictional Discourse." *New Literary History*, 6 (1975): 325, and M.L. Pratt, Toward a Speech Act Theory of Literary Discourse. (Bloomington: Indiana University Press, 1977), p. 94.
2. J.R. Gerrig and A.D. Prentice argue that films are more likely to elicit p-responses. They state that "formal properties of film and particularly, the ability of film to fix the focus of attention make it especially likely that such as if responses will occur…even more than in the experience of text individuals are likely to lose track of the fact that they can't really participate." See J.R. Gerrig and A.D. Prentice, "Notes on Audience Response," *Post-Theory: Reconstructing Film Studies*, Ed. by D. Bordwell and N. Carroll (Madison, Wisconscin: The University of Wisconscin Press, 1996), pp. 389-97.
3. Roger C. Shank and Tamara R. Berman have viewed readers' digestion of stories in the light of how memory restructures itself. They suggest that "we listen to stories with an innate ability to pull apart the details and fill out our memory structures where they are lacking. In essence, our knowledge is constructed of stories in various forms." See Roger C. Shank and Tamara R. Berman, "The Pervasive Role of Stories in Knowledge and Action," *Narrative Impact: Social and Cognitive Foundations*, Ed. by Melanie C. Green, Jeffrey

J. Strange, and Timothy C. Brock (Mahwah, New Jersey: Lawrence Erlbaum Associates, 2002), p. 311.

4. For instance, Michael D. Slater has researched the narrative persuasion of entertainment education. He concludes, "The incidental and cumulative effect of entertainment narratives on beliefs, values and behaviors is one of the most important issues facing communication scientists. Critical and cultural scholars have long emphasized the importance of such effects in understanding the impact of media on contemporary society." See Michael D. Slater, "Entertainment Education and the Persuasive Impact of Narratives," *Narrative Impact: Social and Cognitive Foundations*, Ed. by Melanie C. Green, Jeffrey J. Strange, and Timothy C. Brock (Mahwah, New Jersey: Lawrence Erlbaum Associates, 2002), p. 117.
5. In "Development of Parasocial Interaction Relationship," R.B. Rubin and M.P. McHugh have researched such a readerly identification from the perspective of parasocial relationship, which they think is a one-sided relationship consumers of any media (including books) may establish with characters. For them, such parasocial relationships may be very "intimate, friendlike." A. Burnett and R. Beto's research targets romance novels. In "Reading Romance Novels," they argue that romance novels give "visual stimulation for the reader through language," from which readers' parasocial relationships with characters arise. See R.B. Rubin and M.P. McHugh, "Development of Parasocial Interaction Relationship." *Journal of Broadcasting and Electronic Media*, 31 (1987), 280, and A. Burnett and R. Beto, "Reading Romance Novels: An Application of Parasocial Relationship Theory." *North Dakota Journal of Speech and Theater*, 13 (2000), 30.
6. Certainly, it is not to say that young adult literature, without any exception, has a pedagogically effect on young readers. For example, Amy E. Bonomi, Julianna M. Nemeth, Lauren E. Altenburger, Melissa L. Anderson, Anastasia Snyder, and Irma Dotto survey young readers' response after they have read E.L. James' *Fifty Shades of Grey*. They have concluded that the depictions of violence against women

in this blockbuster series do influence young female readers negatively, "Our analysis showed that young women who read at least the first novel in the *Fifty Shades* series...were at increased risk of having, at some point during their lifetime, a partner who shouted, yelled, or swore at them and who delivered unwanted calls/text messages..." At its worst, *Fifty Shades* have transformed into submissive females in their relationships. See Amy E. Bonomi, Julianna M. Nemeth, Lauren E. Altenburger, Melissa L. Anderson, Anastasia Snyder, and Irma Dotto, "Fiction or Not? Fifty Shades is Associated with Health Risks in Adolescent and Young Adult Females." *Journal of Women's Health*, Vol. 23, No. 9 (2014), 724.

7. For instance, Christopher Palmi, Deborah Augsburger, and Dorene Huvaere target preservice teacher candidates, aiming "to explore the impact of using young adult (YA) literature as a lens to broaden the candidates' understanding of" multiculturalism issues. At the end of their paper, they conclude that they "are confident that YA literature written about microcultures is an effective way to help preservice teacher candidates explore the issue of multiculturalism." See Christopher Palmi, Deborah Augsburger, and Dorene Huvaere, "Transforming Preservice Teachers' Awareness and Understanding of Multiculturalism Through the Use of Young Adult Literature." *Illinois Reading Council Journal*, Vol. 44, No. 4 (Fall 2016), 12, 21.

Works Cited

Allbritton, D.W. and R.J. Gerrig. "Participatory Responses in Text Understanding." *Journal of Memory and Language*, 30 (1991): 603-26.

Bean, T.W. and K. Moni. "Developing Students' Critical Literacy: Exploring Identity Construction in Young Adult Fiction." *Journal of Adolescent & Adult Literacy*, Vol. 8, Issue 46 (2003): 638-48.

Benjamin, Walter. *The Arcades Projects*. Trans Howard Eiland and Kevin Mclaughlin. Cambridge: Belknap Press, 1999.

Bennett, Tony. "Marxism and Popular Fiction." *Popular Fictions: Essays in Literature and History*. Ed. Peter Humm, Paul Stigant, and Peter Widdowson. London: Methuen, 1986. 237-65.

Black, Joel. "(De)feats of Detection: The Spurious Key Text from Poe to Eco." *Detecting Texts: The Metaphysical Detective Story From Poe to Postmodernism*. Ed. P. Merivale and S. E. Sweetney. Philadelphia: University of Pennsylvania Press, 1999. 75-98.

Bonomi, Amy E., Julianna M. Nemeth, Lauren E. Altenburger, Melissa L. Anderson, Anastasia Snyder, and Irma Dotto, "Fiction or Not? Fifty Shades is Associated with Health Risks in Adolescent and Young Adult Females." *Journal of Women's Health*, Vol. 23, No. 9 (2014): 720-28.

Brand, Dana. "From the Flâneur to the Detective: Interpreting the City of Poe." *Popular Fiction: Technology, Ideology, Production, Reading*. Ed. Tony Bennett. London: Routledge, 1990. 220-37.

Bruner, J. *Actual Minds, Possible Worlds*. Cambridge, MA: Harvard University Press, 1986.

Burnett, A. and R. Beto, "Reading Romance Novels: An Application of Parasocial Relationship Theory." *North Dakota Journal of Speech and Theater*, 13 (2000): 28-39.

Butler, Catherine. "Critiquing *Calypso:* Authorial and Academic Bias in the Reading of a Young Adult Novel." *Children's Literature in Education*, 44 (2013): 264-79.

Cohen, Jonathan. "Defining Identification: A Theoretical Look at the Identification of Audiences with Media Characters." *Mass Communication & Society*, Vol. 4, No. 3 (2001): 245-64.

Cohen, Michael. *Murder Most Fair: The Appeal of Mystery Fiction*. Cranbury, New Jersey: Associated University Presses, 2000.

Cole, Pam B. *Young Adult Literature in the 21st Century*. New York: Mcgraw-Hill Higher Education, 2008.

Crowe, C. "Young Adult Literature: The Problem with YA Literature." *The English Journal*, (90)3 (2001): 146-50.

Cunningham, M. Wayne. Rev. of *Eye of the Crow: The Boy Sherlock Holmes,* by Shane Peacock. April 15, 2017 <http://www.mysteriousreviews.com/mystery-book-reviews/peacock-eye-crow.html#.WPI6rFIkq00>

Dadds, M.R., D.H. Bovbjerg, W.H. Redd., and T.R.H. Cutmore. "Imagery in Human Classical Conditioning." *Psychological Bulletin* 127 (1997): 89-103.

Doyle, Arthur Conan. *Sherlock Holmes: The Complete Novels and Stories*, Volume I. Ed. with Intro by Loren Estleman. New York: Bantam Dell, 1986.

Erb, Peter C. *Murder, Manners, Mystery.* London: SCM Press, 2007.

Estleman, Loren D. Introduction. *Sherlock Holmes: The Complete Novels and Stories*, Volume I, by Arthur Conan Doyle. Ed. Estleman. New York: Bantam Dell, 1986. vii-xviii.

Fiscus, Sheila. Rev. of *Eye of the Crow: The Boy Sherlock Holmes,* by Shane Peacock. *School Library Journal*, Vol. 53, Issue 11 (November 2007): 134.

Gerrig, Richard J. *Experiencing Narrative Worlds: On the Psychological Activities of Reading.* New Haven: Yale University Press, 1993.

Gerrig, Richard J. and A.D. Prentice, "Notes on Audience Response," *Post-Theory: Reconstructing Film Studies.* Ed by D. Bordwell and N. Carroll. Madison, Wisconscin: The University of Wisconscin Press, 1996. 389-97.

Gilloch, Graeme. *Walter Benjamin: Critical Constellations.* Cambridge: Polity, 2002.

Green, Melanie C. and Timothy C. Brock. "In the Mind's Eye: Transportation-Imagery Model of Narrative Persuasion." *Narrative Impact: Social and Cognitive Foundations.* Ed. Green, Jeffrey J. Strange, and Brock. Mahwah, New Jersey: Lawrence Erlbaum Associates, 2002. 315-43.

Green, Melanie C., Timothy C. Brock. and Jeffrey. J. Strange. "Insights and Research Implications: Epilogue to Narrative Impact." *Narrative Impact: Social and Cognitive Foundations.* Ed. Green and Brock. Mahwah, New Jersey: Lawrence Erlbaum Associates, 2002. 315-43.

Groves, Derham. "Better Holmes and Gardens: Sense of Place in the Sherlock Holmes Stories." *Journal of Popular Culture*, Vol. 36, Issue 3 (Winter 2003): 466-72.

Helbig, Alethea K. and Agnes Regan Perkins. Preface. *Dictionary of American Young Adult Fiction 1997-2001*. Ed. Helbig and Perkins. Westport, Connecticut: Greenwood Press, 2004. xvii-xxii.

Henderson, Virginia M. "The Development of Self-Esteem in Children of Color." *The Multicolored Mirror: Cultural Substance in Literature for Children and Young Adults*. Ed. Merri V. Lindgren. Fort Atkinson, WI: Highsmith Press, 1991. 15-30.

Jacobs, Ronald. N. "The Narrative Integration of Personal and Collective Identity in Social Movements." *Narrative Impact: Social and Cognitive Foundations*. Ed. Melanie C. Green, Jeffrey J. Strange, and Timothy C. Brock. Mahwah, New Jersey: Lawrence Erlbaum Associates, 2002. 205-29.

James, P.D. "The Art of the Detective Novel." *The Welsh Review*, 2/1 (1989): 4-9.

Jansen-Gruber, Marya. Rev. of *Eye of the Crow: The Boy Sherlock Holmes*, by Shane Peacock. 15 April 2017.
<http://lookingglassreview.com/books/eye-of-the-crow-the-boy-sherlock-holmes-his-1st-case/>

Johnson, Webb J. "Chick lit Jr.: More Than Glitz and Glamour for Teens and Tweens." *Chick lit: The new woman's fiction*. Ed. S. Ferriss and M. Young. New York: Routledge, 2006. 141-57.

Kaufman, G.F. and L.K. Libby. "Changing Beliefs and Behavioral Through Experience-Taking." *Journal of Personality and Social Psychology*, 103 (2012): 1-19.

Kokesh, Jessica and Miglena Sternadori. "The Good, the Bad, and the Ugly: A Qualitative Study of How Young Adult Fiction Affects Identity Construction." *Atlantic Journal of Communication*, 23 (2015): 139-58.

Kutenplon, Deborah and Ellen Olmstead. Preface. *Young Adult Fiction by African American Writers, 1968-1993*. Ed. Kutenplon and Olmstead. New York: Garland Publishing, Inc, 1996. ix-xv.

Labov, W. *Language in the Inner City: Studies in the Black English Vernacular.* Philadelphia: University of Pennsylvania Press, 1972.

Lin, Si Yan. Foreword. *Eye of the Crow: The Boy Sherlock Holmes, His 1st Case.* By Peacock. Trans by Yi Chen, Han. Taichung: Morning Star, 2011. 13-15.

Lu, Ren. Foreword. *Eye of the Crow: The Boy Sherlock Holmes, His 1st Case.* By Peacock. Trans by Yi Chen, Han. Taichung: Morning Star, 2011. 5-9.

Lukens, Rebecca J. *A Critical Handbook of Children's Literature.* Boston: Scott, Foresman and Company, 1986.

MacDonald, Ross. *The Moving Target: A Lew Archer Novel.* New York: Warner, 1990.

Mazlich, Bruce. "The Flâneur: From Spectator to Representation." *The Flâneur.* Ed. Keith Tester. New York: Routledge, 1994, 43-60.

Muse, Daphne. "Detectives, Dubious Dudes, Spies and Suspense in African American Fiction for Children and Young Adults." *The Black Scholar*, Vol. 28, No. 1 (Spring 1998): 33-39.

Nell, V. *Lost in a Book: The Psychology of Reading for Pleasure.* New Haven: Yale University Press, 1988.

Oatley, Keith. "Meetings of Minds: Dialogue, Sympathy, and Identification in Reading Fiction." *Poetics*, Vol. 26 (1999): 439-54.

Palmi, Christopher, Deborah Augsburger, and Dorene Huvaere, "Transforming Preservice Teachers' Awareness and Understanding of Multiculturalism Through the Use of Young Adult Literature." *Illinois Reading Council Journal*, Vol. 44, No. 4 (Fall 2016): 12-22.

Peacock, Shane. *Eye of the Crow: The Boy Sherlock Holmes, His 1st Case.* Toronto: Tundra Books, 2007.

Pederson-Krag, Geraldine. "Detective Stories and the Primal Scene." *The Poetics of Murder: Detective Fiction and Literary Theory.* Ed. Glenn W. Most and William W. Stowe. London: Harcourt Brace Jovanovich Publishers, 1983. 13-20.

Polichak, James W. and Richard J. Gerrig. "'Get Up and Win!': Participatory Responses to Narrative." *Narrative Impact: Social and Cognitive Foundations*. Ed. Melanie C. Green, Jeffrey J. Strange, and Timothy C. Brock. Mahwah, New Jersey: Lawrence Erlbaum Associates, 2002. 71-97.

Pratt, M.L. *Toward a Speech Act Theory of Literary Discourse.* Bloomington: Indiana University Press, 1977.

________. "Emotions and the Story Worlds of Fiction." *Narrative Impact: Social and Cognitive Foundations*. Ed. Melanie C. Green, Jeffrey J. Strange, and Timothy C. Brock. Mahwah, New Jersey: Lawrence Erlbaum Associates, 2002. 39-71.

Pinney, Thomas, ed. *Essays of George Eliot.* New York: Columbia University, 1963.

Pratt, M.L. *Toward a Speech Act Theory of Literary Discourse.* Bloomington: Indiana University Press, 1977.

Raheja, Lauren. "Anxieties of Empire in Doyle's Tales of Sherlock Holmes." *Nature, Society, and Thought* Vol. 19, No. 4 (2006): 417-26.

Rosenfeld, Shelle. Rev. of *Eye of the Crow: The Boy Sherlock Holmes,* by Shane Peacock. *Booklist*, Vol. 104, Issue 5 (November 2007): 44.

Rothfield, Lawrence. *Vital Signs: Medical Realism in Nineteenth-Century Fiction.* Princeton: Princeton University Press, 1992.

Rubin, R.B. and M.P. McHugh, "Development of Parasocial Interaction Relationship." *Journal of Broadcasting and Electronic Media*, 31(1987): 279-92.

Rybakova, Katie and Rikki Roccanti. "Connecting the Canon to Current Young Adult Literature." *American Secondary Education*, Vol. 44, Issue 2 (Spring 2016): 31-45.

Samuels, Barbara G. "Young Adults' Choices: Why Do Students 'Really Like' Particular Books?" *Journal of Reading*, Vol. 32, No. 8 (May 1989): 714-19.

Schank, R.C. and R.P. Abelson. "Knowledge and Memory: The Real Story." *Advances in Social Cognition.* Ed. R.S. Wyer. Vol. VIII. Hillsdale, New Jersey: Lawrence Erlbaum Associates, 1995. 1-86.

Schank, R.C. and Tamara R. Berman, "The Pervasive Role of Stories in Knowledge and Action," *Narrative Impact: Social and Cognitive Foundations*. Ed. Melanie C. Green, Jeffrey J. Strange, and Timothy C. Brock. Mahwah, New Jersey: Lawrence Erlbaum Associates, 2002. 287-315.

Searle, John R. "The Logical Status of Fictional Discourse." *New Literary History*, 6 (1975): 325.

Simmons, Diane. *The Narcissism of Empire: Loss, Rage, and Revenge in Thomas De Quincey, Robert Louis Stevenson, Arthur Conan Doyle, Rudyard Kipling and Isak Dinesen*. Brighton: Sussex Academic Press, 2007.

Slater, Michael D. "Entertainment Education and the Persuasive Impact of Narratives." *Narrative Impact: Social and Cognitive Foundations*. Ed. Melanie C. Green, Jeffrey J. Strange, and Timothy C. Brock. Mahwah, New Jersey: Lawrence Erlbaum Associates, 2002. 157-83.

Stephens, John and Robyn McCallum. *Retelling Stories, Framing Culture: Traditional Story and Metanarratives in Children's Literature*. New York: Garland.

Strange, J.J. and C.C. Leung. "How Anecdotal Accounts in News and in Fiction can Influence Judgments of a Social Problem's Urgency, Causes, and Cures." *Personality and Social Psychology Bulletin*, 25(4) (1999): 436-49.

Strange, J.J. "How Fictional Tales Wag Real-World Beliefs." *Narrative Impact: Social and Cognitive Foundations*. Ed. Melanie C. Green, Strange, and Timothy C. Brock. Mahwah, New Jersey: Lawrence Erlbaum Associates, 2002. 263-87.

Thompson, H. Douglas. "Masters of Mystery." *The Art of the Mystery Story: A Collection of Critical Essays*. Ed. Howard Haycraft. New York: Simon and Schuster, 1946. 128-45.

Thomson, Jon. *Fiction, Crime, and Empire: Clues to Modernity and Postmodernism*. Baltimore: University of Illinois Press, 1993.

Wang, Jian Min. Foreword. *Eye of the Crow: The Boy Sherlock Holmes, His 1st Case*. By Peacock. Trans by Yi Chen, Han. Taichung: Morning Star, 2011. 5-9.

Ward, David. Rev. of *Eye of the Crow: The Boy Sherlock Holmes*, by Shane Peacock. April 15. 2017 <https://www.umanitoba.ca/cm/vol14/no2/eyeofthecrow.html>

Zhang, Zi Zhang. *Realism and Fantasy: A Guided Reading of Foreign Young Adult Literary Works*. Taipei: Mandarin Daily News, 2001.

5

Growing Out of Location

Alessandro Monti and *Carole Rozzonelli*

Fictional young adults either from the subcontinent, India and Pakistan, or from the diasporic lands, the States and England, live in a disturbing condition of maladjustment the former, due to the burden of the excessive requirements imposed by the family, or in isolating non-hyphenated estrangement and perennial miscegenation of failed shared identities the latter.

Domestic alienation and a bitter or resentful feeling of unbelonging are the dominant features in such young adult novels. We should consider, for instance, *Jihadi Jane* (Tabish Khair, 2012), the sad story of two high-school students, the migrants Jamilla and her friend Ameena, both of them living in Birmingham, both of them coming out of an Urdu background.

Jamilla grows up in a squalid tenement building whose "blank windows were staring like the eyes of a zombie and the lift smelled of sweat and deodorant. There were newspapers and wrappers, syringes and used condoms lying about". The brown working class, mostly Muslims, has taken progressively the place in the building of the white working, or drinking, class (Adapted from p. 3).

Jamilla cannot get by with the too easy ways of her school batch, but at the same time stands at odds with the patriarchal order by which her family is ruled. In particular she disapproves them for disinheriting her ("I was just homeless in my father's house—that, by rights belonged to me too—as I was in this city", p. 72).

She refuses the Western ways of life ("the streets seemed filled with tawdriness and noise") and her unsympathetic feeling of depression reaches its highest point when she is going to be caught in the trap of an arranged marriage with a suitable expatriate young man ("The idea of living [...] with that vapid, satisfied-looking man did not appeal to me", p. 72).

The need for a simplified way of life ("The way an orthodox woman wants to dress—and I was a very orthodox woman—the way you want to dress, interact, meet or not meet other people, and live, all of it is under constant assault by ordinary life in the West", p. 82) leads Jamilla and Ameena to join the Caliphat in Syria. They think they will be empowered as a person by living in "a world where things appeared to have meaning, because they were not refracted into a million distorted shapes in thousands of mirrors of perception, sensation, thought", p. 116).

Unfortunately, their need for a blessed simplification against the confusion arising out of double belonging just means the exposure to constant gendered blame and punishment, insomuch as women they are denied any autonomy of thought and action. They just find a new and more severe prisonhouse, instead of a shared and friendly community.

The seclusion to which they are submitted to in the Syrian "orphanage", actually a refuge for Muslim women quitting the West and for the widows and daughters of the Isis fighters, magnifies the authoritarian and violent rule of the migrant domestic circle. Jamilla escapes at last, thanks to the sacrifice of Ameena, but branded a terrorist she is obliged to live in exile.[1]

Arranged marriages in the blind with unknown men from the homeland take often place to subtract daughters from school and the "immoral" ways of the corrupt West. This plight is exposed in *Daughters of Shame* (Jasvinder Sanghera, 2009), a chronicle grounding on a narrative of real broken lives among the Sikh migrant community in England.[2]

To escape an enforced marriage and a stifling domestic seclusion, a sort a preventive or punishing purdah, the "rebellious" daughters are obliged to live on the run, moving from a protected refuge to another, being continuously hunted down by parents, relatives, members of the Sikh community.

They are killed, after being left alone by the police or being ignored by such people as teachers or whatever authorities to which they reported. They are the victims of *izzat*, the honour of the family,

> Asian people don't question it [the concept of honour]: they're swaddled in it from the moment they're born, it's as though they absorb it along with their mother's milk. Honour—*izzat*—is the cornerstone of the Asian community and since the beginning of time it's been the job of girls and women to keep it polished. And that's really hard because so many things can tarnish it, wearing lipstick, owning a mobile phone, cutting your hair; any of those things could be said to bring dishonour on a family because those are all signs that a girl is getting westernised, which is what Asian families fight so hard against. They'd lock up their daughters for months on end rather than let that happen. When I was a girl my mum was always warning me against white people with their dirty white ways. She slapped me once because I said I'd like to buy a pair of jeans.[3]

The perspective is quite different if the narrative focus is shifted to a male character. In *Indian Takeaway*: *A British Story* (Hardeep Singh Kohli, 2008) a would-be "Scottish" migrant Sikh is seen since his boyhood as a fat brown Indian by everyone else in England. When in his thirties he decides to endorse his misrepresented hyphenated identity and sets out on a journey to India, with the purpose to cook for the natives British food.

His cooking is intended to be a condensed biographical recollection of his early years in England and at the same time it would suggest his accomplishment in the quest for an identity born out of fusion, that is the successful melting together of a double, but not partitioned cultural, heritage, "[...] I have decided that my opening foray into the education of the Indian palate should be something straight out of the heart of my childhood; a plate of food that by its ingredients and history alone tells the story of where I come from", (p. 50).

His "British" cooking would "epitomize" all he is, in a sort of emotional synthesis applied to the kitchen. However, his dream of "feeding Bharat" proves itself a sorry failure, a miscegenation rather than a happy meeting of cultures by means of an assimilative process. A confusion of food arises, given the impossibility of finding locally the proper ingredients.

Even a possible fusion (or a hyphenated kitchen) in cooking cannot be achieved. Indian eaters discard dishes like the "toad in the hole" ("Everything is correctly seasoned and I can honestly say that given the circumstances I couldn't have done any better", p. 154) and favour "king prawns in coconut and chilli".

The "onion sauce type gravy *jus* thing" reflects in its lexicon smacking of code mixing (*jūs*, Hindi, broth, soup, the water in which pulses and vegetables are boiled) reflects the divided self of the migrant cook, his attempt to fight his Britishness, to hide his own self (Adapted from p. 155).

His condition of everlasting inadequacy ("Why did I feel the need to apologise for being British when in India, and apologise for being Indian when in Britain?", p. 155) drives him far beyond the by now usual representation of the mimic migrant, but evades at the same time the Lacanian notion of the Other as the ontological mirror that allow us to recognise our inner self.

After coming back home the confused traveller seems to have learnt to cope with "the complexity of belonging". To cope with, not to go through it. When cooking his last meal in India, a goat curry with chopped onions and heated oil, he finally enjoys "a little bit of India in that place called home".

He failed when he tried "to bring a little taste of Britain to all of India", but now he is able to unify the two different locations in his life. If the aroma of frying in Indian oil with Indian spices is the smell of his heritage, it is also "the smell of growing up in Glasgow".

His "mission" of bringing British food to India has finally made it possible to conclude a search about himself and about what he feels about himself. His conclusion is: Home is where he wants it to be.

Indian Takeaway stands before the reader as an uninterrupted dialogue with the childhood of the writer. The novel is purposed to have a biographical background, above all with his father. Here no joint notions of *izzat* and shame harass and trouble family life. Indian migrants do not isolate themselves from Western society, by sticking acritically to excluding customs and vexing ways of life.

The troubled saga of *The Good Children* (Roopa Farooki, 2014) brings the reader back to tyrannical family circle, aptly embodied by an authoritarian and scheming mother, who wants to make obedient and passive respectable puppets of her two daughters and two sons.

The latter are destined to the medical practice following their father's steps, and are sent away to complete their studies in England and the United States. The two daughters are instead doomed to convenient arranged marriages with suitors to be chosen among the affluent families of Lahore.

However the daughters react with a vengeance to the enslaving schemes nurtured by their mother, who would train them to a life of domestic drudgery and imposed conjugal submission, also in the most private duties of marriage.

But one of them countertricks her mother, by marrying astutely of her own an almost unsuitable suitor, just to take refuge in her mother-in-law and get rid of a domineering mother. She will eventually divorce her husband and then marry and divorce again several times.

The other daughter will accept a man chosen by the family and unknown to her: they meet for the first time on the day of their marriage. Her unreactive acceptance of the connubial duties required of a woman at night drives her spurned husband to sexual promiscuity with a servant. She, an artful dodger, takes advantage of his betrayal and leaves him once for all; she goes to see her parents and never comes back. Of course, the gendered current morals consider disgraceful for a woman to quit her husband because of a sexual relationship with a servant, provided the man does not associate himself with a courtesan or a homosexual.

About the two sons, who still live in freedom abroad, one enters into a "scandalous" marriage with a Westernised Hindu expatriate, whereas the other cohabits as a wife with a man. The latter have adopted a raped child mother with her son.

The *Good Children* deals with a diasporic rejection on the part of the young daughters and sons against the joint code of moral behaviour. However, behind the claim for autonomous choices in private life lurks sadly the inability to break the stifling psychological and emotional tie with the mother, who still dominates even in absence.

The daughters and the sons reproduce the uncommunicative course in their family life—the former use husbands to achieve their own purposes and get afterwards rid of them. The latter are the weak ones in their relationships that seem to be marked, as far as partners are concerned, by an underlying feeling of estrangement.

The *Good Children* covers a span of about fifty or sixty years, but the narrative moves continuously backwards and forwards in time, through a sequence of alternate chapters, each devoted to a single character. This fragmentation would lay bare the affective failures within the family group, in a way that suggests the impossibility of a linear development of the narrative: the past is always encroaching upon the present.

A most radical case of estrangement and deranged disaffection from everyday life and its spatial surroundings is given in *A Bad Character* (Deepti Kapoor, 2014). Here an orphaned University student (her mother is dead and her father has moved on his own to Singapore, where he lives with a woman) is with her Aunty in Delhi, who is worrying at finding a husband, possibly a NRI, for her reluctant niece.

The usual frame of inner loneliness and extraneous participation to the social rites of the middle class acquires in the novel an almost uncanny metaphysical quality: Delhi is seen by the young woman through a hallucinatory sequence of shadows with no reality in them.

The turning point in the life of the character takes place when she meets the bad character of the title. He becomes her profane guide and instructs his disciple to sex, liquor, drugs and nocturnal wanderings about a ghastly Delhi, with its filthy suburbs and its dens of cosmopolitan drug addicts.

A nameless female *flâneur*, after the death of the man she wanders incessantly and alone, across and outside herself. Sometimes she shifts from "I" to "she" when writing about her —in the same page, suddenly and with no apparent reason, in a schizophrenic division of confused identities.

Also the chronological order of the narrative is upset: her autodiegetic voice moves up and down through the time sequences, as if she would revive the lost presence of the "bad character". Twenty-one years old, she just lives to remember the past, a shadow herself who moves in-between the tearing remembrance of her love-story and an aimless wandering in the present.

To conclude, it is worth quoting a mildly transgressive *Bildungsroman* concerning the early emotional education of a student. *Mom Says No Girlfriend* (Subhasis Das, 2010) mixes the *dosti* narrative with the usual theme of the overcontrolling mother, who has planned his entire life.

The protagonist is introduced to bouts of drinking and to the vision of porn DVDs, besides being entangled with several girls and young women, all of them unreliable or not really loved by him.

At twenty he gets rid of parental interference: he becomes an acclaimed singer, and his last escapade will perhaps end in marriage, but at the same time he realises he is in love, a platonic one however, with one of his three "disgraces" (that is, his friends), the one who is gay, and who has just consented to an arranged marriage in the blind, to please his unaware parents.

In this novel achieved adulthood means a "happy" compromise between public virtue, the marriage, and a legitimate wish concerning a personal, and not necessarily faulty, standard of behaviour.

Notes

1. In *Jimmy the Terrorist* (Omar Ahmad, 2010), a young man living in a conservative Muslim little town marries the uninterested and uncommunicative daughter belonging to a broken branch of the most prominent family in the *mohalla*. He is doomed to a marginal position in the local élite and his rage bursts finally out when Hindu fundamentalism starts pursuing the Muslims. He will kill a policeman ("I am Jimmy the Terrorist"). The novel is about alienating discrimination.
2. *Daughters of Shame* is a sequel to the biographical novel *Shame* (2007), in which the writer "flees from her family under threat of forced marriage".
3. In the seventies a middle-class Italian mother could forbid the wearing of jeans to a daughter. Quotation in the text from *Daughters of Shame*, p. 25.

References

Ahmad, Omair. *Jimmy the Terrorist*, New Delhi: Speaking Tiger, 2015 (2010).

Das, Subhasis. *Mom Says No Girlfriend*, New Delhi: Rupa, 2010.

Farooki, Roopa. *The Good Children*, London: Tinder Press, 2014.

Kapoor, Deepti. *A Bad Character*, New York: Knopf, 2014.

Khair, Tabish. *Jihadi Jane*, Gurgaon: Penguin India, 2016.

Kohli, Hardeep Singh. *India Takeaway: A Very British Story*, Edinburgh, Canongate, 2009 (2008).

Sanghera, Jasvinder. *Shame*, London: Hodder & Stoughton, 2007.

__________ *Daughters of Shame*, London: Hodder & Stoughton, 2009.

6

Exploring Traditional and Contemporary Conceptions in Young Adult Literature: The Way from the 'Incapable' to the 'Capable' Young Reader

Elena Xeni

Introductory Notes

In this contribution prevalent social conceptions of the young readers throughout the years will be critically visited in an attempt to acknowledge the influence of adults' views on the child and young reader in all relevant choices and decision-making and the significance this influence holds for the future of young adulthood, literature and the arts, and society (Γαβρηλίδου, 2013; Xeni, 2014, Ξενή 2014l, 2014m). Exploring adults' conceptions is a captivating process helping out to understand the context of the child and the young adult as well as decisions and choices made for them, without them, regarding present and future issues in various sectors (e.g., well-being, education, recreation, etc.) (Γαβριηλίδου, 2013).

This contribution, has its basis on a beneficial outcome of a recently conducted research, revealing that the adult-translators' views on child, childhood and children's literature influence their choices and decision-making, and, at the same time, children and young adult-readers' present and future contexts and perspectives (Xeni, 2014). Pouring to the surface the significant role the adults (adult-translators) play in all decisions involving children and young adults, this research in question highlights translators' strategies and behaviours while translating for young readers and the views and conceptions that govern these from simplifying the text because the reader might not understand it, to prettifying the text because the reader may not be able to deal with the bad, the sad, the confusing, and the difficult stuff (*ibid.*).

Leaving no space for second thoughts or interpretations, adults' views and conceptions about the young readers, the young readers' profile they construct, and the picture they have in their minds for the young readers, portrays the reasoning governing all their actions concerning the child and the young adult. This figure—the child/young adults—has always been a creature under adults' protection, supervision, auspices, and care, making the adult's role much more important, influential, powerful and dynamic (Kanatsouli, 2005; Xeni, 2016). Being of high status in society, much acknowledged concerning her/his strong abilities, responsible guidance and care, with a number of rights and benefits, the *adult* in history was a title of honour instead of the *child* and the *young adult* who had always stood by in ignorance due to a number of (mis)conceptions linked to childhood and young adulthood (Corsaro, 1997; James, and Prout, 1990; Gillins in Kehily, 2004; etc.). These conceptions will be critically reviewed below chronologically, from the early to the contemporary years.

Visiting Traditional and Contemporary Conceptions of the Young Reader

In the following lines, some notions concerning the young reader will be explored. Interestingly, although they are traditional in the sense that they chronologically link back to the early years in the history of childhood and society, they can be contemporary at the same time due to their influential presence in the notions of the current years.

The Incapable Young Reader

The conception of the incapable child originates from the classic years and the middle ages, when the young reader was not seen as a capable creature. Being seen in contrast to the adult reader, the young reader was always missing or lacking things and was dependant on the 'capable' adult, the authority with every power and all abilities and rights (Bidon and Lett, 1997; James and Prout, 1990; Kehily, 2004; etc.). From literature perspectives what was chosen for the young reader started from and ended in didactic texts, thus the limited role of literature was strictly moral and didactic, proclaiming readers how to be and behave accordingly (Γαβριηλίδου, 2013; Jenkins, 1998; Mills and Mills, 2000; etc.).

The Inexperienced Young Reader

Part of a child and young reader's inability was the lack of experience in life comparing to adults. The inexperienced child—a notion that links back to the middle ages—disabled the child from attending a large part of the adult's life (and even childhood itself), missing present and future opportunities and involvement. And when the young reader was lucky enough to accompany the adult in experiencing life, it was still that limited life experience that particular adult (mostly mother, father and teacher) would allow him/her to experience. This means that even though some children and young adults could have opportunities to enrich their experience, this was indeed limited and dependant on the adult (Alanen, 2014; Corsaro, 1997; Jenkins, 1998 and James, Jenks and Prout, 1998).

The Innocent Young Reader

Besides limited—or total absence of—experience, participation and abilities, innocence was a characteristic related to the young reader in the early years (Jenkins, 1998; Joosen and Vloeberghs, 2006; and Robinson, 2008). This is why the concept of the innocent child was frequently featured in literature and the arts during the classic years and the middle ages, traces of which can often be found in later years and even today. This particular representation of the young reader in adults' minds, which influences their actions and decisions concerning the young reader (Γαβριηλίδου, 2013; Xeni, 2014), can be said to be the reason, along with the two previous concepts—i.e. the one of the incapable and the inexperienced child—for the construction of one more conception, that of the protected young reader, which will be explored below (Γαβριηλίδου, 2013; Μακυρυνιώτη, 1997).

The Protected Young Reader

Living with an innocent young reader, lacking abilities and experience, the adults' conception of the protected child could not seem illogical in the early years. This conception advances the role of the adult; the adult having power and authority and being experienced and capable, protects the innocent, incapable and inexperienced young reader and is always available and willing to support, guide and defend her/him (Aries, 1973; Gillins in Kehily, 2004; Qvortrup, Sgritta and Wintersberger, 1994b). The adult-protector figure and the protected child or the child in need of protection figure are prevalent in literature starting from the 13th century (Γαβριηλίδου, 2013; Lukens, 1995). In these early years, young readers had access to literature that mainly taught them how to behave themselves at school, in the family and in society, whereas through play they were taught how to socialise and enjoy. In the framework of protection, every effort was made for young readers to access literature that created no problems with language, structure and content and with characters that mainly lived in a world or roses, away from barriers (Γαβριηλίδου, 2013; Kehily, 2004 and Lukens, 1995). Similarly to the previous notions, the conception of the protected young reader, was not being observed only throughout the years it was firstly emerged; it was still prevalent in later years and it is still the case in contemporary societies, where the child has power and authority (Μακρυνιώτη, 1997).

The Capable Young Reader

Interestingly, the young reader was not placed in the centre of all adults' plans, decision-making, actions, and perspectives from the early days of life, as one might guess. It took several years of marginalisation and underestimation before the young reader gained the attention inside and outside the family, the school, society, literature and the arts, etc. It hadn't been until this century—and, at a sense, the previous one—that childhood and young adulthood have gained their rights, have been acknowledged as being capable of doing things, thinking about things, choosing things, have the potential and the right of doing, saying, claiming, negotiating, acting, etc. (Γαβριηλίδου, 2013; Ξενή 2014l, 2014m; Xeni, 2014).

However, being acknowledged is one step towards success, but it does not mean 'winning the fight', as in the context of (mis)conceptions several years are needed for changes and improvements. This means that the current years might not be just there, when it comes to abundantly acknowledging the profile of the capable young reader in theory and practice.

Discussing the Diachronic Nature of the Adults' Conceptions Concerning the Young Reader

It goes without saying that attempts to explore traditional and contemporary conceptions in young adult literature, reveal conceptions that though traditional, old and outdated, are still present in the profile(s) that the adults build for the young reader. Although it is obvious that the way from the 'incapable' to the 'capable' young reader is a long one, one that has taken centuries to be constructed, entrancingly, how adults view and behave towards the young reader frequently reveals the existence of traditional conceptions as they were explored above, i.e., the incapable child, the inexperienced child, the innocent child and the protected child, making these conceptions contemporary ones, due to their diachronic nature and influential presence. Although in many neighbourhoods of the contemporary world the young reader is much acknowledged and respected as an actor, an agent and a personality, and is of a high status in society and other sectors (Lansdown, 1994; Qvortrup, Sgritta and Wintersberger, 1994b; etc.), she/he is still being conceived as innocent, incapable, inexperienced, dependent, etc., and thus may not only be guided and supported by adults, but supervised and protected by them.

These conceptions, that influence behaviours and actions, result in a literature for the young reader in particular and an everyday life in general with simplifications and prettifications. In this constructed-by adults-context and well-protected framework, the young reader, being incapable of handling too much cognitive-load, is prevented from too much thinking, doing, acting, etc. (Xeni, 2014). This is why the language is simple; the plot is simplistic; the characters are easy to be understood, interpreted and remembered; the events taking place are happy, enjoyable and amusing; etc. Everything is simple, clear, easy to understand, nice, mostly familiar and enjoyable. Sadness, disaster, difficult and unknown situations, dilemmas and losses are far away from this protected-by adults-construction, in this framework that creates the need for the adults to protect the young reader and make sure that things move smoothly and effortlessly (*ibid.*).

And although the historical overview makes a last stop to the capable young reader as a contemporary conception and as a view acknowledging all abilities and aspects missing or lacking behind in the traditional conceptions, in reality it may not function as a last one in a number of contemporary societies (Ξενή, 2014l, 2014m). Adults' behaviours in many parts of the world link back to the features describing what young readers are not able to do than their abilities, whereas in other contexts, societies have taken a step further in notions, acknowledging the critical reader and embarking upon bridging the gap between the young and adult reader (and literature)—a development being captivatingly significant for a number of fields (Xeni). These behaviours derive from adults' (mis)conceptions concerning what the young reader can do (or can't do) and may (or may not) achieve and due to these behaviours (translated) literature addressed to the young readers might (or not) lack behind developments and achievements affecting—at the same time—the young reader widely.

Concluding Notes

Adults' views concerning the young reader do not necessarily correspond to reality nor link to or benefit the young reader's authentic profile(s). These views are constructed based on outdated conceptions—at times misconceptions—about the child/young reader and childhood, linking back to early years and previous centuries, where the young reader was concerned by the adult to be innocent, incapable, inexperienced and in need for protection. Such conceptions mainly affect young readers' present and future everydayness, dynamic and potential, imprisoning them into a context of several limitations, less opportunities and minimum potential, all harming knowledge, participation, autonomy, critical thinking, etc. In this context the adult—being her/him the adult-writer, the adult-translator, the adult-editor, the adult-teacher, the adult-parent, etc. (Xeni, 2014)—gains a key role, being the protector, the decision-maker, the constructor of a non-advanced present and future reality, taking away every opportunity for advancement, independence, involvement, and critical ability from the young reader.

In exploring traditional and contemporary conceptions about the young reader, one cannot miss to observe that the way from the 'incapable' to the 'capable' young reader might have taken a number of centuries as a journey and a greater number of adults to construct the (mis)conceptions in question. It will, however, take a lot more to take these conceptions further, especially in years such as the contemporary ones, where besides the improvements detected, in certain parts of the world and for particular groups of adults, there is still a tendency to ignore or underestimate the abilities and potential of the young reader.

References

Greek Language

Γαβριηλίδου, Σ. (2013). Φλυαρία και Λακωνικότητα στους Τίτλους των Βιβλίων για Παιδιά. Ιστορικές Διαδρομές μέσα απσό την Ανάγνωση των Τίτλων της. Θεσσαλονίκη: Ζυγός.

Μακρυνιώτη, Δ. (1997). Παιδική Ηλικία. Αθήνα: Νήσος.

Ξενή, Ε. (2014l). «Το Παιδί, η Παιδικότητα και η Παιδική Λογοτεχνία στο Μυαλό του Μεταφραστή:

Χαρτογραφώντας τις Παιδαγωγικές Προεκτάσεις». Πρακτικά 11ου Συνεδρίου Παγκύπριας Παιδαγωγικής Εταιρείας (ΠΕΚ), Πανεπιστήμιο Κύπρου, 10-11 Οκτωβρίου 2014.

Ξενή, Ε. (2014m). «Ανα-στοχασμός για την Παιδική Ηλικία όπως προκύπτει από μια Βουτιά στα

`Αδυτα του Μυαλού του Μεταφραστή της Παιδικής Λογοτεχνίας». Εισήγηση. Πανελλήνιο Συνέδριο με διεθνή Συμμετοχή: «*Ανα-Στοχασμοί για την Παιδική Ηλικία*, ΤΕΠΑΕ», ΑΠΘ, Θεσσαλονίκη, 31 Οκτωβρίου-1 Νοεμβρίου 2014.

English Language

Alanen, L. (2014). Theorizing childhood. *Childhood*, 21(1), 3-6.

Aries, P. (1973). *L' enfant et al vie familial sous I' Ancien Regime.* Paris: le Seuil.

Bidon, D.A. and Lett, D. (1997). *Children in the Middle Ages: Fifth-Fifteenth Centuries.* Notre Dame, Indiana: The University of Notre Dame Press.

Corsaro, W. (1997). *The Sociology of Childhood*. USA: Pine Forge Press.

Gillins, D. "The Historical Construction of Childhood". In Kehily, M.J. (Ed.). *An Introduction to Childhood Studies* (2nd edition). Maidenhead: Mc-Graw-Hill-Open University Press, 35-49.

James, A. and Prout, A. (Eds.) (1990). *Constructing and reconstructing childhood: Contemporary issues in the sociological study of childhood*. London: The Falmer Press.

James, A., Jenks, C. and Prout, A. (1998). *Theorizing Childhood*. Cambridge, UK: Polity Press.

Jenkins, H. (1998). "Introduction: Childhood Innocence and Other Modern Myths". In H. Jenkins (Ed.) (1998). *The Children's Culture Reader*. New York: New York University Press.

Joosen and Vloeberghs (2006). *Changing Concepts of Childhood and Children's Literature*. Newcastle, UK: Cambridge Scholars Press.

Kanatsouli, M. (2005). "Ideology of Contemporary Greek Picture Books", *Children's Literature*, 33, 209-23.

Kehily, M.J. (2004). *An Introduction to Childhood Studies*. Oxford, UK: Open University Press.

Lansdown, G. (1994). Children's Rights. In B. Mayall (Ed.) *Children's Childhoods: Observed and Experienced*. London: Falmer Press.

Lukens, R.J. (1995). *A Critical Handbook of Children's Literature*. New York and London: Longam.

Mills, J., and Mills, R. (2000). *Childhood Studies: A Reader in Perspectives of Childhood*. London: Routledge.

Qvortrup, J., Sgritta, G. and Wintersberger, H., (Eds.). (1994b). *Childhood Matters: Social Theory, Practices and Politics*. Avebury Aldershot, UK/Vienna, Italy: European Centre.

Robinson, K. (2008). In the name of childhood innocence. A discursive exploration of the moral panic associated with childhood and sexuality. *Cultural Studies Review*, 14(2): 113-29.

Xeni, E. "The way to the critical child/young reader: An Overview". 2nd International Conference on: "Literacy and Contemporary Society: Bridging sociocultural, philosophical, pedagogical and technological dimensions". Nicosia, Cyprus, 24-25 November 2017.

Xeni, E. (2016). *Contemporary Profile(s) of Childhood*. Oxford, UK: Inter-Disciplinary Press.

________ (2014). Investigating the Process of Translation: Humour Translation Norms, Strategies and Approaches in Children's Literature. MPhil Thesis. Aston University, Birmingham, UK. Available at: https://research.aston.ac.uk/portal/en/theses/investigating-the-process-of-translation(04c5d744-2191-46ca-986b-aa49ddde9030).html [accessed 1 August 2017].

7

Environmental Education through Fiction: A Study of Deepak Dalal's Vikram-Aditya Series

Shobhna Ramaswamy

One of the offshoots of postcolonial criticism is the rise of ecocriticism which studies the relationship between literature and the physical environment (Glotfelty and Fromm xviii). It seeks to counter the anthropocentric view which spells inevitable doom for the planet by trying to justify the exploitation of natural resources. The creators of Indian fiction in English for the young have always been keenly sensitive to the need for providing a value-based experience to their young readership and so have aimed at imparting ecological literacy. "Ecological literacy refers to conscious awareness and understanding of the relationships among people, other organisms, and the environments in which they live. Texts themselves work toward ecological literacy, whether specifically or tacitly" (Dobrin and Kidd 233).

Deepak Dalal is one of the foremost writers of Indian young adult fiction today. A chemical engineer by profession, Deepak Dalal set out to write "Indian tales for Indian children" in 1995 (Gupta). Thus was born the *Vikram-Aditya* series of adventures, set in some of the most picturesque places in India, with a strong focus on environment and travel. With an idea towards connecting young people with the wilderness, his stories highlight issues of conservation of forests and wildlife. The books, drawn from his own travels and observations, are to date: *Ranthambore Adventure* (1998), *Lakshadweep Adventure* (2000), *The Snow Leopard Adventure* (2000), *Ladakh Adventure* (2013), *Andaman Adventure: The Jarawa* (2013) and *Andaman Adventure: Barren Island* (2013).

Deepak Dalal takes immense care to authentically research the environment in which his adventures are set. He has personally travelled to Ladakh, the Andamans, Lakshadweep, Ranthambore and to the other places he describes. He meets the locals and brings out the problems and the eco-friendly lifestyles of the traditional communities. He makes a realistic assessment of the impact of 'civilization' on their lives and also on the ecosystem of which they are a part. He is keen to expose poaching—the poachers, their markets and their network. Dalal's heroes are fearless but well-trained nature adventurers who save the ecology of the endangered regions through their sharp wits and timely actions. They also go on expeditions amidst the beauty of nature and indulge in adventure sports. The flora and fauna of the varied ecosystems—be they mountain, high plateau, coral reef, sea, volcanic island, lush forest—is authentically portrayed, with ecological concepts woven seamlessly into the stories.

Rachel Carson's words: "The predator and the preyed upon exist not alone, but as part of a vast web of life, all of which needs to be taken into account" (253) seems to form the basis of *Ranthambore Adventure*. In this book, Dalal addresses the issue of tiger poaching which is carried on with impunity in India's wildlife sanctuaries. He exposes the operational tactics and network of poachers as well as the potential market for tiger bones. Dalal also portrays the noble work of dedicated forest officers.

The story is humanized by following the story of Genghis, the king of the Ranthambore tigers. Mr. Reddy, Chief Forest Officer of Ranthambore National Park, records through photographs a tigress and her cubs. The story follows birth of the tiger cub Genghis in the cold season in the valley in between steep cliffs. The care taken by the tigress to ensure the safety and happiness of her offspring is touching. The mother tigress looks after her new-born and teaches them to take their first steps. She took many great precautions to avoid predators, especially those of the two-legged variety. "She trusted humans seated in vehicles, but humans on foot were another matter altogether" (*RA* 9). She would be very still until they passed.

Deepak Dalal alternates chapters devoted to the tiger's narrative to that of the youngsters Vikram, Aditya Khan and Aarti. Vikram's father heads a wildlife conservation organization, Wilderness Conservation India (WCI) where they learn about India's Tiger Crisis. Tiger bones are valued in Chinese medicine and so poaching is rampant in the sanctuaries. The poacher-smuggler nexus depletes wildlife. Aditya tells Aarti that killing wildlife for meat is forgivable; hunting for fun is unpardonable; but the worst offenders are those who hunt for profit (*RA* 15). Deepak Dalal includes information about animal behaviour and human-animal conflict supported with statistical data in an ideal combination of fictitious narrative backed with solid facts in order to imbue the minds of his readers with environmental awareness.

The intrusion of people into the sanctuary disturbs its peace. Cattle-grazing is a bane to wild animals. "The presence of humans and their cattle disturbed the forest equilibrium" (*RA* 72). Since the tiger's natural prey disappeared when they saw humans, the tiger was forced to hunt domestic cattle, and this caused humans to invade forests to hunt the tiger, which they perceived as the enemy. The vicious circle which was actually initiated by human beings led to the vilification of a beast which was by nature reclusive.

Dalal reveals that the human and the animal are not so very different "Recognised as a cornerstone of deep ecological thinking, identification constitutes an awareness that humans are inextricably enmeshed in broader bio-social relations" (Curry 161). One of the most pathetic episodes in the book is the discovery by Genghis of his dear mother's skin and flesh, abandoned near an unused human dwelling in the forest.

> On one side of the dwelling, he came upon portions of crumpled tiger skin. The smell of the skin had been unmistakable; the familiar, comforting, all-enveloping odour of his childhood—the scent of his mother Whoever had killed her had sliced her body apart. Her flesh was a bloodied mess on the ground, but her bones were missing. (*RA* 73)

Two of the tigress's cubs had been slaughtered along with their mother. The third had possibly escaped, but "the death-dealing humans had ensured its demise. The tiny animal was too young to hunt and there was no mother to provide for it anymore. The cub would die a slow, lingering death by starvation; or, if it were lucky, suffer a quick end at the claws of an opportunistic predator" (*RA* 73). As Huggan et al. warn, "The ultimate concern about species is that they may become extinct due to human activities.... The death of an individual is also the death of its kind" (177).

The cruelty of poaching is graphically illustrated by Dalal when he describes how a trap, "a murderous mechanism" slices into Genghis's leg: "It was as if a million ants were digging pincers within. Blood pumped forth, staining the grass red. The tiger collapsed, his calls of distress shattering the peace of the night" (*RA* 74).

Early next morning, two men enter the reserve with a sack, a gun and a spear. They follow the blood trail of the wounded tiger. They had been promised ₹10,000/- for procuring tiger pelt and bones. For this paltry sum, the equivalent of the biblical thirty pieces of silver, they are willing to deprive the country of its national animal.

The encounter with Genghis is something the poachers would never forget. The magnificent terror of the powerful beast stuns them. Still, the tiger does not strike. "Some inner sense-instilled by his mother prevented the tiger from ever attacking humans". The man drops his gun when "the tiger's flaming eyes were locked with his, reflecting a terrible anger." He seemed "unable to withstand the animal's accusing glance" (*RA* 75).

The enormity of poachers' perfidy is exposed. Even though Genghis escapes being killed by the greedy men, he cannot fend for himself. Dalal describes the tiger's plight very accurately through the words of Chief Forest Officer Mr. Reddy: "Can a limping tiger bring down fleet-footed deer and antelope? Even healthy tigers, with four good legs, rarely succeed" (*RA* 77). The forest officials had to attempt to capture the tiger and treat him for his injury. But since traps were designed to bring about permanent disability, the tiger's chances of recovery were slim. He would have to be taken to a zoo. A wild tiger who had lost his freedom would not survive long. It would be a delayed death sentence for him.

Meanwhile, Genghis, with the tenacity inherent only in tigers, somehow overcomes his terrible pain and tries to hunt. But he is by and large unsuccessful and has to subsist on very small animals and birds. Nearing starvation, he does not care anymore and prepares to die.

The forest officials try to bait him with live prey. It is a difficult task, since, "like all wounded animals, Genghis had sought deep cover" (*RA* 78). They manage to shoot a tranquillised dart at him. But Genghis disappears, causing the officers much anxiety. Dalal informs the young reader of a little-known fact—the temperature of a tranquillised tiger shoots up abnormally and unless he is caught and treated, he could die. A thrilling encounter with the injured Genghis who has sought refuge in a cave follows. The drugged tiger falls down while in pursuit of a forest official and is examined and treated by a veterinarian before being released into the wild. It is due to Mr. Reddy's intervention that he is not sent to a zoo. Genghis soon regains his position as the king of Ranthambore, but not before inadvertently giving the poacher, Shakar Chand, the shock of a lifetime. The tiger survives to live a life of dignity in the sanctuary.

In Deepak Dalal's *Andaman Adventure: The Jarawa*, Dalal's adventurous duo, Vikram and Aditya, along with the athletic and independent girl Chitra embark on a voyage along the fabulous Andaman coastline. In the introductory letter written by Vikram's father, there is a detailed description of the islands, their fauna and flora as well as of the elusive natives. Vikram's father asks the trio to meet his friend, Dr. Sankaran, an ornithologist who is residing on the islands in order to ensure the survival of a small bird called 'edible nest swiftlet' which surprisingly secretes the material for its nest. Unfortunately, its nest is considered to have medicinal properties by the people in the Far East and hence the nests are stolen. The youngsters encounter various types of nest-thieves as well as a sea-snake which inhabits the mangrove swamps on the islands. Chitra is excited and picks up the highly poisonous snake fearlessly and explains its distinct characteristics. They cross the mangroves with their spear-sharp ariel roots and the waters are phosphorus Chitra has plans to pursue research at the Crocodile Bank in Chennai and has already learnt how to move safely among the fearsome reptiles. For example, she can stun them temporarily with a powerful torchbeam.

The highlight of their adventures is their encounter with the Jarawa, who resent outside contact and fiercely protect their culture. However, the Jarawa are friendly towards them after they make it clear that they detest Burmese intruders. However, the outside world has made some impact on Jarawa lives in the form of plastic buckets, bottles and nylon fishing nets. Ominously, some of the westernized tribesmen sport colourful shorts and hats, Deepak Dalal, with his penchant for accurate recording of fauna and flora is evidenced in course of the story. Along the coast, the young nature-lovers spot the mighty white-bellied sea eagle, the serpent eagle and the brown eagle. Diving underwater, they see stunningly beautiful sea fans, clownfish, sea anemones, parrotfish, butterfly fish and encounter a sting ray. The food chain and predator-prey relationship is explained with regard to birds and fish. The book warns the readers about the overwhelming nature of "modern civilization" which had made the Greater Andamanese extinct and appreciates the valiant efforts of the Jarawa to resist it. The Andaman Trunk Road was built through the forest despite the efforts of the Jarawa to stop its construction. The traffic arouses the curiosity of the tribesmen who, till then, had hidden themselves in the forests. When they began to become visible, "Jarawa tours" were conducted by unscrupulous businessmen. Measles, which was hitherto unknown in the region, attacked the Jarawa and they nearly all died. Dalal's message to save the Jarawa is: "Leave them alone!"

Andaman Adventure: Barren Island is a continuation of *The Jarawa*. The preface traces the intrusion of the British into the island to build a prison. They cleared the forests and deprived the Andamanese of their livelihood in the name of 'development.' The children encounter goats on Barren Island which had learnt to survive on seawater, a recent case of evolutionary adaptation. They admire the volcano of Barren Island, which acquired its nomenclature from the fact that no vegetation grew among its ashes. The landscape around the volcano is carefully described. The trio foils the efforts of poachers from Burma who come to steal *trebang* and also other poachers who steal lapwing nests.

Lakshadweep Adventure takes Vikram and Aditya far out into the Arabian Sea to crystal-clear lagoons and coral reefs. They enjoy adventure sports such as windsurfing and scuba diving and encounter sharks and sea turtles. The Author's Note at the beginning of the story explains the geography of the islands and highlights their unique features. Vikram warns Aditya about the angers underwater. Any fish more than two feet long can seriously injure a human being. The descriptions are accurate and pleasing: "Vikram could now see that the coral reef was not really a wall, instead it was a complex jumble of various types of exquisitely shaped clumps of coral. In front of them—stretching across their path like a quivering blue curtain—was a shoal of little pale blue fish, each no bigger than Vikram's little finger" (*LDA* 14). They watch the graceful underwater movements of the great turtles and are fascinated by the ugly and dangerous Moray Eel. Vikram encounters reef sharks, but his knowledge that they do not attack unless they see a weak or injured person, reassures him. The boys learn the to-dos and not-to-dos of scuba diving from Mr. Koya.

Dalal expresses his feelings about coral reef through Vikram: "The reef was an eerie place. Vikram felt uneasy—as if he were trespassing on a forbidden zone.... The reef was not for humans. It belonged to the sea and all its myriad creatures which lived and died within its unique life-sustaining embrace." On the beach surrounding the lagoon, "the sand between them and the water appeared to be alive with creatures" (*LDA* 113). They happened to be hermit crabs, which inhabited different varieties of shells, since they had none of their own. Dalal shows the reader that it I man who interfere with nature; nature rarely does. "None of the crabs came towards them. They went about their own business, purposely waddling across the sand" (*LDA* 113). Vikram reflects: "It was fascinating how each creature adapts differently to its environment. Each species had to develop mechanisms to survive. The Clownfish had its sea anemone, the Porcupine Fish had its poisonous spines, Stonefish had its brilliant camouflage and the Hermit Crab stone shells" (*LDA* 114).

Vikram and Aditya acquire a friend, Shaukt, who has never set foot on the mainland since he was fifteen finds a great contrast between the rude behaviour of the people on the mainland and the calm, peaceful island life, where crime is unknown. He asserts that no islander would want to leave: "Our lagoons, our palm trees, the coral sand, the fishes, the reef—it is all part of us. You can never separate them from our souls" (*LDA* 115). The author includes an endnote about volcanic islands and the fragile coral ecosystem.

Ladakh Adventure takes Vikram and Aditya to the land beyond the Himalayas, to the lofty Changthang Plateau. The boys camp with *Meme* Chacko, who is there to observe black-necked cranes. The sheer cold in the hottest month of August strikes Vikram, as does the vastness of the Himalayan landscape, where everything is on a grand scale. Vikram learns that the local Changpa dogs are a menace to the bird population, since each pair of the latter has only one chick a year. "The loss of even a single chick has a bearing on the future of the species," says Meme Chacko (*LA* 8). Vikram breathlessly witnesses the miraculous escape of a nestling. Higher on the mountains, they see hundreds of marmots on the slopes. Aditya laughs: "Marmot locomotion is always comical. The animals are fat, squat balls of fur. Their movements are funny indeed: a kind of rolling, twisting motion, more like a frantic waddle" (*LA* 30). The marmots enjoy the summer and hibernate during the winter.

On the high altitude desert of Tso Kar, they see the magnificent golden eagle, redshanks, greenshanks, sand plovers, river terns, brahmini ducks, and, surprisingly, gulls. They also see bar-headed geese migrating over the Himalayas at an altitude of 25,000 feet, far higher than any other bird could fly. Vikram is mesmerized by the primeval songs of the cranes at sunset, which he remembers a poet describing as 'the trumpet in the orchestra of evolution' (*LA* 36). Vikram sees 'scree' slopes, which are covered with a crumbling material which does not fall.

Dalal waxes poetic over the beauty of the Himalayan mountainscape:

> In a chameleon-like manner Vikram had never witnessed, the mountains kept changing colours. In some sections they were shaded brown, in others they were purple; sometimes they appeared orange and sometimes golden. It was a grand wilderness they drove through, hostile ad inhospitable to the extreme, yet magnificent to behold. Sheer mountainsides; windswept peaks; boulder-strewn slopes; tones of delicately balanced scree; twisting gorges; a frothing river—the images piled one upon the other, moving Vikram deeply, evoking in him a profound sense of desolation. (*LA* 57)

The group passes through the Indus valley into Leh where they learn that western influence has begun corrupting the youth of the region. Vikram and Aditya encounter the Indo-Japanese smuggler Akira, who is to feature as Dalal's prominent villain. The boys join Dr. Raghu on his expedition to photograph and document the elusive snow leopard.

In Deepak Dalal's *The Snow Leopard Adventure,* Vikram and Aditya, joining a team of ecologists and explorers, set off on an expedition to the Zanskar Mountains of Ladakh to search for the fabled leopard. The snow leopard is a rare animal of immense beauty but so elusive that it is called the 'Grey Ghost of the Himalaya.' The book is the result of the author's own experiences as part of ecologist Raghu Raman's annual snow leopard expedition.

The team members are Dr. Raghu Raman, expedition leader and dedicated wildlife scientist, Tina Kuruvilla, second-in command, Julia and Caroline Austin, from the USA, Kathy and Richard Smith, a British couple, both wildlife lovers, Yuan Lee, a computer engineer from Singapore, who loves the mountains, the Australian, Roger Allen, Anders and Eva, a Swedish couple on a bicycle tour, and Tsering Ringmo, young reincarnated lama.

The company travels along the Indus River. Vikram is aware of the great historical and geographical significance of the region. The landscape, with wide fields of barley and stands of popular trees is striking. "But this was the only visible greenery. Everywhere else the landscape was so stark and barren that it resembled the surface of the moon" (*LA* 1), says the author.

Ladakh is a high altitude desert. It lies to the north of the mighty Himalaya mountains. Vikram recollects:

> My mind boggled at the star scenery about us. It was a fantastic wilderness, so desolate and so strange that I felt threatened by it. Crumbling peaks sprouted amidst vast barren plateaus. Visibility was perfect and we could see for miles, but there was no sign of human habitation. The thundering presence of water seemed at odds with the desert like landscape around us. (*LA* 2)

They follow the course of the Rumbak, a tributary of the Indus, into the mountains. *Bharal*, or blue sheep, graze in the high altitudes, above the snow line. "Unlike any sheep I have seen they possessed no fleecy wool. They were grey and stood much taller than domestic sheep" (*LA* 4), says Aditya and continues, "The goat-like creatures were about the same size as Ladakhi ponies and their predominant colour was a greyish-brown which merged well with their surroundings" (*LA* 41).

They are easily able to negotiate the treacherous mountain paths. Blue sheep are an important prey species of the snow leopard, so there was always a possibility of spotting a leopard when they saw *bharal*. In the summer, blue sheep, *argali* and *urial* the animals which are the natural prey of the snow leopard, move into the higher pastures and the predator follows them. When the mountain sheep sense the presence of the leopard, they go to the edge of the cliff, because the animal would hesitate to spring on them for fear of going over the edge. From the way the sheep watch a pile of boulders nearby, the team understands that a snow leopard is hiding there. They could not see the animal, which "had the talent of melting into the mountainside" (*LA* 30).

"The Ladakh Mountains are very different from my Nilgiri ones. There are no trees to soften their edges and their slopes are bare and naked" (Gupta 34), says the author, who did his schooling in Uthagamandalam in the Nilgiris. As they travel higher, Vikram and Aditya find glacier-smoothened mountainsides. They come across leopard scats or excretions, which they collect in order to analyse the snow leopard's diet. They also meet Anders and Eva, the Swedish couple on a bicycle tour.

The landscape, the author writes, recalling his personal experience: "Every peak that soared above the campsite was bathed in sunlight, but lower down the valleys were filled with shadows. Vikram gaped in awe at the scale of the shadows. They were gigantic, some stretching several kilometres" (*LA* 38). The level ground they walked across was huge. "There was enough space here for fifty cricket grounds," thought Vikram. "The valley ahead was crawling with bharal; there were well over a hundred of them" (*LA* 40). The positive effect of the huge Himalayan range helps the American girl, Caroline, who accompanies her mother on the expedition. She is the victim of a fragmented family and is so deeply upset that she wants to die. It is her near escape from death that cures her. She later tells her companions:

> Crazy things were going on inside my head. But when I found myself dangling on the edge of the cliff and my death wish about to be fulfilled, something snapped inside me. It was a wake up call. My life, everything I was, everything I wished to be, flashed before my eyes and I discovered that I did not want to die. (*LA* 63)

The landscape cures her of depression and she grows to love the place. "At first all I noticed in Leh were the power failures, the crummy hotels, the lousy plumbing and the terrible food. Now I remember the smiles on the peoples' faces, their warmth and their hospitality. The mountains appeared forbidding...I was frightened of them then. But the truth is that they are grand, infinitely beautiful..." (*LA* 63).

The tiger bone and shahtoosh trade is rampant in Ladakh. The story begins with a report prepared by the Wildlife Society of India with regard to this. The magnitude of the poaching in the region is seen from the fact that the Tibetan antelope or the Chiru, as it is locally known, once roamed the northern plains in huge herds but their numbers have been dramatically reduced due to hunting for its dense undercoat, called shahtoosh. The wool spun from it is considered the finest in the world. Its name means 'king wool.' The wool is woven into luxurious shawls that are prized the world over. In the past, hunting was minimal, but today the demand from the fashion industry has pushed up the value and killing of the animals has become an extremely profitable venture. Though the trade in shahtoosh has been banned worldwide, it still persists. A barter system exists along the border of Ladakh and Tibet, where shahtoosh wool is exchanged for tiger bones. The bones are from tigers killed in the sanctuaries of India. The nomadic Changpa people carry them on the backs of yaks, across remote Himalayan passes, into Tibet. Besides spurring the slaughter of the antelope, this trade also threatens the survival of the Indian tiger. Mr. Akira Singh, a half-Indian and half-Japanese smuggler is behind the trade. He is the main villain of the story.

Vikram argues with Akira the smuggler in an effort to make him give up his trade. "What right do we have to destroy these species and wipe them off the face of the planet?... They too have a right to live!" (*LA* 79).

Akira contends that he is simply a businessman. The people who want medicines made from tiger bones and those who wear shahtoosh shawls are to blame:

> I don't use tiger bone medicines and I personally don't care for shahtoosh shawls. Get it clear in your head that it is not Akira who is driving these animals to extinction. It is those *educated* people with money in their pockets who are responsible.... If they catch me, someone else will take my place. You arrest him, and somebody else will take his place. The killing will go on. Tell your precious organisations to focus on the *cause* of the problem. Their money can be better spent on educating people not to use tiger bone medicine and not to aspire for shahtoosh shawls. (79)

The argument between Vikram and Akira forms the crux of the story. It provides the reader with new insights into the problem:

> "Seriously," said Akira earnestly, "I have always liked animals. I have visited all the sanctuaries in this country. . . . I have been to Kanha, Kazhiranga, Ranthambore and Corbett. Dealing in animal products doesn't mean that I do not appreciate the creatures. I believe that people should be clear about their priorities, like I am. I am fond of animals. But I will not let that override my business instincts." (*LA* 85)

The highlight of the story is Dalal's descriptions of the snow leopard. Caroline, looking at them from afar with binoculars, calls them "silver ghosts". "The leopards walked in single file, the cubs following in the tracks of their mother." When in danger, they stop. Caroline recalls Raghu, words: "when a snow leopard freezes, it vanishes into the mountainside" (*LA* 115).

Vikram's encounter with the snow leopard is an almost mystical experience:

> It was a silver shadow against a backdrop of glittering stars. It had wonderful fluffy fur. Vikram couldn't help admiring it magnificent coat. The animal wasn't very tall and it had a long tail, almost as long as itself. The tail was silvery too. Two ears protrude from its head and he saw delicate whiskers on its snout.... For a carnivorous cat its face was rather small, much smaller than that of a tiger.... It had thick, furry paws and rosettes. The cubs were cute and cuddly, not adjectives usually associated with carnivorous cats. The animals were balls of smoky fur, exquisite and delightful. (*LA* 109-11)

Deepak Dalal's well-researched books, based on his actual experiences carry the message of Lawrence Buell that the non-human is not a mere framing device but a presence and that the human interest is not the only legitimate interest in this world. Therefore, human accountability to the environment should be a part of the text's orientation (7-8).

His descriptions of nature are breath-taking photographs and these, along with his environmental messages, will instill national pride and protective instincts in the young reader.

Works Cited

Buell, Lawrence. *The Environmental Imagination: Thoreau, Nature Writing and the Formation of American Culture.* Cambridge, MA.: Harvard University Press, 1996. Print.

Carson, Rachel. *Silent Spring*. London: Penguin, 2000. Print.

Curry, Alice. *Environmental Crisis in Young Adult Fiction: A Poetics of Earth*. New York: Palgrave Macmillan, 2013. Print.

Dalal, Deepak. *Andaman Adventure: Barren Island.* Pune: Tarini Publishing, 2000. Print.

_______. *Andaman Adventure: The Jarawa.* Pune: Tarini Publishing, 2000. Print.

_______. *Ladakh Adventure.* Pune: Tarini Publishing, 2000. Print.

_______. *Lakshadweep Adventure.* Pune: Tarini Publishing, 2000. Print.

_______. *Ranthambore Adventure.* Pune: Tarini Publishing, 2010. Print.

_______. *The Snow Leopard Adventure.* Pune: Tarini Publishing, 2010. Print.

Dobrin, Sidney I. "It's Not Easy Being Green: Jim Henson, the Muppets and Ecological Literacy." Dobrin, Sidney I. and Kenneth B. Kidd, eds. *Wild Things : Children's Culture and Ecocriticism.* Detroit: Wayne State University Press, 2004. 232-53. Print.

Glotfelty, Cheryll and Harold Fromm. Introduction. *Ecocriticism Reader*. Athens, Georgia: University of Georgia Press, 1995. xv-xxxvii. Print.

Gupta, Atula. "Interview: Deepak Dalal, Penning of Nature and Adventure." *India's Endangered.com.* 18 Dec. 2012. Web; 14 Aug. 2014.

Huggan, Graham and Helen Tiffin. *Postcolonial Ecocriticism: Literature, Animals, Environment.* New York: Routledge, 2010.

8

Reading *Frankenstein* and *The Strange Case of Dr. Jekyll and Mr. Hyde* in High-School: The Oscillating Worlds of 'Beautiful' and 'Ugly'

Sharmistha Chatterjee Sriwastav

(.................) I see him there
Bringing a stone grasped firmly by the top
In each hand, like an old savage armed.
He moves in darkness as it seems to me,
Not of woods only and the shade of trees.
He will not go behind his father's saying,
And he likes having thought of it so well
He says again, "Good fences make good neighbours".

("Mending Wall" Frost ll. 38-45)

Amusement and wit, as characterized in the quoted lines, make Robert Frost's poems enduring still at the high school level, but they come laced with ambivalences and food for thought, making the young readers think and reflect. In "Mending Wall", Frost essentially mulls over the dichotomies of 'nature' and 'nurture'—nature which propels human beings to be selfish, barbaric and a seeming philistine like the 'old savage armed', keen to keep away neighbours from his well corseted orchards. In a way therefore 'humans' essentially emerge as selfish beings—In Frost's America this being sugar coated as 'self—preservation'. No matter how much Frost the modernist, would like to break down the literal and metaphorical fences (foreseeing globalization of today), the neighbours insist on walling out Frost.

Children read Frost's poems to understand complexities of human nature and the problems of choices. What is kept at bay in Frost, is the potential of the 'stone grasped firmly', to be hurled most forcefully at the speaker who proposes such edification. It seems to Frost that his neighbour 'moves in darkness', whereas in fact, he actually does, as Robert Louis Stevenson was to elaborate in 1886 in his popular novella, *The Strange Case of Dr. Jekyll and Mr. Hyde*, also taught in many countries of the world at the high school and undergraduate level. A same tendency is studied by Mary Shelley in her celebrated novel *Frankenstein* (1818), read by both young and old. In India, this novel is a part of the undergraduate syllabus.

Grappling with the darkness of the human beings has been an obsession with authors since the days of European Enlightenment, as evident in the writings of Shelley, Stevenson and Frost. However, the chronology of dates of publication interestingly reveal a phenomenon—that of trying to understand the human psyche and the 'id' in Shelley and Stevenson, almost corresponding with Freud and Breurs' subsequent theories and findings in *Studies in Hysteria* (1895). Interestingly, in Frost we identify a drive to study the tendencies of modern individual to overcome the 'Id', again traceable the studies of the post-Freudians ranging from Donald Winnecott (1931) to Erik Erikson (2002).

It is the potential capacity to become latent resources of edification in subjects of morality, ethics and choice that *The Strange Case of Dr. Jekyll and Mr. Hyde* and *Frankenstein* become powerful learning materials for classroom full of young learners. They are equally potent as materials for pleasure reading. The tremendous popularity of the texts may be gauged by viewing the range the adaptations or comic strips both of them have generated and the commercial success of each of these adaptations. Some of the popular films based on *Frankenstein* are: *The Rocky Horror Picture Show,* Mel Brooks' *Young Frankenstein* starring James McAvoy and Daniel Radcliffe, *Dean Koontz's Frankenstein.* In the world of comics Stan Lee introduced Frankenstein's Monster into Marvel Comics—the comics pick up where the book left off: After Victor dies in the Arctic, the Monster is frozen for centuries.

He gets thawed out to fight the avengers (in one decade) and team up with Spider-Man (in modern-day). Because it's comic books, there are multiple versions of the Monster in existence: a robot, two Nazi clones, and an intelligent clone. On the other end of the comics spectrum, the Wachowskis (behind *The Matrix*) wrote the short-lived series *Doc Frankenstein.*

No less is the popularity of *The Strange Case of Dr. Jekyll and Mr. Hyde.* Some examples are: *The Strange Case of Dr. Jekyll and Mr Hyde: The Graphic Novel* (Campfire Graphic Novels) by CEL Welsh (Adapter), Lalit Kumar Sharma (Illustrator), Classic Comics No. 13: *Dr. Jekyll and Mr. Hyde,* DC Comics—World Famous Comics No. 173, *Jekyll-Hyde Heroes.* In this number, a potion gives Batman and Superman split personalities, Batman turns into his old foe. Other adaptations are: No. 1. *Dr. Jekyll and Mr. Hyde* (Marvel Classics Comics, 1976) where the art is done by Nestor Redondo and the adaptation is by Kin Platt. In this series, the first transformation is shifted forward (it takes place on the second page); as in the Hollywood tradition, Jekyll also does saintly work in a charity hospital; the film tradition also provides the fight in the music hall and the faint allusions to sexual desire linked to the transformations into Hyde; the narrative is mainly based on the last chapter of Stevenson's work with first person narration in italics, which then changes to third-person for Hyde's visit to Lanyon up until the end, with Utterson and Poole breaking down the door and finding Hyde and Jekyll's statement. The last frame is of Utterson who has just finished reading the statement, saying 'Poor Jekyll' and with the faces of Jekyll and Hyde in a cloud behind him. Then there are the Marvel Comics Supernatural Thrillers, No. 4. *Dr. Jekyll and Mr. Hyde*, June 1973, with the script by Ron Goulart and art by Win Mortimer. The cover shows a huge hairy Hyde bursting out from clothes; and the young, good-looking Jekyll works for a charity hospital. These are only a selected few, to mention in a seemingly endless list.

Although the list of adaptations can be awfully long, properties which allure the young readers to *The Strange Case of Dr. Jekyll and Mr. Hyde* and *Frankenstein* are the eerie world of science fiction, the graphic descriptions contrasting the world of the beautiful and the ugly, the classic Aristotelian symptom of the feeling and participation in the forbidden world of fear and guilt, riding on the excitement with a curiosity and the final cathartic effect with the unraveling of the mystery.

It is worth noting that like most pleasure readers for children, *The Strange Case of Dr. Jekyll and Mr. Hyde* and *Frankenstein* do offer a sneak peek into the world of adults and therefore a forbidden world they would like to grow up into. Anti-heroes like the monster Frankenstein and Mr. Hyde wield a considerable influence on the young minds in spite of their detestable ugliness. This is an emotion as old as Adam and Eve, who had tasted the forbidden fruit of Paradise.

The famous philosopher Emmanuel Swedenborg had once opined, "without contraries is no progression", *The Strange Case of Dr. Jekyll and Mr. Hyde* and *Frankenstein*, also therefore become sites of conflict and resolution, but definitely a resolution veered towards the 'good' and the 'just'—the 'good' because Mr. Hyde (the evil in the self) is killed, although Dr. Jekyll is killed with him too, and 'just' because Victor Frankenstein (the scientist) is punished by being robbed off his own people by the monster whom he had created but had subsequently deserted.

Sigmund Freud in his *Civilization and its Discontents* (1930) had once asserted:

> Men are not gentle creatures, who want to be loved, who at the most can defend themselves it they are attacked; they are, on the contrary, creatures among whose instinctual endowments is to be reckoned a powerful share of aggressiveness. As a result, their neighbour is for them not only a potential helper or sexual object, but someone who tempts them to satisfy their aggressiveness on him, to exploit his capacity for work without compensation, to use him sexually, without his consent, to seize his possessions, to humiliate him, to cause him pain, to torture and to kill him. (24)

Elsewhere, in the same essay Freud was to assert, man is a 'savage beast' to whom consideration towards his own kind is something alien (24).

Thought in this way, Victor Frankenstein's, apathy and anger towards the monster, Mr. Hyde's trampling over a child in chapter one who happened to collide with him, or later his killing of Sir Danver Carew with a heavy stick for irritating him (Mr. Hyde) with polite enquiry (Chapter Four) are acts which are instinctive but normal.

It is precisely for this reason, psychologists find these books as fertile grounds for negotiation and interrogation by young minds. What if they go by the instincts, tempting and easy to follow? Freud would call these desires, 'Thanatos',—the outward manifestation of the aggressive instincts as opposed to 'Eros'. Taken, at their face value, *Frankenstein* and *The Strange Case of Dr. Jekyll and Mr. Hyde* lays bare a world which follows the 'pleasure-principle'—two 'overreaching' (following Harry Levin's description of Marlovian heroes) scientists follow their unbridled desires to create an alternative but dangerous reality, waiting to suck the humble, social ordinary humans out their ordinary world, all drawn in the vortex of the storm created by their extraordinary ambition. Just when the young readers gloat in a feeling similar to the 'wanton boys' who kill the flies for sport, the ethical considerations pull them back. An example of this is the eloquence of the monster who is well read in Plutarch's *Lives*, Goethe's *Werther* and *Paradise Lost* by Milton. "Remember, that I am your creature, I ought to by the Adam, but I am rather a fallen angel, whom thou drivest from joy for no misdeed" (98). The monster unerringly discovers language to be on the sense of 'culture' rather than 'nature', and to imply the structures of relation at the basis of culture. The discovery is a vital one, for the side of 'nature' is irreparably marked by lack, by monsterism (Brooks 331).

This 'nature' is not Rousseau's nature—the pristine, gifted one, but Frost's 'nature'—where men move about in darkness with stones in their hand.

As Peter Brooks comments, "In his essay on the 'Unheimliche' (translated into English as—'sinisterly'), Freud speculates on the special capacity of literature to evoke and to control the feeling of the uncanny. Literature appears to be a kind of controlled play with the daemonic" (341). With the dialectics arising from the doubling or polyphony of voices, the young reader is compelled to move from the relish of the 'eerie', the 'natural' to the awe of the 'nurtured' the 'civilized'—the movement from individual to society with the symbolic order of Language. In 1925, Freud had proclaimed:

> Psychoanalysis has never said a word in favour of unfettering instincts that would injure our community, on the contrary it has issued a warning and an exhortation to us to mend our ways. But society refuses to consent to the ventilation of the question, because it has a bad conscience in more than one respect. In the first place it has set up a high ideal of morality - morality being the restriction of instincts and insists that all its members shall fulfill that ideal without troubling itself with the possibility that obedience may bear heavily upon the individual. (219)

Freud goes on to describe this tendency of suppressing instincts as 'cultural hypocrisy' (219). Young minds need to therefore know and explore instinctive behaviour and the consequences in a way only literature can allow them to do (as Freud himself has said earlier). Dr. Jekylls full statement of his own case would prove how 'cultural hypocrisy' could lead to abnormal and more importantly, self destructive behavior:

> hence it came about that I concealed my pleasures; and that when I reached years of reflection, and began to look, round me and take stock of my progress and position in the world, I stood already committed to a profound duplicity of me [...]. (www.gutenberg.org)

The realization of this duplicity within himself leads Dr. Jekyll to give free reign to his instincts. He creates Mr. Hyde who is the manifestation of his own ugly 'id' and particularly his 'thanatos', because Mr. Hyde can only harm and hurt.

Victor Frankenstein in his own way manifests his ambitions and his unbridled desires by creating a monster outside his self. Although Ellen Moers chooses to call and read Frankenstein as a 'birth myth', it might also be interpreted as one's inability to manage and control ones latent desires in a productive manner. Both in *Frankenstein* and *The Strange Case of Dr. Jekyll and Mr. Hyde,* there are births (of course, but) of monsters (of desire) who wreak havoc in society.

In both the texts, therefore, the reader is carefully weaned away from a world of desires and ambitions, to consider the repercussions of self centredness—more importantly, into the realization that how selfish lives can seriously upset the sense of courtesy, decency and good relations in a society—in other words the social equilibrium.

Philip Reiff (1959) argued that these kind of texts presented a 'moral challenge' to the readers although they denied any direct normative, prescriptive thought. The core of the Freudian praxis as seen in the texts "had no message to preach, no ideology, no morality, but his thinking contained an implicit set of ideas and ethical connotations that could be shaped into such a message" (17). These ethical connotations are there floating in the texts of *Frankenstein* and *The Strange Case of Dr. Jekyll and Mr. Hyde.* The figures of Victor's parents, Elizabeth, Clerval and even the monster with his eloquence provide the other side of reality, just like Mr. Utterson, the lawyer, Poole the servant and Dr. Lanyon are important links between Dr. Jekyll and the ordinary reality. Among these characters many of them in their own prudent way are successful—Clerval, Victor's father, Mr. Utterson or Dr. Lanyon. Young readers can thus, make choices of their own.

Donald Winnicott (1963) gives a lot of importance to psychological development as an aspect of moral development. In so far as healthy psychic development contributes to healthy moral growth, psychic development involves assimilation of moral attitudes and orientations derived from caretaking figure, parents, educational influences, and the surrounding culture. He drew our attention to issues fundamental to all ethical concerns, the task of establishing an authentic sense of self and the capacity to relate meaningfully and productively with others, both other persons and society. One of the significant and underlying themes of *Frankenstein* and *The Strange Case of Dr. Jekyll and*

Mr. Hyde is the danger of isolation or 'solipsism' (probably best illustrated in the figure of Kurtz in Joseph Conrad's novella, *Heart of Darkness*). Deliberate breaking away from friends, from society, like Victor Frankenstein in the initial years (while making the monster) or Dr. Jekyll who stopped talking to Mr. Utter son and Dr. Lanyon (when Mr. Hyde took the better of him), could therefore potentially drive humans towards self destruction.

Winnicott writes:

> Your adult moral code (the texts under discussion) is necessary because it humanizes what for the child is subhuman. The infant suffers talion fears. The child bites in an excited experience of relating to a good object, and the object is felt to be a biting object. The child enjoys an excretory orgy and the world fills with the water that drowns and with fifth that buries. These crude fears become humanized chiefly through each child's experiences in relation to the parents, who disapprove and are angry but who do not bite and drown and burn the child in retaliation related exactly to the child's impulse or fantasy. (101)

Winnicott, however, disapproves forced compliance in children and in the process the chance of aborting discovery of the true self, driving that self into hiding and substituting a form of conformity that falsifies its whole life experience.

As discussed earlier, Frosts poems do explicitly allow a scope of this self discovery, but *Frankenstein* and *The Strange Case of Dr. Jekyll and Mr. Hyde* also do so without the overt edification which might come as an abomination to high schoolers or undergrads.

As an extension of the thoughts of Winnicott, Erik H. Erikson centred his argument on the need of mutuality and loving acceptance as essential for growth to mature identity and ethical integrity. Erikson distinguished between morality and ethics. Morality was a result of fear, responding to threats of abandonment, punishment, exposure, or inner threats of guilt, shame and isolation. Most young readers would identify this kind of morality in the monster Frankenstein who definitely uses his eloquence to align him to culture and society, but cannot take away the obvious incongruity of such attempts. Even the De-Lacey family cannot accept him because of his horrible appearance. At the end of Volume II, Chapter V, the monster's lamentation definitely reminds one of the need of the family and society for a child's proper psychosexual development:

> But where were my friends and relations? No father had watched my infant days, no mother had blessed me with smile and caresses, or if they had, all my past life was now a blot, a blind vacancy in which I distinguished nothing, ... I had never yet seen a being resembling me, or who claimed any intercourse with me. What was I? (93)

The monster therefore, can pick up morality but not ethics, for according to Erikson, ethical rules were based on ideals to be striven for. Without an identity, in an absence of interaction with one's own people, ethics cannot develop. To the young reader, Frankenstein inevitably endorses the need and significance of family and a social system, just as in *The Strange Case of Dr. Jekyll and Mr. Hyde* adolescent readers might feel the absence of a heroine or a family who might have tempered the budding yet aggressive scientist.

The primitive morality of fear and retribution however is necessary. They exist in the adult mind as remnants of childhood. The child's morality precedes the adults ethical sense not only developmentally but in a sense that the earlier stage is necessary for the emergence of the later.[1]

Erikson impinged that the development of the ego in an adolescent which is to become his identity as an adult, was not only,

> a matter of intrapsychic vicissitudes of inner psychic states, but also a matter of interaction and 'mutual regulation', between the developing human organism and significant persons in its environment. Even more strikingly, it was a matter of mutual regulation evolving between a growing child and the culture and traditions of his or her society. (Meissner 23)

It is remarkable that Sigmund Freud and his followers (often accused of limiting themselves to the diagnosis of psychological ailments without being able to suggest remedies) are able to reiterate the importance of social systems, culture (and literature as a part of culture) to contribute to the sound development of a child.

It is no wonder that *Frankenstein* and *The Strange Case of Dr. Jekyll and Mr. Hyde* have achieved immense popularity as rapid readers among the high schoolers since they are carefully graded and suited to the level of users. The wide range of issues that they bring forth to their young readers make them veritable treasure houses of options—options which could make or mar individual's lives, could give wings to their talents or toss them to purgatories. It is up to the readers to choose between the two.

Note

1. Erik. H Erikson's ideas have been borrowed from the first chapter of W.W. Meissner's book, *The Ethical Dimension of Psychoanalysis: A Dialogue*. Albany: State University of New York Press, 2003. Web. The first chapter is titled: "Freudian and Post-Freudian Ethics".

Works Cited

Frost, Robert. "The Mending Wall" <https://www.poetryfoundation.org/poems-and-poets/poems/44266> downloaded on 25.5.2017.

Shelley, Mary. *Frankenstein*. ed. Maya Joshi. Delhi: Worldview Publications, 2008. Print.

Stevenson, Robert Louis. The Project Gutenberg EBook of *The Strange Case Of Dr. Jekyll And Mr. Hyde*. www.gutenberg.org June 25, 2008. Last updated: September 14, 2016. Produced by David Widger. Web.

Brooks, Peter. "Godlike Science/Unhallowed Arts". *Frankenstein* by Mary Shelley. ed. Maya Joshi. Delhi: Worldview Publications, 2008. Print.

Freud, Sigmund. *Civilization and Its Discontents*. Buckhamshire, England: Chrysoma Associates Limited, Publications Division-Electronic Books Library. 1929. Web.

"The Development of the Capacity for Concern." Winnicott, D.W. Bulletin of the Menninger Clinic; Topeka, Kan. 27.4 (July 1, 1963). Web.

Meissner, W.W. *The Ethical Dimension of Psycho Analysis: A Dialogue*. Albany: State University of New York Press, 2003. Web.

9

Postmodernism and Indian Adult Literature: A Study of Shiva Trilogy

Arpa Ghosh

Indian young adult literature is experiencing a market boom as witnessed never before. Whereas the pre-millennial generation was dependent on English and American genre fiction like Enid Blyton, Hardy Boys and Nancy Drew for their reading needs, the current generation has happily turned to the local market replete with names like Amish Tripathi, Ashwin Sanghi, Ravindra Jain and Chetan Bhagat for their reading needs.

This paper concentrates chiefly on Amish Tripathi's *Shiva Trilogy* to point out certain key features in young adult reading habits.

Though teens are a time of rebellion and iconoclasm, it is surprising how predictable and pattern-oriented teen reading habits can be. Teenagers may occasionally dress and act in weirdly, but when it comes to reading they like to go by formula. Genre or formulaic fiction is possibly most popular among teenagers. Young, enthusiastic and hopeful, they like their temperament reflected in the fiction they read. Fantasy fiction meets a major portion of their needs:

> Fantasy more than ever performs its priestly prophetic function, alerting readers to the social and spiritual dangers of apathy and cynicism; while offering reassurance and hope for a better tomorrow. Of all genres, fantasy offers healing, a glimpse of the human potential to overcome evil, and strong motivation to fight for the good and to strive

> for the Grail, whatever we perceive it to me. Perhaps after all, the skepticism of this century has managed to provoke the writers to fantasy to wear their priestly robes with pride. (Filmer 137)

Challenging the still centre of humanism Jacques Derrida in his celebrated essay, "Structure, Sign and Play in the Discourse of Human Science" states:

> Besides the tension between play and history, there is also the tension between play and presence. Play is the disruption of presence. The presence of an element is always a signifying and substitutive reference inscribed in a system of differences and the movement of a chain. Play is always a play of absence and presence, but if it is to be thought radically, play must be conceived of before the alternative of presence and absence. Being must be conceived as presence or absence on the basis of the possibility of play and not the other way around. (Derrida 369)

Derrida refutes the Humanist concept of "Being as *presence*" (Derrida 353). He says:

> The event I called a rupture, the disruption I alluded to at the beginning of this paper, presumably would have come about when the structurality of structure had to begin to be thought, that is to say, repeated, and this is why I said that this disruption was repetition in every sense of the word. Henceforth, it became necessary to think both the law which somehow governed the desire for a center in the constitution of structure, and the process of signification which orders the displacements and substitutions for this law of central presence—but a central presence that has never been itself, has always already been exiled from itself into its own substitute. *The substitute does not substitute itself for anything which has somehow existed before it.* Henceforth, it was necessary to begin thinking that there was no center, that the center could not be thought in the form of a present-being, that the center had no natural site, that it was not a fixed locus but a function, a sort of nonlocus in which an infinite number of sign-substitutions

> came into play. This was the moment when language invaded the universal problematic, the moment when, in the absence of a center or origin, everything became discourse—provided we can agree on this word—that is to say a system in which the central signified, the original or transcendental signified, is never absolutely present outside a system of differences. (Derrida: 353, 54)

Derrida's thesis on the absence of centre and nonlocus of systems that can be endlessly and perpetually rearranged to create new permutations, combinations, not to mention new centres, sits very well on the playfulness and postmodern irreverence of genre fiction fantasy novelists. Not only are known myths being reread, they are playfully combined with other genres like espionage, gothic mysteries and war thriller fiction.

Rosemary Jackson writes: "fantasy characteristically attempts to compensate for a lack resulting from cultural constraints: it is a literature of desire, which seeks that which is experienced as absence and loss" (qt. in James and Mendlesohn 2012). For the young and hopeful, fantasy literature often provides the way to comprehending the world in a manner that is excluded in historical studies.

The unprecedented and phenomenal success of Amish Tripathi's *Shiva Trilogy*, Book 1 published in 2010, Book 2, 2012 and Book 3, 2013, has no doubt opened gates for imitators. Amish, an MBA from IIM Joka, Kolkata, and presently living in Mumbai, self-confessedly, an aggressive and innovative promoter of his text, took book publishing and book sales to new heights. He not only got book-sellers to distribute the first chapter of *The Immortals of Meluha* free to shop-clientele increasing the buzz and visibility of his book, but he also got a promotional video made that had all ingredients of a popular Hindi action film trailer. An ardent believer in publicity, he firmly holds the view that excellent books have sunk into oblivion for want of good marketing. Therefore aggressive marketing is as important if not more, than the superiority of book content.

Readers of *Shiva Trilogy* have been struck by the detailed paratext; that undefined zone between the inside and outside of the book, in Philippe Lejeune's words "a fringe of the printed text which in reality controls one's whole reading of the text". Serrated and coloured maps with incremental detailing, reminiscent of Tolkein's map sketches in *The Lord of the Rings* trilogy adorn the left inside cover of each book to guide us through the rough terrain traversed by Shiva in his long, arduous journey to uproot evil. Book 3 ends with the incantation:

> Om Namah Shivaiy.
>
> The Universe bows to Lord Shiva. I bow to Lord Shiva.

At the end, Amish promises to return another day with the "unadulterated story" of the *Mahabharat* if the Neelkanth allows it. The authorial mediations, the neat and delicious, colour-coordinated, low-priced paperback get-up, rich words of praise for Amish's work all go towards a persuasive packaging that readers will presumably find irresistible.

Authors of fantasy literature in Kurt Vonnegut Jr's words play a priestly role. They not only initiate readers into a new, stylized world that touches and takes off from the real at significant points but also provide consolation for readers in a meaningless world. The first book of a fantasy trilogy therefore is Dickensian in its eye for detail. With loving meticulousness the writer carefully lays out the locales usually static and picture-perfect as in children's literature. The paratext with its elaborate hints and indications that we are about to enter a parallel and more primal, ordered world that is complex but never random nor existential goes a long way to fortify our flagging energies and confidence. The discourse of fantasy is presented in the same forms as those used in religious scriptures—metaphor, myth and symbol. The pattern is a quest pattern. These devices appeal to reason, imagination and emotion, and allow for the same kinds of experience in reading as do religious texts.

Moreover, fantasy and science fiction are no less didactic than sacred texts. Since energy never dissipates, but merely changes its form; so the linguistic expression of the most profound human needs for ordered beauty and ordered truth is displaced from religion to literature. Fantasy literature therefore satisfies the deepest aesthetic and spiritual needs of man; needs in the present-day world that religion, weakened by its repeated clashes with science and technology, is unable to satisfy. Amish's text goes an extra mile by combining mythology with the conspiracy novel, made the current rage after the world-wide affirmative reception of Dan Brown's *Da Vinci Code*. Like revisionist history the conspiracy novel too rereads a given set of codes unlocking it with a new cryptographic-historical key, unearthing the 'truth' from a thick cobweb of lies. However unlike revisionist history, the conspiracy novel erects a substitute edifice of intriguing codes and conventions. Therefore while Amish's attempt to re-present Shiva as soldier-hero instead of Almighty God is revisionist, the new set of quasi-mythopoeic, quasi-scientific explanations that replace the age-old interpretations of Shiva's blue-throat, Sati's death by fire or Ganesh's elephant-head engender a new rubric of myths. In significant portions the old is merely replaced by the new.

At the same time, Amish's logical explanations for *daivi astras* (explosives), *brahmastra* (atom bomb), *pashupatiastra* (an explosive that works by fusion rather than fission and is therefore more benign and eco-friendly than *brahmastra*) and Somras (an immortalizing and anti-aging drink initially thought to be miraculously good, but gradually found to contain harmful oxidants and toxins that are responsible for congenital defects, diseases and ecological imbalance) is a time-honoured tradition to popularize science by using it as an imaginative ingredient in literature carried forth from the Renaissance. In Book 2 Brihaspati, chief scientist of the Somras manufacturing unit in Mandar proudly admits to Shiva:

> I believe in science. It provides a solution and a rationale for everything. And if there is anything that appears like a miracle, the only explanation is that a scientific reason for it has not been discovered as yet.

Francis Bacon's essay on Pan in his treatise *Wisdom of the Ancients* where he seeks the scientific explanation of Pan's biform is one such example. Other examples closer to home are the noted scientist Acharja Jagadish Chandra Bose's book of essays intelligently titled *Obyekto* or Unarticulated and Bankim Chandra Chatterjee's *Krishnacharitra*. *Krishnacharitra* is a long essay in which as a part of Bankim Chandra's agenda to enhance the national pride of the Indian the Bengali intellectual interprets Sri Krishna's miracles in logical and scientific ways and conveys the impression that far from being a part of the strange, timeless, racially stereotyped, feminine and degenerate Oriental culture, Indian mythology is actually capable of being interpreted by the same logic and ratiocination that is associated with Occidental ways of life.

Apart from popularizing science and attempting to decomparmentalize and glamorize scientific thought patterns this strategy also instills national pride in the reader, in its apparent updatation of the Orient with the West while embracing and giving primacy to Oriental mythological history and also in its efforts to connect the mythological past and the actual present. Bankim Chandra's effort gains potency in that he uses Western ratiocinative methods to refute the Western allegation that the East is a teeming, chaotic, amorphous, non-scientific discourse ruled by passion and whim rather than science and common sense. Through his writings Bankim Chandra was able to infuse hope and pride in a subjugated nation. Amish's agenda is very different from Bankim's. But hope and pride are intrinsic components of his authorial vision in Shiva trilogy.

It is in the articulation of hope that fantasy literature has displaced religious discourse in the twentieth century. Fantasy more than ever performs its priestly prophetic function, alerting readers to the social and spiritual dangers of apathy and cynicism; while offering reassurance and hope for a better tomorrow. Of all genres, fantasy offers healing, a glimpse of the human potential to overcome evil and strong motivation to fight for the good and to strive for the Grail, whatever we perceive it to be. Perhaps after all, the skepticism of this century has managed to provoke the writers of fantasy to wear their priestly robes with pride. Whereas in Tolkein, there is a specific mission to destroy the ring of pride, Amish further queers and contemporizes the pitch by turning the quest into a quest for knowledge. What begins as a mission to destroy evil ends as a mission to *comprehend* evil which often resides in the best and most sterling parts of a society.

In "novels for men", authenticity, adventure and heroism are given value. Male readers are interested to see how heroism works and how masculinities are constructed. War and conflict are therefore the favourite themes. Description of war, war strategy, one-to-one combat, suspenseful twists that settle battle outcomes are undeniably the best passages in the Shiva trilogy. Also, only bold and heroic characters, irrespective of their gender, like Sati, Shiva, Kali, Bhrigu, Parvateshwar, Ganesh and Kartik are given importance. The rest are merely undefined props. Amish doesn't bother overmuch with complex characterization. His characters are drawn in broad, simple strokes. Various examples of male behavior: dandyism (Dilipa), cowardice (Daksha), valour (Sati, Shiva, Parvateshwar, Parshuram), intellect (Bhrigu, Shiva, Ganesh), saturnine plotting (Bhrigu, Vidyunmali), etc. are held up for inspection. Shiva's career in this text is that of a soldier and sailor and his contribution to history is the hero's contribution through combat and battle strategy. A set of possible masculinities within a relatively conservative nationalistic narrative is studied as models of heroism. They are largely straightforward, dutiful, resourceful, violent and homosocial. The conflict at the end of the day is between good and evil. Details are mainly military, martial and technical. The outcome, whether tragic or happy (in this case both), is deeply satisfying. All questions are fully and finally answered within the framework of the text. Finally history is presented in a way in which the central character is repeatedly tested in some way before achieving some form of martial success. It is the eagle's point of view, the history of the hero, the god, the superman who comes at a cusp period to annihilate an era so that a new way of life can begin.

Writing in and for the globalized, free, techno-rich and techno-savvy world of the 21st century, Amish clearly sets his goals. His target readership is the huge army of English speaking and English reading young adult urban Indian readers. The charm and appeal of Amish's text can best be appreciated by readers who have a smattering of Hindu mythological knowledge, say the Shiva-Sati-Daksha myth, a working knowledge of the relations between gods and goddesses, a knowledge of the Ganga and Saptarshi myths and so on. Since Amish's narrative strategy is a delicious mix of linear and cyclical, abstract and reified, readers are wonderfully intrigued by a simultaneous sense of continuity—old wine being served in new bottles—and discontinuity—revisionist history where Ganesh and Kali with their aberrational physiological features become representatives of the wronged and downtrodden. The adventure story genre dependent on a swiftly unfolding plot propels us forward. But the anti-aging formula of the Somras partaken by almost all characters, Shiva included, cannily fits everyone—mother (Sati), sons (Ganesh and Kartik), Mausi (Kali), father and villain (Daksha)—in roughly the same age-bracket, thereby neatly replacing timebound realism with mythological fantasy played out at leisurely pace in a ageless, unchanging background. Also, the cyclical time rhythms, an integral part of Hindu mythology and culture, are referred to repeatedly. Shiva is constantly compared to his antecedent Lord Rudra. Towards the end of Book I the comparison becomes extremely strong. Shiva, a mirror of Lord Rudra, teeters on the verge of making the same mistake, that is externalizing evil, when evil actually lies within. Just as Rudra destroys Asuras only to recognize that by doing so he has in fact destroyed a way of life with all its precious components. Shiva desists from making the mistake of favouring Suryavanshis over Chandravanshis just in time. Thus the text attracts both older and younger readers by treading the middle path of the linear and cyclical.

Till now we have been discussing the strengths of the text. The threat and the opportunity of the text stem from the same crux, Amish's recasting and remoulding rather than rereading of Indian myth. The text dangerously and unconscionably flattens the content very much in the tradition of cartoons and video games. This is aggravated by Amish's use of ancient Greek war models, like the tortoise formation of battalions for example and the Egyptian challenge of Aten thrown by Sati. While Sanskrit verses are liberally smattered all over the text, Americanisms abound too. The flat facile quality of language used is perhaps Amish's greatest weakness. In this he falls short of reaching the excellence and sublimity of Tolkein who reworks diction with every species and category of character.

By tying India myth to western genre literature modes, especially the fantasy and conspiracy adventure literary models, Amish could be charged with seriously trivializing the multi-layered, psycho-social character of Hindu mythology. Myth is loosely and interchangeably confused with fantasy, but myth is definitely not fantasy. Each myth has a definitive character. The Shiva myth of yore is a myth of regeneration and resurrection with Sati returning to Shiva's life as Parvati to fulfill the promise made to the Devas. By turning a regeneration myth into hero myth that focuses relentlessly and exclusively on the martial qualities and endurance powers of Sati and Shiva, Amish could be interfering with the core substance of the Shiva myth.

Amish has been compared time and again to J.R.R. Tolkein. According to Tolkein what Fantasy literature does then is to instigate a process by which "Suspended" belief can be accommodated, and if belief is not fully recoverable from the experience of reading, than at least it can be compensated for by the articulation of hope. It is with the articulation of hope that Amish wins over his readers. The adventure story pattern presents two types of heroes: the infallible Superman and the fallible, vulnerable, yet extraordinarily valorous entity. The Shiva trilogy characters are a mix of both categories. They are supermen in that they are chosen and special with the aura of mythological grandeur constantly surrounding them. But at the same time the human angle is explored repeatedly. The curious flaws and vulnerabilities of Sati, Shiva, Kartik and Daksha make the trilogy a deeply human story. While Amish's wonderfully written book has reignited a love for reading in countless school-going and college going readers and draws attention to such contemporary socio-political issues as the evil of war, misuse of atomic explosives, honour killings and widow remarriage thereby holding the attention of young and old (strength, opportunity), his representation of the Shiva myth unfortunately is a far cry from the original myth and may be viewed by purists as distortion, trivialization and flattening of same (weakness and threat).

References

Derrida. *Writing and Difference*. NY and GB: Routledge, 1978 (translation in English). First Indian Reprint 2003. First published 1967 by Editions du Seuli.

Filmer, Kath. *Scepticism and Hope in Twentieth Century Fantasy Literature*. Ohio: Bowling Green State University Popular Press, 1992.

James, Edward and Farah Mendlesohn. *The Cambridge Companion to Fantasy Literature*. Cambridge University Press, 2012.

Tripathi, Amish. *The Shiva Trilogy*, Westland Limited.

_______ *Immortals of Meluha*, 2010.

_______ *The Secret of the Nagas*, 2011.

_______ *Oath of the Vayuputras*, 2013.

10

Pedagogical Curiosity in Young Adult Literature

Mehar Fatima

Can young adult literature offer suitable way to meet literary standards in our English classrooms, in schools and universities, or is it destined to a marginal function of leisure reading for adolescent learners outside English classrooms? The purpose of pedagogy is much beyond setting canonical and literary standards in rigidity. In fact, the usefulness of the study material is crucial to a holistic development of both teacher and the taught in a conscious society. Compatibility between the changing time and the development of the learners ask for more contemporary literary study materials which can be found in young adult literature (YAL) meant for adolescents. Young adult literature is to deal with the issues of giving and taking perspectives. Its purpose is to deal with construction of societies, homes and personal affairs in a democratic world.

Pedagogy is defined as the discipline that deals with the theory and practice of education; in other words it elaborates the study of how best to teach. It is concerned with the general development of human latent as well as imparting and acquisition of particular skills. Johann Friedrich Herbart's educational philosophy and pedagogy stressed upon the connection between personal development and the following benefits to society as productive citizens. Pedagogy is the method and practice of teaching, particularly as an academic subject or theoretical concept. However, the need of the hour is Critical pedagogy.

Critical pedagogy is one of the philosophies of education that has been established as a social movement developed and applied concepts from critical theory and related traditions to the field of education and the study of culture (Kincheloe and Steinburg, 1997). Critical pedagogy is the term used to describe what emerges when critical theory encounters education. It scrutinizes teaching as an essentially a political act, refusing the neutrality of knowledge, as well as maintains issues of social justice and democracy, infusing the acts of teaching and learning. The purpose of critical pedagogy is liberation from domination through stirring of the critical consciousness of the people, which encourage them to bring change in their world through social critique and political means. Freire Paulo supports students' capacity to reflect critically about their education situation; in order to give them enough space to identify connections between their problems and experiences and their social frameworks in which they are set in. Changes in our pedagogical practices can compel us to occupy the world in essentially new and special ways.

Anti oppressive education is another means that includes multiple approaches to learning that actively confronts different forms of oppression. It is based on the belief that many traditional and commonsense ways of engaging in education essentially contribute to oppression in schools and society. In addition many "commonsense" approaches to education reform disguise or aggravate oppressive education methods. (Kumashiro, K. 2000). The work of anti-oppressive education includes a profound dedication to changing the notion and action of educators in engaging in curriculum, pedagogy, classroom management and school culture. (Kumashiro, K. 2004). It also suggests that institutional structure and policies must be changed. Exploring perspectives on education that are not conventional to what has become "commonsense" must be partaken as well. This type of education expects to be different, uncomfortable, and controversial Lang 2007). In Paulo Freire's *Pedagogy of the Oppressed* (1968 and 1970), he stated that education is suffering from "narration sickness" (Freire 1993). It implies that students simply memorize mechanically the narrated content transmitted by the educator. This is called "banking concept" of education, in which the possibility of action allowed by the students broadens only as far as receiving, filling and storing the deposits. Thus, projecting an absolute ignorance onto others, a characteristic of the ideology of oppression, negates education and knowledge as a process of inquiry. Consequently, the more students work at storing these deposits entrusted to them, the less they develop the critical consciousness that would result from their intervention in the world as transformers of that world. As a result, oppressive social controls are never questioned and remain as an integral part of our culture thus, perpetuating oppression in our education systems (Freire 1993).

Anti-bias curriculum is an activist approach to educational curricula which tries to combat prejudices like racism, sexism, ableism, ageism, homophobia, and other forms of kyriarchy. The aim of the anti-bias curriculum is to raise awareness of bias and to reduce bias. Anti-bias curriculum transgresses the limitations by vigorously providing learners with a concrete understanding of social problems and issues while providing them with strategies to fight bias and improve social conditions. It is put into practice as an active way of reducing social oppression in order to achieve social justice. Balanced learning should be the goal of pedagogy today.

For years, studies have proved that young adult literature should be integrated into English classrooms for the reason that such literature can help improve students' reading skills, encourage young adults to read more books, thereby improving their abilities to read, facilitate teachers' abilities to incorporate more books of interest to adolescents into the curriculum, thereby avoiding the non-reading curriculum or workbooks and lectures, and support the development of an inclusive curriculum (Reed 1994).

However, teachers often believe that young adult literature does not have sophistication and literary merit; the qualities present in canonical texts and, therefore, it fails to meet the curricular objectives. Most teachers are of the opinion that YAL's function in the curriculum is most appropriately peripheral, and can be used for motivating struggling readers. Stover points out that good YAL "deals with themes and issues that mirror the concerns of the society out of which it is produced. It does so in ways that help readers understand the complexities and shades of gray involved in dealing with these issues" (119-20). Young adult literature comprises multiple genres and themes apart from being the novels of teenage anxiety. Over the years, YAL has developed comprehensively to incorporate genres such as biographies, memoirs, poetry, informational texts, and science fiction and fantasy, etc.

Louel C. Gibbons, et al. (2006), investigate that while teachers complain that students in their classes struggle with difficult texts and, hence, with the presented literary concepts, YAL provides an excellent vehicle for introducing students to literary concepts through engaging texts that are written at an appropriate reading level. As Joan Kaywell points out in her series Adolescent Literature as a Complement to the Classics, "Part of the problem, as most teachers are fully aware, is that the classics are often too distant from our students' experiences or the reading level is too difficult" (ix) (Kaywell 1993). We are having young adult literature throughout the English language arts curricula proves a strategy for making the curricula more engaging for students (Stover 2001). Over the years, the studies have found that the most students would read books provided they are given literature that shares their interests and their lives. Young adult literature appeals to adolescent readers for numerous reasons. Firstly, it is written about characters with whom they can identify with, on issues such as age, differences, and wider world perceptions. It is fast-paced and will hold students' attention in a fast growing technological society where their world accurately opens before their eyes. YAL also includes a growing body of work that represents different ethnic and cultural groups, reflective of our ever-growing diverse society (Donelson and Nilsen, 2004).

In order to combat the time constraint a prescribed crowded curriculum poses, it is for teachers to look for creative ways to integrate YAL into their existing curriculum, such as Reading aloud, book study groups, project works, and so on. In this way, young adult literature would help struggling and hesitant readers to build literacy skills. It presents students with more chances to read for pleasure and contentment, thus strengthening their reading and literacy skills. Additionally, as Louise Rosenblatt (1991) asserts, "Few teachers of English today would deny that the individuals' ability to read and enjoy literature is the primary aim of literary study" (64).

Teaching students to truly love literature, but to remember that performance on tests does not necessarily demonstrate what learners have gained from simply reading literature. Competency exams may determine the content students could draw from the text read; conversely they do not measure what students actually learned from reading literature, what they thought, and what questions it raised (Bushman and Haas 1997).

Classics are not always significant to our students' lives. However, pairing of contemporary literature such as YAL with canonical texts can at least bridge the distance between students' lives and the textual world of their classrooms. Choosing to teach age-appropriate literature can better serve readability as well as relevance.

Why do adolescents look for relativity and connectedness in a book to read? The answer maybe their sensitive growing stage where they feel quite disconnected to the world of adults who are seen to be in power. They are aware of their disadvantage of the particular stage they live through and they strive to live through this stage in semi secrecy. It is therefore, most important to examine pedagogical implications and the effectiveness of teaching young adult literature in the present day. Reader response practices of teaching students help to identify with or "relate to"—a character in the text. But to identify with the similarities may not suffice, as learning to identify with the differences analytically is to incorporate YAL in our pedagogy. We often fail to ask learners how they enjoy those characters that are nothing like them, recognizing the difference. It is for YAL teachers to help identity and to extend his or her identity theme into a new sphere—into a fresh intensity of response that enhances the literary experience and broadens the learner's cognitive and emotional response to it (Alsup, 2010). In a response to literature, the learner-readers can share their understanding and reaction to a piece of literature. They can write about; their feelings about the characters, impression of the story read, ruling out similarities and differences of the story to their own lives and of others they know. Students can write down their personal responses to the text read. They can record their reactions, feelings, thoughts, ideas, actions, characters, plot, themes, ask questions, instead of summarizing the text. They can as well react to the differences they find, state the unusual, make predictions, and relate to personal experiences.

Students have to deal with difficult problems in their lives. They are growing up in an increasingly complex world where they will need to be able to work with others, solve problems, and communicate well (Windschitl, 2002). Young Adult Literature (YAL) could be the best way to engage students with real life issues and problems which can as well teach social justice and tolerance. Unfortunately classical books featured in the curriculum have been the same texts that one would find in the present English curriculum. This lack of change between the 1980s and the 21st century motivates us to promote teaching YAL in the classroom. Young adult literature continues to grow in popularity outside of school, becoming more and more critically acclaimed literature, and yet it continues to be controversial material in school (Cart 2003).

Miller (2005) National Council of Teachers of English found that reading controversial violent texts in his classroom that were labeled as young adult literature profoundly raised the motivation of reluctant readers in the classroom. Young adult literature in our classroom has been controversial and therefore remains the second choice after canonical texts, but recent scholarship in reading and literacy shows the benefits of building student motivation, and the clear connection between heightened motivation and young adult literature.

It is rightly suggested that teachers can implement other collaborative methods such as reading aloud, games that involve cooperation between groups or classes of students, chats or readings hosted by the author, dramatizations, teacher-student dialogue journals, letters to the author, and other purposeful writing assignments to conjure student motivation to read (Arthur and Burch 1993). The agreement among researchers suggests that students profit when they are given chance to choose texts to read that they can relate to, concerning themes that they find interesting. There has been a wide gap between what is taught in classroom; the traditional canonical texts and budding literacy practices among young adult readers. (Burns & Botzakis, 2012) note: The International Reading Association has highlighted the fact that 'traditional definitions of reading, writing, and communication, and traditional definitions of best practice instruction—derived from a long tradition of book and other print media—are insufficient in the 21st century (p. 23). With the rapidly changing world the readers of this millennium should evolve. Curriculum should include complex texts, teaching to analyze and synthesize information existing in various media, literary text, print text, visual text, and latest technology. Young adult literature can be an effective way to make relations and inspire readers. Young adult literature that deals with controversial topics can be used to teach social justice and encourage positive action in our educational institutions and societies. Incorporating subjects relating to social justice such as genocide, bullying, sexual harassment, suicide, and dysfunctional relations and families makes students the problem solvers in our democratic scenario.

Critics have argued well that in order to help young adults through the difficult time of being adolescents, teachers must provide literature that speaks to the issues facing our students: problems in their physical, intellectual, moral, and reading development. It would seem that the classical literature (the canon) of which most, if not all, was written for the educated adult community, does not provide the answers that young people are seeking (John H. Bushman 1997). Erik Erikson (1984) suggests that the major task of adolescence is the formulation, or reformulation, of personal identity. Robert Havighurst (1972) outlines developmental tasks for healthy individuals that include a series of tasks that confront adolescents. In his view, the principal needs of adolescence are emotional and social development, rather than intellectual growth.

Age-appropriate literature is the major decisive factor for emotional and social development. For a successful classroom teachers should be willing to look outside the classics. Reading decreases as the students move from freshman to senior level for reasons as common as ever; they find no spare time to read. No opportunity to enjoy reading. With a knowledge-based curriculum, reading stops as the curriculum culminates. It seems to be beyond Teachers' responsibility to help create reading culture. Students fail to carry reading habit into adulthood.

Our educational institutions have failed to choose literature that facilitates students to become emotionally and cognitively drawn in their reading. When students are asked to read books that are inconsistent with their developmental levels, they are not being able to interact effusively with the books. Consequently, students who do not relate to the literature are left with learning only about literature-information, that does not help students attach with their aspiration, level of development, and experience.

It can be called 'Graveyard situation' when students are trapped in their prescribed university courses. They cannot come out of it. Lifting the imposed curriculum may give a suitable opportunity to learners to recognize their crucial role in the wider pedagogical scenario. The felicitators must create choices for the learners. There should be a paper in the curriculum that gives choice to the students to select novels or texts for study and exam. In fact, every literature paper should extend choices to the students to select books for study and exam. Choose a text and also create a text can be new challenges for students. Teachers should define their teaching goals and so should students. Any gap between the two should be bridged through proper implementation of newly desired curriculum.

Quality young adult literature caters to moral development and is positively proper for discussion and study by adolescents. Lawrence Kohlberg (1984) suggests that the development moves along a line from self-centeredness, unable to consider the interests and claims of others doing right to avoid punishment to adopting principles for moral reasoning and action, recognizing that these moral principles occasionally conflict with social rules (Kohlberg 1984). Young adult literature presents hope to the young readers for change, improvement, and success. They are mirror images to the young adults, teaching them to deal with their present and more contemporary situations. Such young adult literature presents responsibility by equipping them with courage to deal with the consequences of their own choices and simultaneously meet an appropriate level of pedagogical curiosity.

References

Alsup, Janet, ed. (2010). *Young Adult Literature and Adolescent Identity Across Cultures and Classrooms: Contexts for the Literary Lives of Teens*. New York: Routledge.

Arthur, B., and Burch, A. (1993). "Motivation for Reading is an Affective Concern". *Intervention in School and Clinic*, 28 (5), 280-87.

Burns, L., and Botzakis, S. (2012). "Using the Joy Luck Club to Teach Core Standards and 21st Century Literacies". *English Journal*, 101(5): 23-29.

Bushman, John H., and Kay Parks Haas. (1997). *Using Young Adult Literature in the English Classroom* (3rd ed.). Upper Saddle River, NJ: Merrill Prentice Hall.

Bushman, J.H. (1997). "Young Adult Literature in the Classroom—Or Is It?" *John H. Bushman English Journal*. March, 45-40.

Cart, M. (2003). "Bold Books for Innovative Teaching: A Place of Energy, Activity, and Art. *The English Journal*, 93 (1): 113-16.

Donelson, Kenneth L., and Alleen Pace Nilsen (2004). *Literature for Today's Young Adults*. 7th Ed. Boston: Pearson/Allyn and Bacon.

Erikson, E.H., ed. (1963). *The Challenge of Youth*. Garden City, NY: Anchor Books.

Freire, Paulo (1993). *Pedagogy of the Oppressed*. New York City, USA: The Continuum Publishing Company.

Havighurst, R. (1972). Developmental Tasks and Education. New York: David McKay "Kids Closing the Book on Reading for Fun," 1995. Wichita Eagle (Sept. 24): 16A.

Kaywell, Joan F. ed. (1993). *Adolescent Literature as a Complement to the Classics*. Norwood, MA: Christopher-Gordon Publishers, Inc.

Kincheloe, Joe and Steinburg, Shirley (1997). *Changing Multiculturalism*. Bristol, PA: Open University Press. p. 24.

Kohlberg, L. (1984). "Essays in Moral Development". Vol. 11: *The Psychology of Moral Development*. San Francisco: Harper and Row.

Kumashiro, K. (2000). "Toward a Theory of Anti-Oppressive Education." *Review of Educational Research*. 70(1), 25-53.

______. (2004). *Against Common Sense: Teaching and Learning Toward Social Justice*. Routledge: New York.

Lang, Pete. (2007). *Six Lenses for Anti-Oppressive Education: Partial Stories, Improbable Conversations.*

Miller, S. (2005). *Shattering Images of Violence in Young Adult Literature: Strategies for the Classroom.*

Reed, Arthea J.S. (1994). *Reaching Adolescents: The Young Adult Book and the School.* New York: Merrill.

Rosenblatt, Louise M. (1991). *Literature as Exploration.* 4th Ed. New York: Modern Language Association of America.

Stover, Lois T. (2001). "The Place of Young Adult Literature in Secondary Reading Programs." *Teaching Reading in High School English Classes*. Bonnie O. Ericson, Ed. Urbana, IL: National Council of Teachers of English. 115-38.

Windschitl, M. (2002). "Framing constructivism in practice as the negotiation of dilemmas: An analysis of the conceptual, pedagogical, cultural, and political challenges facing teachers." *Review of Educational Research*, 72 (2): 131-75.

11

The Fair and the Foul: Reading the Journey of the Narratives of Agatha Christie's *Murder on the Orient Express* and Satyajit Ray's *Sonar Kella*

Maitree Deb

The unfolding of a detective fiction often parallels the reading process, with a criminal writing a hidden 'text', in the form of a crime and the detective seeking to read that text and decode the truth of the crime. In contemporary study however, the continued appeal of the detective fiction owes its existence mainly to the study of the genre's conservatism. As William W. Stowe explains in his article "Critical Investigations: Convention and Ideology in Detective Fiction",

> Politically, morally, and epistemologically, detective fiction tends to affirm rather than to question, to take social structures, moral codes, and ways of knowing as givens, rather than subjecting them to thorough, principled criticism.... The truth in these novels may be elusive, but it is ultimately knowable and always worth knowing. The hero's goal, simply put, is to right wrongs by uncovering facts. (570)

Though much of this view is proven, it often eradicates the contribution of detective fiction in holding taut a reader's undisputed attention through the length of the story and intriguing the human mind to instigate and investigate its chambers of passion and thrill along with an exploration of the dark psyche of the human cognizance. The formula of detective fiction lends itself as an admirable critique of personal, social and cultural fallacies. A critical reading of the conventional versions of detective narratives skillfully highlights an understanding of the cultural and social issues of the time along with an effective understanding of how the narratological tools bring alive "self-conscious works of literary art" (Stowe 571). This paper, for a brief study of the narrative of detective fiction, has engaged one text each from two of the widely accepted classifications of detective fiction namely Agatha Christie's prototype whodunit *Murder on the Orient Express* and Satyajit Ray's classic thriller *Sonar Kella.* The paper will try to examine the course of the narrative structure of the two texts, through the primary trope of physical and psychological journey, which form a significant part of both the narratives, to explore how two generically opposite and contrasting forces unravel the fair and foul corners of the human mind.

Agatha Christie, often referred to as the queen of whodunit fiction, has enjoyed an unparalleled popularity for her great success at satisfying her readership. In her quintessential whodunit *Murder on the Orient Express,* Christie employs her setting as the closed compartment of the Stamboul-Calais coach of the Simplon Orient Express. The train journey begins with the onset of the narrative. A murder takes place in the coach, and soon after, the train is stopped in its tracks by a snowdrift. The physical journey gets stalled but the narrative allows a seasoned exploration of the psychological journey in the detective Hercule Poirot's mind where, a common trope of the whodunit, one where everyone looks guilty, is employed. Stuck in the Calais coach, Poirot travels back in time, to a long discreditable case of a child's brutal murder which eventually helps him solve the present crime by the end of the journey. In Satyajit Ray's *Sonar Kella*, we embark on a journey with Ray's exquisite sleuth Feluda and accomplices Topshe and Jatayu to the antique lands of Rajasthan to unearth the truth of the past life of Mukul, a *jatishwar*, someone who is able to recount the events of his past life. It is Mukul's remembrance of his past life and a probable existence of hidden treasure, as related by him, that initiates the various journeys in the story. The two ruffians, Mandar Bose and Bhobanondo alias the fake Dr. Hazra, take Mukul along a long way in quest of credible wealth. This gives rise to three parallel journeys in the story. Feluda takes the primary charge of commencing on an expedition to save Mukul and prevent the perpetrators from performing any personal or social misdemeanor. Mandar Bose enters a separate journey, that of pursuing Feluda and his accomplices, to stop them from reaching Mukul to help his partner in crime carry on the felony. The actual Dr. Hazra tries to follow the criminals to ensure Mukul's safety, unaware of Feluda's presence. Towards the climax, this complex web of linear journeys intersects with each other after there is an effort to suspend Feluda's journey to ensure the survival of the journey of the robbers. Like Christie's novel, this one too projects a major psychological journey in Mukul's mind that forms the bedrock of Feluda's physical itinerary. Both the fictions engage an interruption in their central theme of travelling. While the majority and indeed the most crucial revelations are made after the stalled journey of the Orient Express in Poirot's well-sculpted thinking mind, Ray's thriller encounters all its riveting and exotic aspects during the journey and its re-initiation after several interruptions. The journey within the mind and the physical journey of deciphering the truth, become united into one and through powerful strokes of narration, itself becomes a narrative in its quest for meaning and fulfillment. As we look into the narrative, we seek to grasp meaning not only in space but also in time. Our narrative perception stands ready to be activated and in our reflex to learn and know, not only what is there but also what happened, we give fruition to the universality of narrative.

Like most conventional whodunits, in Chistie's *Murder on the Orient Express*, the writer is the authoritative voice of the narrative. Written in the third-person narration, it is the author and not the reader who chooses the murderer. It is Christie's aforetime construction of the plot with its selected criminal and victim that is related by the omniscient narrator. Employing this narrative voice is a total negation of Roland Barthes' emphatic argument in "Introduction to the Structural Analysis of Narratives" that "The (material) author of a narrative is in no way to be confused with the narrator of that narrative" (282). Much of recent study has emphasized on mystery being used as a metaphor for hermeneutic reading of conflicting information, given to both the readers and the detective to reconstruct a systematic analysis. While the author, through the omniscient narrator provides various enigmatic clues and evidence concerning the true nature of the criminal to both the reader and the detective, the latter moves steadily ahead in the journey of discovering a coherent pattern in and resolution of the vicious mystery. Christie's whodunit novels owe their success to the non-arbitrariness of most of her solutions. The suspects are often the most likely but the straightforwardness of the crimes are submerged in the presumption that the mystery is complex and the hermeneutic creation of an alternative gateway of clues makes the simple and like insignificant, diverting the reader's reason. Miss Marple explains in *The Moving Finger*, "Most crimes, you see, are so absurdly simple...and quite understandable in an unpleasant way of course" (180). Eliot A. Singer in his essay "The Whodunit as Riddle: Block Elements in Agatha Christie" states

> What Dame Agatha Christie consciously and insidiously does is *close the reader's mind*. The clues themselves, then, become insignificant, and the solution lies not in untangling their pattern, but in discovering the mechanism by which the reader's mind is closed. (160)

In *Sonar Kella*, the narrative shows a clear contrast between authorial persona and the third-person narrator, Feluda's nephew Topshe. Though Topshe accomplishes the adolescent charge of a mature assistant like Conan Doyle's Watson or Sharadindu's Ajitesh, it is through him that the narratorial journey reaches its fruition. Though he seems an omniscient narrator, his narration is far from it. The predetermined plot by Ray enfolds in front of Topshe's eyes much like in front of the audience's, only a little ahead and he only narrates the plethora of thrilling experiences and episodic plots which unlike the whodunit is an adventure along with an investigation. Topshe is not given the privilege of the all-knowing narrator and much like the audience, he meets the reality of the thriller when the authorial persona wishes its acknowledgement through the immaculate detective expertise of Feluda. The narratorial voice belongs to Topshe but he remains with the audience while Feluda travels ahead of the narrative in his deciphering of truth.

Tzvetan Todorov in *The Poetics of Prose*, distinguishes a true whodunit from other forms of detective fiction in that "it contains not one but two stories: the story of the crime and the story of the investigation. In their purest form these two stories have no point in common" (44). The crime often takes place right after the beginning of the story, as in Christie's novel where it occurs as early as the fifth chapter. Like conventional whodunits, there is no attempt to prevent the crime and the entire novel runs along the generic format of discovery of crime, followed by investigation into whodunit, discovery of culprit and the motive of crime. Lucy Sussex in her book *Women Writers and Detectives in Nineteenth-Century Crime Fiction* observes,

> Two narratives are interwoven: the story of the crime, in the past, which is gradually uncovered by the story of the investigation, in the present. The text is structured as a puzzle...until the two plots merge at the conclusion, becoming one. (11)

The uncovering of the Daisy Armstrong murder-case and a recapitulation of all the probable people involved with the deceased family answer the motive of the crime linking the present journey to the past one. The narrator's reliability is a definitely positive perception since in relating a detective fiction, it is the narrator who devises the plotline with a definite thought behind the criminal, the victim and the motive. Though all the passengers of the coach are denied any reliability since each of them deliberately conjures up a false information, the audience reads and is either satisfied or dissatisfied with the outcome of the completion, thereby depending on the reliability of the narrator. Ray's fictitious work too engages several journeys that remain intertwined. As a *jatishwar*, Mukul has an access to his past and journeying through the memories of his past, enables him to originate a quest in the present, in both of which he is primarily involved. When all the journeys in Sonar Kella merge into one, there is a completion of the investigation of the crime and a judgement of the validity of Mukul's former life in the fortress of Jaisalmer. The narration travels through the complexities of the adult world to ultimately illuminate a fantastic world of imagination of a child who acquires the security of his thoughts amidst the architecture of the tangible world. Once again, the audience accepts the narrator's reliability since the authorial persona has already etched the story and the narrator is not given a superior position in answering the investigation of the crime.

The extent to which the narrator participates in the story being narrated often controls our assessment of the information presented. *Murder on the Orient Express* follows a heterodiegetic narration where Christie's voice, situated outside the action, accomplishes the narration. Outside the world of the story, Christie formulates clues and contradictions that are secondary devices and should not bother the experienced reader until the narrative intends it to. During interrogation Colonel Arbuthnot exclaims, "I couldn't say. I don't remember anyone passing except the conductor. Wait a minute—and there was a woman, I think" (Christie 173) which is a pure mechanical construction by Christie to elide the actual clue, only to be taken up later in the narrative. An acute contradiction takes a mature form in Christie's *Murder at the Vicarage* where Lawrence Redding, the victim's wife's lover is quickly cleared on evidence and it becomes easier for Poirot to later establish him as the actual murderer. Topshe narrates a story that he is essentially made a part of by the author. Playing the role of a homodiegetic narrator, Topshe presents all the episodes of which he is a part and later the events which have actually unfolded parallely concealed from his knowledge. Topshe is inside the story and through his narrative, Ray proposes the prospects, attitude of and reactions to all the characters involved in the journey.

Foculisation, as a specific device of narration refers, as H. Porter Abbott states in his *Cambridge Introduction to Narrative*, "specifically to the lens through which we see characters and events in the narrative" (66). Frequently in Christie's whodunits, the narrator is our foculiser. It is through Christie's authorial voice as the third-person narrator, that we are equipped with the background and information that links all the twelve passengers of the Calais coach to the Daisy Armstrong murder-case and helps us analyse the culmination of the narrative and the reason behind Ratchett's victimization. No voice is given to Ratchett to talk of his guilt or innocence except a feeble attempt to seek Poirot's help to save his life. His character is built solely on the foculisation of all the passengers and Poirot. Positioned outside the narrative of the text, Christie engages Poirot to read all the anomalies and lies that every character resorts to and in turn richly contributes to the way the audience thinks or feels about the characters. It is also Christie's expertise of narration that guides the reader's thoughts in favour of Mr. Bouc's interpretation while the final solution is provided through Poirot's foculisation in the end. Though a majority of the action of the novel is provided by the narrator Topshe, *Sonar Kella* admits information through the child Mukul, the actual Dr. Hazra as well as the forged one. Mukul blurts out, "No. This is an ugly fortress. This is not Sonar Kella" ([translation mine] Ray 36), which forces Feluda and the readers to abandon this fortress and move towards a new one. The vantage point of deception and truth provided by the rogues and actual Dr. Hazra respectively, guide Feluda and help him reveal the truth in his mind and provide a resolution which through the narrative of Topshe becomes the audience's foculising point.

The appeal of the narrative of detective fiction lies in its "ability to prey upon the reader's tendency to confuse expectations with norms" (Singer 166) to create a complex mystery. Christie's novel applies the trope of too much information to mislead the reader. Running into a snowdrift, the plan of the twelve murderers needs amendments which come in the form of a red kimono, description of a short man with a woman's voice and a blood-stained knife in a sponge-bag, all employed to misguide Poirot. The suggestions and half-truths employed, prolong the delays and gaps in the narrative, slowing down the process of comprehension of the reader, something that Abbas Lightwalla explains as a crucial requirement of detective fiction. Though *Sonar Kella's* narrative seems to be initially devoid of any hostility and antipathy when much of the journey happens pleasantly, it is not free from the presence of shadows in the form of a mysterious man who seems to be pursuing a journey not disparate from that of Feluda's. Coded instructions and letters become a strong presence in the latter part of the novel with an excellent strength of narrative that keeps the reader's access to the thoughts of the detective perfectly distant. This narrative, guarding the detective's outlook also involves the opposition between "force and finesse" (Stowe 579) and establishes an intricate link between knowledge and power. The prominent French philosopher and historian, Michel Foucault, believed that knowledge is always a form of power. He took his belief a step ahead when he stated that knowledge can be gained from power, where the former does not prevent but produces power. It is this idea of knowledge's discursive connection with power that is exploited throughout the narrative of detective fiction. Knowledge linked to power becomes the authority of truth. It is through the knowledge of the felons that the actual Dr. Hazra is reduced to the background, while they take the reins of truth in their hands. They are able to manipulate Feluda initially and themselves become the producer of reality. Quite similarly, all the passengers of the Orient Express engage in a collective use of knowledge and revenge and gain the power to make their assumed identities real and true. However, as Foucault states, power is everywhere, working as a regime of truth that pervades society and is in constant flux. The power that the narrative gives to the accused is ultimately transferred to the detective figure which transcends politics and sees power as an everyday, socialized phenomenon. Ray and Christie, through their narratives portray how power becomes more efficient through the mechanisms of observation. Feluda and Poirot utilize their panopticon gaze, which Foucault describes as a mode of power and knowledge, for constant observation that results in internalized coercion where the accused are denied any knowledge of the observation of the detective. Like the prisoners of the panopticon, the felons are aware of a constant vigilance on them but are unable to trace the nature of the surveillance imposed on them. This disciplinary power of the detective over the corrupt is constant, unnoticeable and internalized.

This crucial relation is meticulously revealed by Mandar Bose's journey, whole sole aim is to keep Feluda at bay. His agency of power looms superior over their knowledge. Knowledge betokens the kind of power to the felons which through Michel Foucault's idea of 'gaze' exercises a sadistic power over the victims. First introduced in his 1963 book, *The Birth of the Clinic*,

Foucault's 'gaze' includes both the object of knowledge and the knower. The actual Dr. Hazra, despite being the proprietor of parapsychological knowledge and the knowledge of the authentic danger, is reduced to ineffectual power after the ruffians employ their 'gaze' on him. It is however again a turning of the 'gaze' by Feluda that ultimately disempowers the felons. Similarly, all the twelve passenger-murderers try to misguide Poirot with their deception but the power of the latter's 'gaze' peruses their lies and aids knowledge and power to the assistance of the detective. This swapping of the power of gaze has much to contribute to the thrill and overwhelming nature of the narrative along with building and breaking the power dynamics inherent in it. The sociological understanding of the examining gaze has its manifestation in the understanding of power and knowledge throughput the narrative.

Joseph Campbell coined the term 'monomyth' in *The Hero with a Thousand Faces*, which in narratology has come to demonstrate a hero's journey following the trajectory of an adventure, a decisive crisis and a victory with a return journey home. The hero of a detective fiction, namely the detective, too traverses this journey which is often a journey from the known to the unknown. Feluda departs from his familiar boundary of Kolkata to the alien land of Rajasthan, initiated by Mukul's psychological journey from the past to the present. Mukul's presumed known journey to his ancestral sonar kella turns into a kidnap which goes through an ordeal to finally return to the threshold of his accepted world. Poirot's physical from Syria to London is interrupted in an unfamiliar space and though rooted to a closed surrounding, Poirot introspectively undertakes Campbell's journey where he travels to the past to unearth the unknown from the known. The murderers' journey however is a familiar quest of the past with an unexpected culmination in the end. The narrative's movement from the known to the unknown territory and vice-versa design much of the observation of the innocent as guilty and the ultimate revelation of the real guilt and consciousness.

The formal structure of the detective fiction genre becomes complete with the detection of the crime which ideally makes up the narrative of the fiction which is always already pre-crafted before the onset of the novel. This makes the narrative of a detection fiction its primary tool to hold the description and organization of the story. Both Agatha Christie and Satyajit Ray elevated the prominent hermeneutic devices in their fictions representing two cultures through two genres of different generic origin. Using the motif of journey to display the conventional narratological journey, both these authors juxtapose popular art with the cardinal rules of the genre and use this crucial narrative function to account a story of detection of crime while maintaining suspense and the confrontation between reader and author in solving the crime.

Bibliography

Abbott, H. Porter. *The Cambridge Companion to Narrative*. New York: Cambridge University Press, 2008. Print.

Barthes, Roland. *A Barthes Reader*. Ed. Susan Sontag. New York: Hill and Wang, 1982. Print.

Campbell, Joseph. *The Hero with a Thousand Faces*. California: Princeton University Press, 1968. Print.

Christie, Agatha. *Murder on the Orient Express*. London: HarperCollins Publishers, 2007. Print.

________ *The Moving Finger*. New York: Dell Paperback, 1968. Print.

________ *Murder in the Vicarage*. London: HarperCollins Publishers, 2012. Print.

Lightwalla, Abbas. "The Theme of Narrative and Narrator in Detective Fiction." *Innervate Leading Undergraduate Work in English Studies* 2 (2009-2010): 299-303. Web.

Ray, Satyajit. *Sonar Kella*. Kolkata: Ananda Publishers, 1997. Print.

Singer, Eliot A. "The Whodunit as Riddle: Block Elements in Agatha Christie." *Western Folklore* 43.3 (1984): 157-71. JSTOR. Web.

Stowe, William W. "Critical Investigations: Convention and Ideology in Detective Fiction. *Texas Studies in Literature and Language* 31.4 (1989): 570-91. JSTOR. Web.

Sussex, Lucy. *Women Writers and Detectives in Nineteenth-Century Popular Fiction The Mothers of the Mystery Genre.* London : Palgrave Macmillan, 2010. Print.

Todorov, Tzvetan. *The Poetics of Prose.* Trans. Richard Howard. New York: Ithaca, 1977. Print.

Worthington, Heather. *The Rise of the Detective in Early Nineteenth-Century Popular Fiction.* New York: Palgrave Macmillan, 2015. Print.

12

Retreat to Primordial 'Id': Reflection on the Marooned Boys' Transposition from R.M. Ballantyne's *The Coral Island* to William Golding's *Lord of the Flies*

Jyotirmoy Sil

Robert Michael Ballantyne's *The Coral Island: A Tale of the Pacific Ocean*, published on 1884, is a tale of three adolescent boys—eighteen years old Jack Martin, Ralph Rover, the narrator, aged fifteen, and Peterkin Gay, thirteen—survived the shipwreck and somehow were led to an uninhabited island with a coral base. The teen boys faced several hurdles and through them they traverse a journey from innocence to experience but always, quite unnaturally, exhibiting the utmost 'British'/European civilized shadow and perfection in their acts—they learned to cope up with the moody 'raw' nature of the island, fought with Cannibals and saved their victims, involved in the fighting between the native Polynesians, defeated the pirates and played a pivotal role in the pagans' conversion into Christianity—and, quite unnaturally, a minimal account of childishness or immature boyish folly is traceable in their way of accomplishing tasks. Now, this text has been considered the major inspirer in the formulation of William Golding's *Lord of the Flies* (1954), considered to be one of the Postmodern canonical fiction, where the author transposes the very scope of the Robinsonade story from Ballantyne's *The Coral Island* set in the Victorian times—an era ruled by the Imperialist temperament—to the War-stricken Modern context and deviates from the story's orientation confirming/justifying Victorian British priggishness to reveal the unethical bestial kernel or, in terminology of Sigmund Freud, 'id' active underneath the façade human civilization. Here he adeptly re-envisioned the three Ballantyne characters—Jack, Ralph and Peterkin, here re-Christened as Piggy imposing them similar conditions that of *The Coral Island* but with dire consequences. In Golding's novel, a group of boys—all of whom were the student of a British military school—survived a plane crash and fell over the sea. The boys along with their ailing supervisor/captain swam to a nearby unknown island. Sooner, in the unavailability of the ailing captain's supervision, Ralph was chosen as leader. But while in Ballantyne's text the boys grew more mature and civilized, in Golding's novel, most of the boys retreated to the archaic barbaric and chaotic behaviour identical to primitive humans and barbarians.

Now, Sigmund Freud, in the seventh chapter of *The Interpretation of Dreams* (1900), has defined human psyche to be constituted of two basic factors—'conscious' and 'unconscious' and later based on this conscious-unconscious components, Freud in *The Ego and the Id* (1923) divided human mind topographically into three sectors: the 'id' (the contour of the mind possessing libidinal cravings impervious of ethicality), the 'superego' (the ethical and societal consciousness) and 'ego' (the inter-mediatory domain of human mind engaged to maintain the inherent link between the 'id' and 'superego'). In the opinion of Freud,

> ['Id'] is the dark, inaccessible part of our personality, what little we know of it we have learned from our study of the dreamwork and of course the construction of neurotic symptoms, and most of that is of a negative character and can be described only as a contrast to the ego. We approach the id with analogies: we call it a chaos, a cauldron full of seething excitations.... It is filled with energy reaching it from the instincts, but it has no organization, produces no collective will, but only a striving to bring about the satisfaction of the instinctual needs subject to the observance of the pleasure principle. (Freud, *New Introductory Lectures on Psychoanalysis,* 105-06)

Freud in *An Outline of Psychoanalysis* has explained that the 'id' is constituted of 'every-thing that is inherited, that is present at birth, that is, fixed in the constitution—above all, therefore, the instincts, which originate in the somatic organization and which find their first mental expression in id unknown to us' (Freud, 18). The 'libido' inherent in 'id' constitutes the instinctual cravings untamed by the societal norms and ethicality.

The 'superego' of the marooned boys, in Ballantyne's text, acutely suppressed their 'id'—Jack, Ralph and Peterkin's behaviour always reflected their modesty, ethical conscience and wit and even in their killing of pigs and mirth. But like Kurtz of Joseph Conrad's *The Heart of Darkness*, in Golding's text, most of the boys except Ralph, Piggy and few others cannot deter themselves from yielding to their 'id'—they started behaving like primeval humans in their wild persuasion of animals for food. However, here hunting pigs was not just for food but became an obsession perishing the natural human sentience; they had made it a ritual—wild dance, as witnessed by Ralph and Piggy on one night, surrounding the fire and feigning pig-killing:

> Jack leapt on the sand.
>
> "Do our dance! Come on! Dance!"
>
> He ran stumbling through the thick sand to the open space of rock beyond the fire. Between the flashes of lightning the air was dark and terrible; and the boys followed him, clamorously. Roger became the pig, grunting and charging at Jack, who side-stepped. The hunters took their spears, the cook took spits, and the rest clubs of firewood. A circling movement developed and a chant. While Roger mimed the terror of the pig, the littluns ran and jumped on the outside of the circle. (Golding, 138)

Here, the feigning of pig-killing in this manner seems quite like a wild carnival sanctioned/organized by the 'government' of the boys that had been unofficially formulated under the leadership of vicious Jack. In *Rebelais and His World*, Bakhtin has elucidated the concept of 'carnivalesque' existing in the contour of certain literary works. According to M.H. Abrams, this carnivalsque literary 'mood' 'parallels the flouting of authority and temporary inversion of social hierarchies that, in many cultures, are permitted during a season of carnival. The literary work does so by introducing a mingling of voices from diverse social levels that are free to mock and subvert authority, to flout social norms by ribaldry, and to exhibit various ways of profaning what is ordinarily regarded as sacrosanct' (Abrams, 74). The adolescent boys' adherence to the (European) civilized manners and Christian faith even in the hardest times, in Ballantyne's text, have been counterpointed in *Lord of the Flies*. The carnivalesque nature of Golding's text is unmistakable since the British boys' wild ribaldry discloses the hollowness of Christianity and directly or indirectly mocks the British/European priggishness carrying the heavy 'White men's burden' of civilizing the non-European 'savages'.

Desire for 'power', as Michel Foucault often etched in his philosophical works, is one of the basic human 'instincts' (a cluster of 'id') and in Golding's *Lord of the Flies*, Jack's dark desire for power became one of the major catalysts in the boys' psychic degradation. In Ballantyne's *The Coral Island*, Jack was a humble and mature leader with common sense and foresight but not adept in hunting pigs necessary for food. In Golding's *Lord of the Flies*, Jack snatched the power to command from Ralph with his sly perception—power from the knowledge of the boyish imaginative mind. Here, while Ralph desperately tried to manipulate other boys with civility and order, Jack craved power and that is why when the question of the ghastly presence of the beast came in, he utilized the opportunity and vowed to assassinate the 'beast' and hastily was chosen to be the leader by transposing Ralph. Jack's crave for power became so gigantic that he did not deter to snatch away Piggy's indispensable eye-glasses, showed no remorse when sadistic Roger killed Piggy by dropping a boulder from a vantage height, and would never falter before exterminating his old-friend Ralph. Here, however, Erik Erikson's view on the turbulent adolescent years can be upheld. According to Erikson, a child between six and eleven would tend to ponder over the disparities they have with the children of their age, and the teenagers between twelve and eighteen would strive to establish their own identity. Quite similarly, as Golding's text explores, Simon suffered in 'inferiority complex' while Jack became desperate to establish his 'identity' as a leader.

The deferral nature of the signifier of power is also noticeable in Golding's *Lord of the Flies*. When the boys first arrived in the island, initially, the conch that Ralph started to summon the boys was considered as the symbol of authority, but later in signifier has been changed to the spectacles of Piggy. Significantly, the change of 'signs' and their signifieds are considerable in both texts and their reconfiguring factors too. To follow Ferdinand de Saussure's idiosyncrasy, as elucidated in *Course in General Linguistics*, meaning of the signs are generated by asserting their differences with other 'signs' signifying some other signifieds. Therefore, signs indicate to some other signs, Roland Barthes too proclaimed in *Writing Degree Zero*, that language can never be innocent and always suggestive. In *The Coral Island*, the three boys first found in the island are—a rusty penknife, German silver pen-case without any lead, a piece of whip-cord about six yard long, a sail-maker's needle and ship's telescope. Obviously, these things suggest hope for survival, and telescope provides the scope of salvation and the power to measure/create the hopeful future. And, in Ballantyne's novel, the most intangible abstract power is signified by the Christianity—from a very impartial perspective—it can be visualized how the Christian missionaries were actually colonizing the natives of the Mango and of those belonging to the Polynesian community in the name of preaching Christianity. Although the readers are convinces that those natives were defined to be cannibals and usherer of superstitions, here, in this respect, however, the question of reliability upon the narrator's voice would come since Ralph Rover, now a grown-up, is recounting his tale—

> I was a boy when I went through the wonderful adventures herein set down. With the memory of my boyish feelings strong upon me, I present my book specially to boys, in the earnest hope that they may derive valuable information, much pleasure, great profit, and unbounded amusement from its pages. (Ballantyne, web)

So thereby, there is a possibility that his personal empathy for British imperialism and Christianity have got entwined with the original facts. In Golding's *Lord of the Flies*, on the other hand, the first useful thing found by the boys is a conch which has been utilized to summon the boys. Again, the telescope in Victorian text marks the advancement of humans, but the conch Modern texts signify a possibility of retreat to the pre-historic era in the text. In *The Coral Island*, it was the Christian faith that had been pervaded throughout the text, but in *Lord of the Flies*, the Christianity withered away from the psyche of the boys and instead they imagined a new god—'the lord of the flies'. The rotten severed pig's head swarming with flies reminds one of the primordial gods worshipped by 'uncivilized' wild humans. Thus the severed rotting pig's head symbolize the rotting of the ethical conscience and learned civilized manners within the boy's psyche.

'Id' is the source of our physical and mental desires and impulses—basically that of sexual and aggressive. It is driven by the 'pleasure principle'—aims to the immediate gratification of sudden impulses being impervious to societal limitations. The 'superego' strives to tame the 'id'. In *The Coral Island*, Jack was more mature and farsighted but lacked the skill of Peterkin to kill pigs for food. In Golding's text, although Jack initially hesitated to kill the pig more than Ralph, but the lust for blood, that had its roots in the necessary butcherings of pigs for food, and the sadistic pleasure drawn out from painful bloody assassination slowly encroached the boys' psyche and metamorphosized into impulses—the 'pig-killing' became an obsession for Jack and his group rather than necessity and the lethal bloodshed became the source of some primordial 'sadistic' pleasure to the boys. The sinister sign of evil entwined in human psyche is latently revealed in Ballantyne's text, when Peterkin wantonly butchered a non-eatable old sow, and rationalized by stating the need of leather. But in *Lord of the Flies*, the devilish crave started with pig killing and ended up by appeasing its demand of the life of Simon, Piggy and even Ralph, who was rescued by the naval officer on the brink of his life.

Golding's *Lord of the Flies* parodies the tag of the British as the flag-bearers of the civilization and the prospect of British Imperialism as the civilizing mission. While in Ballantyne's text, the boys, following the British imperialistic spirit(/hypocrisy?) triumphantly bore the 'White man's burden' by saving humans from savage cannibals, and converting rogue pirates into Christianity, in *Lord of the Flies*, the British boys succumbed into their inner 'darkness'—the unruly bestial human instinct, the 'id'. The geographical alienation from the civilized society and the primitive surrounding of the island decorated only by the raw nature also played a crucial role in boys' growing wild attitude—their 'superego' became ineffective in a space where no circumscribing ethical/societal limitation is palpable. The British naval officer's miraculous appearance, that actually saved Ralph from being brutally assassinated in the hands of his frenzied fellow-mates, became the *ex machina* in restoring of the civilized consciousness in the boys' psyche. The boys, who like the frenzied blood thirsty beasts, were pursuing Ralph to get his flesh as the oblation to the 'lord of the flies' were suddenly pacified seeing the militant. At this point, the officer, amazed at the fierce barbaric looks of once-civilized British school boys echoed the prospect that Ballantyne developed in his text—the civilized British boys taming nature and deplorable situations with 'order':

> I should have thought that a pack of British boys—you're all British aren't you?—would have been able to put up a better show than that—I mean—(Golding, 184)

But in Golding's island, the Dionysian instinct prevailed and Ralph and Piggy's Apollonian adherence to order and civilized temperament proved to be too feeble in front of the earlier.

Although, Piggy showed wisdom and rationality, he often tended to follow his 'id' when he would see pig's meat; and it was Ralph who continuously resisted Piggy from joining Jack's fanatic troupe only for pig's meat. The youngest boy, Simon, who used to faint frequently, is a mystifying enigmatic character because of his complex nature comprising of curiosity, powerful imaginative capabilities and intelligence. Simon is the one who conducted an imaginary dialogue with the rotting pig's head swarming with scavenging flies which introduced itself to be the 'lord of the flies'. It mockingly disclosed to Simon that the beast is never an actual entity that can be hunted, but exist within every boy on that island including Simon—a part of them: 'You knew, didn't you? I'm a part of you? Close, close, close! I'm the reason why it's no go?' (Golding, 130). But as Simon did not mingle with other boys (Jack's group) and thereby never would let his inner beast to come out, he, as the 'lord of the flies' warned, might be killed by others:

> I'm warning you. I'm going to get angry. D'you see? You're not wanted. Understand? We are going to have fun on the island. Understand? We're going to have fun on this island! So don't try it on, my poor misguided boy, or else— (Golding, 131)

Then Simon dared to climb the mountain and approached near to the thing the boys thought to be beast earlier and revealed that it was actually a rotting corpse of a parachutist hanging from the robes of the parachute which was somehow trapped on the mountain. Then he, in his desperation to share this revelation, rushed to the boys, but the boys were then frenziedly involved in the wild ritualistic dance and mistook Simon approaching through darkness as beast and killed him with strange fanatic bloodthirsty enthusiasm: '*Kill the beast! Cut his throat! Spill his blood!*' (Golding, 139)

Simon stands here as a miniature of the Christ figure who sacrificed his life in his desperate attempt to enlighten his peer; but unlike Christ's blood, which salvaged humanity from sin, Simon's innocent blood aggravate the homicidal instinct already sprouting in the boys' psyche and the cold-blooded ruthless murder of Piggy is the exemplary of it. Piggy, on the other hand is like some sightless sage and a worthy advisor of Ralph always urging his friend to follow rationality and logic to survive in that island where others were immersing into more and more darkness—he was the one who advised Ralph not to mourn over Simon's death as this happened in a terribly confused state. Jack can be visualized as the embodiment of human 'id' and Ralph as that of the 'superego', but Ralph also, unconsciously, followed his 'id' when he took part in the killing of Simon mistaken to be the demonic 'beast'. Evidently, as the 'lord of the flies', the figment of Simon's imagination, itself disclosed to Simon, the 'beast' resided within the contour of the boys' mind, invisible, unconsciously suppressed yet likely to be awaken anytime. When this 'beast' became apparent, it emerged with enormous savage barbaric lust for blood that would not be appeased solely with Simon's blood—it also craved Piggy's, Ralph's and would, perhaps, demand more if the situation had not been altered with the miraculous appearance of the naval officer. Undoubtedly, this 'beast' is a form of, what Sigmund Freud has delineated, 'id'—the unethical human instinct lying unconsciously underneath of the human ethical consciousness and always striving to unleash and fulfils its 'dark' desires.

The 'Coral', in R.M. Ballantyne's text, links the nature with Christianity. The enigmatic self-beautifying ways of nature is signified by the Coral reef created by the tiny coral insects; and again the 'coral' as a jewellery had a 'pious' Christian connotation, as Katherine Anderson claims in her article "Coral Jewellery", in the Victorian England. The framing of a grand coral reef was considered to be an 'evangelical' work. The boys' invention of the Coral island and their 'civilized' activities including saving the innocence and conquering over the barbarians in 'the Coral Island' can be compared, as Anderson has suggested, to the Christian missionaries' dubious 'civilizing' mission of converting the 'barbaric' societies of the Pacific Islands. The pirates' conversion into Christianity, the Christian missionary's success of converting the pagans into Christianity in the island of Mango and thereby, as implied, making them 'humane' clearly indicates Ballantyne's attempt to glorify the mystical power of Christianity that made the Whites the superior humans. In this text the victory of Christianity over paganism and the pagan superstitions is indicated by the conversion into Christianity of Avatea, the daughter of Tarao, the chief of one of the Polynesian community, whose people were saved by these boys from being devoured by the Cannibals, against his father's wishes and then the burning of the 'false gods' by the societies of the Mango Islands. As the priest himself delineated to the boys:

> I now remembered having heard that it is a custom among the Feejee islanders, that when the reigning chief grows old or infirm, the heir to the chieftainship has a right to depose his father; in which case he is considered as dead, and is buried alive. The young chief was now about to follow this custom, and, despite my earnest entreaties and pleadings, the old chief was buried that day before my eyes in the same grave with his four strangled wives! Oh! my heart groaned when I saw this, and I prayed to God to open the hearts of these poor creatures, as he had already

> opened mine, and pour into them the light and the love of the gospel of Jesus. My prayer was answered very soon. A week afterwards, the son, who was now chief of the tribe, came to me, bearing his god on his shoulders, and groaning beneath its weight. Flinging it down at my feet, he desired me to burn it! (Ballantyne, web)

But in Golding's *Lord of the Flies*, the British boys, ironically, deferred from the Christianity and acted like the worshipper of some primitive god offering pigs as the sacrifice and performing the wild ritual of 'pig killing' circling the fire. In this context, it is noteworthy that Golding's title, apart from signifying the rotting pig's head swarming with flies, which revealed itself to Simon as the "lord of the flies", also refers to Beelzebub, the devil—according to Catholic myth, one of the seven princes of hell. In *Dictionnaire Infernal* by Jacques Auguste Simon Collin de Plancy, Beelzebub has been referred to as demonic fly and the 'lord of the flies'. Golding's text digs out the subdued devilish darkness—the Beelzebub—in the boys' wild activities in an mystique island where, unlike Ballantyne's 'Coral Island', the boys became the worshipper of satanic evil and the once-taught Christian or Civilized creeds seemed to be too feeble to suppress the unethical primitive 'id', the evil incarnation within human psyche.

Immanuel Kant in his "What is Enlightenment?" has defined 'maturity' ass one's ability to judge or accomplish things without the guidance of another:

> Enlightenment is man's emergence from his self-incurred immaturity. Immaturity is the inability to use one's own understanding without the guidance of another. This immaturity is self-incurred if its cause is not lack of understanding, but lack of resolution and courage to use it without the guidance of another. The motto of enlightenment is therefore: *Sapere aude*! Have courage to use your own understanding! (Kant, 54)

In Ballantyne's *The Coral Island*, the marooned boys' 'superego' and overwhelming intellect at such a young age and philanthropy, quite like the boys of R.L. Stevenson's *The Treasure Island*, always subjugated their 'id' and they acted like the true 'British' adhering to the civility. As if, as implied in this text, British boys are inborn 'mature' and civilized and even the extreme geographical and worse socio-cultural alienation cannot deter them from bearing the 'burden' of civilization and civilizing the barbaric ones. But the adolescent boys in Golding's *Lord of the Flies* succumbed in the hideous darkness of evil existing in their own psyche in their courageous 'immature' attempts to form their own clan with unique rules and rituals without any 'mature' man's intervention. Golding's text parodies this frail facade of the British Civilization and pride of superior race and also the prospect Christianity—utilized as the tool of civilizing(/colonizing) project directly or indirectly revealed in Ballantyne's text simply by exposing the raw human 'id'—the unethical pleasure-seeking instinct and by etching how even a transient geographical estrangement from the civilization can erase the signs of civility from humans' psyche and the boys belonging to the superior race like British are not exemption in this respect. And Golding's intention of distorting the 'Europe-idolizing' prospect of Ballantyne's text is further clarified when the Military officer seeing Ralph pursued by a wild fanatic group of boys uttered:

"Jolly good show. Like the Coral Island." (Golding, 184)

Works Cited

Abrams, M.H. *A Handbook of Literary Terms*. New Delhi: Cengage Learning, 2009.

Anderson, Katharine. "Coral Jewellery", *Victorian Review*, 34 (1): 47–52, 2008. 28th Jan, 2017<https://www.jstor.org/stable/pdf/41220397.pdf>

Ballantyne, R.M. *The Coral Island: A Tale of the Pacific Ocean*. London: Thomas Nelson and Sons, 1884. 2nd Jan., 2017 <https://www.gutenberg.org/files/646/646-h/646-h.htm>

De Plancy, Jacques Auguste Simon Collin. *Infernal Dictionary*. Trans. Michael Coles, Natalia Zasadzinska, Jean-Christophe Dufau, Anna Dorzhieva, Piero Mng, Giby Joseph & Cristian G, Francis Rodrigues. Madison: Abracax Press, 2014.

Freud, Sigmund. *New Introductory Lectures on Psychoanalysis*. New York and London: Penguin Freud Library, 1993.

________. *An Outline of Psychoanalysis*. Wiltshire: Redwood Press Ltd, 1940.

_________. *The Egoand the Id*. Ed. James Strachey. Trans. Joan Riviere. New York: Norton & Company, Inc, 1962.

Golding, William. *Lord of the Flies*. USA: Wideview/Perigee Book, 1966.

Kant, Immanuel and Hans Siegbert Reiss. "An Answer to the Question: 'What is Enlightenment?'" *Kant: Political Writings*. 2nd, enl. ed. Cambridge England; New York: Cambridge University Press, 1991. 54-60.

Nayar, Promod K. *Contemporary Literary and Cultural Theory*. New Delhi: Pearson, 2013.

Waugh, Patricia. *Literary Theory and Criticism*. New Delhi: Oxford University Press, 2006.

13

Girlhood—Construction of a Female's Childhood in the 21st Century

Ibha Gupta

When I was introduced to the theory of Feminism for the first time at 18, I didn't find it to be a sort of divine revelation that opened up the floodgates of my mind. Instead, I'm one of the lucky few who found herself thinking how natural it all sounded. Was it because I came from a privileged, upper-class, nuclear, liberal family? Yes. But I'm sure some of it had to with certain literary role models that had given me ideas of who I should be. And once I became more nuanced with the intricacies of what feminism was, its history and its modern manifestations, I decided it was time to revisit these heroines of my childhood and to see whether the reverence I'd carried into adulthood, was justified.

It was definitely a good omen when on 21 January 2017 as thousands of women took to the street in Washington to represent the newest wave of feminism, a little girl was photographed holding a sign that said 'When Voldemort is president, we need a nation of Hermiones'. The implication of this simple sentence was that Hermione, the girl character from *Harry Potter* was strong, able, and equipped for fighting a tyrannical, xenophobic, racist and sexist male leader which is quite a leap from the roles assigned to Hermione's predecessors.

For Hermione's predecessors belonged to the ironically named 'Golden Age' of children's literature where texts were obsessed with vehemently defining gender and constructing the idea of a distinct boyhood and girlhood. The two opposing gender binaries as girl/boy were articulated as passive/active, domestic/

adventurous, introvert/extrovert, weak/strong and follower/ leader. From the colour of their nursery, to what toys children were given to play, what clothes they were made to wear to hobbies that were encouraged and activities they were allowed were all dependent on an imaginary, oppressive construction—gender. In our need to define, somewhere we had confined gender. But as the millennium set in, so did the realization of the senseless indoctrination that children were subjected to since birth and that they were dictated on who they ought to be instead of allowing them to be who they were.

What this paper is interested in is, whether we have come a long way from this define and confine attitude? Whether after reading these characters, would young readers normalize the idea that anyone can do anything? Will they understand that interests, opinions and actions are not forbidden, restricted or abnormal just because one may identify with a certain set of traits? And that no one is lesser because of the choices they make. In other words, will girlhood stop being an ideologically loaded word of definition and confinement and start being a state of mind where these heroines and their readers are empowered to be their true, authentic selves without fear, subjugation and compromise? Like Bob Dixon says "There's no foundation at present for any of the fierce sex-role indoctrination we've seen in children's fiction. Nor need it to go on in life. There is no reason why girls shouldn't play football, climb trees and get dirty, no more than there is any reason why boys shouldn't play with dolls if they want to and take active interest in cookery. Why shouldn't boys, or men, for that matter, cry?" (Hateley 89).

Simply inverting hierarchical conventions and power relations is not enough. We need to resignify or adapt conventions in new ways. Such resignifications and adaptations rely on innovative and creative approaches if change is to be effective. Change in discursive practices of speaking, writing, and behaving inevitably involves transgression, crossing boundaries and re-imagining new situations where past prohibitions and preclusions are dissolved (Mallan 2). In other words, if definitions are changed then confinements will be lifted.

And Hermione, Holly and Annabeth are characters who redefine girlhood. As opposed to passive, submissive, and traditional roles they are pictured as positive, active, and intelligent persons who are interested and capable of being emotionally and physically able and strong. They take on active and non-traditional female roles without fear of losing their femininity. They are independent thinkers who are given thoughtful consideration, fair criticism, and appreciated for their mental contributions. Their place is outside the home, beyond the roles of husband's help-mate, mother, laundress, housekeeper, and interesting and seductive lover-wife. They don't hide their intelligence and they definitely do not believe that it is a man's world and in order to get along in it, a female must be devious and make the male think he's the hero (Pyle 117).

Hermione is described as the 'cleverest witch of her age' and there cannot be a truer sentence about her. She is the researcher, the sleuth and the solver. She is the brains behind every plan be it solving the mystery of which creature is attacking students or teaching Harry important survival skills so that he can compete in a dangerous tournament. Without her to inform, plan, and navigate the dangers, Harry and Ron would be dead in a week. But her role doesn't end at this two-dimensional bookish girl who is happy to pass on information and then sit in the safety of the common room, as Harry and Ron face the real dangers of the world. Unlike Narnia's Susan and Lucy who are very conveniently excused from the battlefield, Hermione stands strong alongside Harry and Ron in each battle against Voldemort.

But it's not only the battlefield where she proves her bravery. Hermione is brave also because she is unafraid to put forth her opinion, even if she knows it won't be liked by her male friends. She is often described as 'bossy' but I like to read that as her having some very strong opinions that she commits to at the risk of losing her male friendships. She is proud of her intelligence and she'd rather be alone than agree with something that she believes is wrong. The disapproval of her male friends doesn't faze her. In other words, she doesn't dumb herself down to please her male friends. The real success is that the boys don't feel threatened by Hermione. To them, it is very natural to know that she is the smartest of the lot. Not even romantic love can persuade her to compromise on her principles. Ron Weasley turns from antagonizing boy to best friend to soul mate. And yet, twice she chooses to do the right thing and use her talents to fight the good fight instead of following Ron's misdirected, mistaken decisions.

Hermione is ambitious and her ambitions are encouraged, so much so that she's given official permission to manipulate time in order to make more hours for her studies. She is often called boring, an 'insufferable know-it-all' (Rowling, *Prisoner of Azkaban* 129) to be more precise, but studying is her one true passion which is revealed when after escaping a life-threatening situation, she admonishes Harry and Ron saying "I hope you are pleased with yourselves. We could all have been killed—or worse expelled" (Rowling, *Philosopher's Stone* 120). Hermione's priorities are sorted. And she never gives up on her passion and is the only one who goes back to finish her last year of schooling after saving the entire wizarding world. She is an initiator and an activist, be it starting a society for the rights of a slave-race or an underground rebel army training to overthrow the government. And she is a feminist for she is the only one who thinks that a powerful, anonymous book could possibly have been written by a female, as opposed to the general opinion of a male writer.

But being the smartest, she doesn't underestimate the talents of her male friends. She doesn't dominate them or scare them into submission. There is egalitarianism where she respects them for who they are. Her world isn't an Amazonian society of inverted hierarchy. If Harry and Ron owe their lives to her, she owes her personality and friendship to them. Without them she'd be only thinking about books and cleverness, and not about things like friendship and bravery. There are times when she lets them take the reins because she knows they'd do a better job. She allows them to save her too and to influence her into being a better person.

Finally she doesn't feel the need to subdue her femininity in order to be accepted. She doesn't play sports at all and finds them boring. Her emotional range is definitely more than that of a teaspoon and while she isn't vain, she cares about how she looks at a school ball. And most importantly, she gets along with other girls. Unlike Enid Blyton's sleuth Georgina who hates to be identified as a girl, asks everyone to call her George and does everything in her power to erase anything remotely feminine about her, Hermione doesn't feel the need to emulate traditional masculinity in order to be active, assertive and accepted. And her friends are more than happy to comfort her when she cries and admire her when she saves their lives.

But if in Hermione we can still find remnants of an older version of feminine qualities, Holly is completely changing the definition of a girl. Holly is a brilliant character from a brilliant series Artemis Fowl, which, over the course of eight books, narrates the redemption of a 12 years old criminal mastermind. She is a female soldier elf. She is the first woman officer in the police force of the underground, secret race of fairies and all her actions are informed by the awareness of her breaking a norm and the fear of being relegated to the background, if she fails. Her superior, Commander Root reminds her and the reader in the very beginning that "You are the first girl in recon. Ever. You are a test case. A beacon. There are a million fairies out there watching your every move. There are a lot of hopes riding on you. But there is a lot of prejudice against you too. The future of law enforcement is in your hands" (Colfer, *Artemis Fowl* 37).

Of course as a girl reader, the only thing I had difficulty in believing was that this fairy race, which was so advanced technologically, almost a century ahead of humans in terms of gadgets and machinery still thought that women on the force was a taboo. Which just goes to show scientific advancement is no guarantee of social reformation.

Nevertheless, Holly is on the force. Unlike J.R.R. Tolkien's passive, invisible, female elf, she is a gun-wielding, combat trained military soldier. Holly gives 'like a girl' an entirely new meaning. She is an excellent pilot, a great field agent and feels most alive in life-or-death situations. On the other hand, her arch enemy turned best friend is a 12 year old boy-man Artemis Fowl who is the passive planner, plotter and thinker. He can neither drive nor throw a punch and is always very conscious about his perfectly manicured nails and his expensive suits. The subversion is glaringly apparent.

Fowl has the talents and IQ of a mythical genius and prefers to come up with plans that have the ability to fool the most conniving of villains and tilt odds in his favour during the most hostile of situations. But he depends on his friends to execute the plans. Holly is not the dumb muscle carrying out orders. Her battlefield instincts, her skill in flying, her ability to be loyal and just are what make Artemis's plans possible. There are always instances where it isn't time for clever deductions; it is time for action (Colfer, *Arctic Incident* 126). It is not only Artemis's IQ but also Holly's nerve and experience that save them.

As can be guessed, Artemis is not very fond of active participation. "Artemis struggled to keep up. This was not for him. Running and sweating. Combat for heaven's sake. He was no soldier. He was a planner. A mastermind. The hurly burly of actual conflict was best left to Butler and people like him" (Colfer, *Arctic Incident* 133). "If you wanted someone to type Paradise Lost in under twenty minutes, then Artemis was your man. But as for hanging on to carriage roofs in a blizzard. Dead loss" (137).

And dead loss he is. Girls were excluded from war and action because they are not strong enough. They would be a liability instead as they would have to be taken care of. Here is a brilliant subversion. The boy is the liability; dare I say the weaker sex?

Artemis over the series tries very earnestly to refine his combat skill but never lasts in the training. He gets bored and leaves. Hyper masculinity is not Artemis's style. He prefers to relinquish control without objection as he realizes there is no time for macho argument. "Holly was undeniably ten times the pilot he would ever be and also several times more macho than he was" (Colfer, *Last Guardian* 253). Artemis doesn't feel insecure or ashamed of who he is. Neither does he resent Holly for having talents he doesn't. He "could properly appreciate how fierce and beautiful his best friend was" (254).

Artemis's language is of poetry, arts and culture. "Artemis generally spoke in sentences that were almost poetic" (Colfer,

Atlantis Complex 45) and by traditional role, feminine. Holly speaks in warfare terms and technical language, discussing fire power, targets and plan of attacks.

She is also the archetypal woman who is the moral compass, the redeemer of a man who sins. The first time Artemis ever feels a tinge of guilt is when he realizes he has abducted a 'girl'. And of course, as the series progresses the guilt transforms into redemption. But Holly doesn't do this by being kind, accepting, sacrificing and forgiving. She literally punches Artemis into being a good human.

Both Artemis and Holly share an equal space in the narrative, with every alternate chapter told from Holly's point of view. We get to know Holly as much as Artemis, which is important because she is telling girls that to 'run like a girl means' to pick up the guns, sprint and hunt down the bad guy. To get up and fight. That there are no gendered activities, no male prerogatives, no 'that's a boy's job'. She says "my father always taught me to do what's right, no matter what the cost. And that's what I do. Rules are important, but the right thing is more important...I can never keep my mouth shut if I see someone being bullied or punished unjustly. It's just the way I am" (Colfer, *Fowl Files* 51).

Neither is Holly less of a girl for being a soldier nor is Artemis less of a boy, for being more cerebral than physical. There truly is a breakdown of constructed gender identity as Artemis's namesake is a female goddess of the hunt, and Artemis is quite proud of the name for he doesn't consider being named after her an insult, but an honour.

Another Greek demigod is Annabeth Chase. The Percy Jackson series brings the entire canon of Greek Mythology into the 21st century. The Olympians are well and alive, covertly influencing modern day phenomenon and the Greek heroes are now 12 year olds fighting monsters and going on quests. One such hero is the daughter of Athena and a war history professor, Annabeth Chase. Though Percy Jackson, son of Poseidon is the narrator and protagonist, Annabeth is, like Hermione and Holly, a character without whom the series would be hollow and meaningless.

The Greek myths don't exactly treat women well. Nor do they have a single female Greek hero with a story and quest of her own. The absence has of course continued for ages as Charles Temple, in his insightful study, proved that though Joseph Campbell claimed that the hero cycle could be applied to both males and females, there simply weren't any females in children's literature that the cycle could be applied to (90). But this was of course in 1993. In 2017, we are lucky we have Annabeth Chase—a girl and a hero.

Annabeth's mother is the goddess of war and wisdom, and in that sense, Annabeth is a true sibling of Hermione and Holly. Borrowing from both, she makes the battle plans and executes them herself, loves reading and is an excellent fighter and finally, like them is unashamedly, unapologetically herself.

Her fatal flaw is revealed to be Hubris or excessive pride. She tends to believe that she can do everything, from fixing her parent's marriage to redeeming a traitor's soul. She wants to create a much better world, more perfect and beautiful than what already exists. On the other hand, Percy's fatal is loyalty to a fault. I bet traditional patriarchal values are not too happy that the female is proud and the male is loyal.

She goes on quests handed out by the Oracle of Delphi, and does most of the tasks that were traditionally done by a male hero like fighting Polyphemus, navigating the Labyrinth and holding up the earth for Atlas. However she is not just a relative of ancient heroes, but also of little girls like Dahl's Matilda and Burnett's Sara Crewe who at the age of 6-7, had abusive childhoods. But while they were passive-aggressive and are finally rescued by an adult, Annabeth, at age seven, takes control, abandons her dysfunctional family and reaches Camp Half-Blood, where she is free to be her authentic self.

This willpower and life-affirming attitude is seen again when twice she is offered immortality and twice she turns it down. Immortality can mean stagnation and Annabeth would rather live a life, facing pain and celebrating joys than give in to an eternal but meaningless existence. When Circe, the misandrous sorceress tempts Annabeth by reminding her that "Men get all the glory. The only way to power for women is sorcery. Medea, Calypso, now these were powerful women. And me, of course" (Riordan 172), Annabeth firmly declines. Circe, Medea and Calypso were women who were cast as manipulative, evil, and immoral in order to survive in a man's world. But Annabeth's female role model is Amelia Earhart—a woman who made it on her own talents and ambition.

Annabeth's general demeanor has often been described as though she was calculating a million things at once and simultaneously thinking of the best way to bring a target down in a fight. She is both cerebral and muscle, both her brains and body are very capable.

Girlhood, once upon a time was a space of conformity and restriction. A girl could, like Alice, have an adventure, but only if it was a dream. Reality would never allow such a thing. Or if she did fly away to Neverland like Wendy, she'd have to take on the role of a mother and caretaker. If she was sent to boarding school, like Blyton's St. Clare, she'll only be successful if at the end of her education she has shed her individuality and become a conforming female. Or if she is an orphan and is sent off to live with a distant relative like Burnett's Mary, her struggle will be taken over by the story of a sick boy and his miraculous recovery.

But Hermione, Holly and Annabeth have redefined girlhood into a space of authenticity and freedom of self-expression. All three of them break rules—rules set by society, rules set by adults and rules set by gender to find their identity and purpose. There is a famous meme on the internet that imagines the book titles of the Harry Potter series as renamed after Hermione instead, and the truth is they don't seem very impossible. These girls are not sidekicks of the main boy-heroes. They are their own persons, independent, intelligent and incredible in their abilities. You can imagine them as adult women; taking up the cause of gender equality, fighting for causes like the glass ceiling, equal pay, FGM and rape culture.

Artemis confesses to Holly "I want you to know, my dear friend, that without you I would not be the person I am today....I was a broken boy and you fixed me. Thank you" (Colfer, *Last*

Guardian 273). Just as Hermione saved Harry and Annabeth saved Percy. Both the boys and the girls complete the plot, the story and each other.

Girlhood in the 21st century is all about empowering one self and others. Because that is essentially what New Feminism is to me—empowering all genders to be the best versions of themselves through equal opportunities, education and law. If girls have been victims of an unrelenting patriarchy, so have boys. So have transgender youth, and the LGB adolescents. Gender needs to become a more inclusive term. A new feminist cannot treat gender as two extreme polarities, but must view it as a mixed basket of characteristics, interests and abilities, where every combination is the right combination. And though social media campaigns like 'Let Toys Be Toys' started in 2015 are actively challenging the rigidity of gender and demanding gender-neutral marketing from children-oriented companies, as I turn to the last page of a Penguin Publication and see the texts used in the study are "Puffin's Adventure Books for *Boys*", I realize that we sadly still have a long way to go.

Works Cited

Colfer, Eoin. *Artemis Fowl*. Penguin Group, 2011.

________. *Artemis Fowl and the Arctic Incident*. Penguin Group, 2011.

________. *Artemis Fowl and the Atlantis Complex*. Disney Hyperion Books, 2010.

________. *Artemis Fowl and the Last Guardian*. Penguin Group, 2013.

________. *The Artemis Fowl Files*. Disney Hyperion Books, 2004.

"Gender." *Keywords for Children's Literature*, 2011.

Mallan, K. *Gender Dilemmas in Children's Fiction*. Palgrave Macmillan, 2009.

Pyle, Wilma J. "Sexism in Children's Literature." *Theory Into Practice*, vol. 15, no. 2, 1976, pp. 116-19, www.jstor.org/stable/1475780.

Riordan, Rick. *Percy Jackson and the Sea of Monsters*. Penguin Group, 2008.

Rowling, J.K. *Harry Potter and the Philosopher's Stone*. Bloomsbury Publishing, 1997.

________. *Harry Potter and the Prisoner of Azkaban*. Bloomsbury Publishing, 1999.

Temple, Charles. "'What If Beauty Had Been Ugly?" Reading against the Grain of Gender Bias in Children's Books." *Language Arts*, vol. 70, no. 2, 1993, pp. 89-93, www.jstor.org/stable/41482067.

14

The Overly Sentimental Musings in *The Perks of Being a Wallflower*

Saloni Prasad (Mrs. Kumar)

The Perks of Being a Wallflower, a contemporary modern coming-of-age novel by Stephan Chbosky, succeeds primarily and solely on the strength of its writing where the author brilliantly captures the perspective of an introvert, socially challenged individual who observes life rather than participating in it. The novel is by turns hilarious, heartbreaking, incisive—a feat which is difficult to accomplish, but a rarity indeed in the realm of young adult fiction. *The Perks of Being a Wallflower* definitely deals with the controversial subject matter at varying times—date rape, homosexuality, drug and alcohol abuse with a stark sense of detachment. These themes are handled in a mature manner, but they never become titillating. The novel evokes no desire to engage in teenage vices and though it refrains from explicitly endorsing or condemning various behaviours, it does not shy from depicting the consequences of bad decisions. Moral judgements are eventually left up to the reader. It is truly a story of a strange course travel through the unknown territories of high school drama and the roller-coaster days of family drama, sex, drugs and other variants of growing up. Chbosky's voice is no doubt a new voice in contemporary fiction.

Many of the cliché employed by Chbosky are already familiar to readers like identity crisis, its struggles, first sexual awakening. It endeavours to capture the totality of the contemporary adult experience, like Salinger's 'Catcher in the Rye', which is drawn on the teen-angst tradition. The titular 'wallflower' is narrated by

Charlie, in a series of letters which he writes to a stranger, before he starts his freshman year of high school. His letters show his attempts to participate as he wanders wide-eyed through a series of house parties and Rocky Horror Picture productions with his friends. Chbosky intelligently explores themes such as mental health, abuse and sexuality, whilst reminding us how exciting it is to be young and idealistic. Chbosky demonstrates Charlie's deteriorating mental health by having him see sadness wherever he goes. His approach is always unflinching, even when the content is upsetting. Underpinning everything is a desire to acknowledge the completeness in other people, an understanding that nobody does bad stuff because they are innately bad. The novel, though at times very upsetting, is ultimately uplifting and life-affirming.

Sexual abuse and suicide feature heavily in *The Perks of Being a Wallflower* which does contain some additional drugs/sex/swearing content that would make the text unsuitable for young readers but then it is a befitting example of adult fiction. Many of the parents complained against the novel being on the school board because of the inappropriate language and sexual content that they felt was not proper enough for their children to read. On the other hand, many stood for the book with the explanation that the children are young adults and they can't be kept protected all the time. Ultimately, after complaints and censorships, it was decided that the book demonstrated education value and young adults should be allowed to read it. Even Chbosky states that his original purpose was to connect with many troubled and misguided youths as possible. He claims that "the whole book is a blueprint for survival. It's for people who have been through troubled things and need hope and support". Never had there been such a beautiful representation of adolescence before Chbosky's *The Perks of Being a Wallflower*. This is the strength of his writing, for he crafts Charlie's voice in a way that defies context. Charlie is inside every lonely teenager and every adult remembers him fondly. He is an outsider in his school who gets bullied by the insiders and thus prefers to be a loner by taking the forty minute walk home instead of the school bus. He is only sixteen years old and when he starts high school, his life changes forever.

Charlie is a mystery—a person who has mental problems, gets angry, sees things and then passes out. His best friend shot himself just before Charlie started high school and this worsened his problem all the more. But the worse in his life was yet to come. Charlie meets Patrick and Sam, who are also outsiders and they introduce him to quite a lot of things—parties, drugs, and rock music and it is for the first time Charlie comes to know what it is to have good friends. Charlie is indeed one of the most vulnerable, raw, real and honest literary characters that one can encounter within the realm of young adult fiction. Throughout the book, Charlie lets others take control over him. He never makes his own choices and constantly makes sure that everyone is happy with him. To him, making friends mattered a lot, so that he felt a sense of belonging. Charlie shows symptoms of Post Traumatic Stress Disorder (PTSD) and anxiety. He is mentally unstable because of being sexually abused as a child by his aunt. He tried to block and repress all such memories that he refused to remember and more importantly, refuse to believe such as his aunt molesting him which caused him some serious trauma. Charlie is incredibly compassionate, sheltered by introversion and social awkwardness. Much of what he displays is simply adolescence as many normal people experience it. He has only disassociated himself from the world probably because he does not know how to feel and how to respond. He sees people and situations differently. He was able to read other people's emotions and felt a great deal himself. Although it was hard for him to express himself at times, he was still capable of doing so, even though it was through his writings.

The novel is one of the instances in which people have the opportunity to witness the uncensored perspectives of a male character who is not afraid to share his thoughts and sentiments. Charlie, the protagonist, depicts his own developmental process through his writings, and given that the novel is written vis a series of letters, it is imperative that the reader becomes attuned to how the process of writing and the process of *bildung* work together to fulfil and challenge the nuances of development within the literary scope. Fascinatingly, Charlie's writing is very much reflective of his own development as a person, and the writing that we encounter in the first letters of the novel is more scrambled, disorganised and immature in comparison to the prose found in his final letters. Charlie develops a clearer sense of the world through this arduous process of integration, and through his immersion in new experiences such as drug use, masturbation, visits to the Rocky Horror Picture Show, and through his exposure to different literatures. It is when Charlie combines his writing skills with the experiences that he has obtained that allows him to develop a richer image of who he wants to be. Interestingly, the more Charlie writes, the more he understands himself, and it is easier for the recipient of the letters to develop a more defined snapshot of. Charlie's mind. In other words, the more Charlie begins to understand himself, the more others begin to understand him.

Charlie is exposed to many social extremes—gay bashing, group violence, rape, drug use, etc. Chbosky argues in favour of realization of trauma as potential for growth. Charlie was a molestation victim as a child, a fact he repressed until urged to enter into a sexual situation he could not deal with. While his breakdown places him into a mental hospital, he comes out of the whole thing as a fuller individual who is more self actualized that he would have been without realizing the sexual trauma of his youth. The provider of Charles's drama—an aunt he looked upto and loved dearly, is a symbol of the death of loyalty; those who love you will inevitably betray you.

The theme of betrayal is brought up again as a fact of the relationship between Charlie and his girlfriend Mary Elizabeth. Mary defines herself as a sexual object and desires to be lusted after to gain validation as a woman. Mary initiates various sexual situations and is so much desperate for male attention that she becomes a living contradiction. Charlie breaks up with her after realizing this and as a result, Mary speaks ill of him, saying that he had no personality and no soul and that he did not challenge her. This acts as a formative realization for Charlie and he realizes that people see a situation as it affects them, and not so as its effect on the people around him.

The Perks of Being a Wallflower thrives on conflicts. The idea of submission in love is a lingering element which Charlie experiences with his aunt. He sees the molestation by his aunt as an expression of platonic love only because he did not have a closeness with his parents. So he willingly took part and let her control him for her own whims in the guise of the growth of a relationship. Raised by a stereotypical father and an emotionally damaged mother, Charlie gained the submissive tendencies and overdrawn reactions due to them. His siblings are similar too, taking after their parents. His sister is unwilling to dismiss her abusive boyfriend, eventually getting away from Charlie. But by the end of the novel, she makes a pro-choice statement and rejects her boyfriend. This enforces the idea that abusive relationships can be ended and triumphed through the strength of will alone.

The novel is reflective, is certainly about growing up, about sexuality, about substance abuse, falling in love and learning to accept yourself as you are. Charlie is introspective, anxious and a loner. Finding acceptance through older students at his new school gives him the opportunity to break out of his self-protective shell bit by bit. Charlie gets to be an actor in his own story but along side, he's also reflecting upon it. Chbosky doesn't sanitize Charlie's story, but chooses to highlight real teen issues. The novel resonates because it has timelessness to it and offers nostalgia. It is indeed a voice-driven, realistic young adult fiction which definitely evokes a sense of emotion and nostalgia from the reader. It is one of the most honest portrayals of teenage life and is considered an influential text for young readers across the world due to its sincere and candid depiction of contemporary teenage life. But it gained infamy for being one of the most banned books because of its depiction of controversial themes. In spite of all this, the novel's realistic tone and depth of the issues discussed in the pages have assured its position as a contemporary young adult and literary classic. The novel appropriates and transmutes the conventions of the formation novel. Although the novel is written in an epistolary fashion, the overarching themes of these musings create a social awareness in which the protagonist can record, evaluate and deliberate his own position within his social context. These epistles also provide clarification about the pains and tribulations of achieving reconciliation between personal desire and social demand. "You see things. You keep quite about them. And you understand" (Chbosky, 1999, p. 37). These three sentences manage to encapsulate how Charlie, the protagonist, approaches his world. He is a passive participant, a wallflower, who observes and learns from the people around him. He describes himself as a writer and a reader, focussing on the development of internal thoughts and ideas. Thus his attempts to adapt to the world and eventually understand it, are limited to the analytical capabilities of his awareness rather than on pragmatic experiences and interventions. He is constantly forced to leave behind the ideologies and viewpoints that he held as a child. Between his drug experimentation and LSD and the suicide of his close friend, Charlie realizes that the world is not as innocent or easy as he initially thought it was. Cleverly, rather than teaching external issues directly, he focusses on the internalization of his problems, turning to writing as a therapeutic way of soothing the tension between the pressures of the outside world and his inability to cope with them. The letters are not peppered with angst prose, but offers a vivid and illustrative written record of the protagonist's mind.

Charlie's letters provide him with a space in which he can reflect and construct his own way of thinking, a space necessary for human development. It is in these letters where he constructs his particular demons—the letters do not allow Charlie to repossess anything he has written because he cannot reclaim his words after they have been sent. He is writing letters for a new purpose, as a means of distancing himself from his thoughts as a way of draining his worries away from his mind. He begins to realize that life does not have to be lived according to other's expectations, he has to find a way to balance his desires with social demand. Despite his attempts and small victories, Charlie's progression from a passive to an active participant is not an overnight change, but rather a very difficult and gradual process. Throughout the entire novel, Charlie's willingness to be active in life and his desire to remain in the background as a passive observer were ostensibly fuelled by his repressed childhood memory. Although he spends most of his time trying to understand how people's personalities are shaped, he finally comes to the realization that people are not bound to the past and that they eventually have the authority to break away from these binds. He realises that the way that he used to view the world no longer dictates the way he will view it from that moment forward. Mary Beckerman of Word Riot says that "The Perks of Being a 'Wallflower', connects with young people because the incidents are so universal and happens to so many teenagers." Many of the parents complained against the novel being on the school board because of the inappropriate language and sexual content that they felt was not proper enough for the children to read. But many stood for the book with the notion that they're young adult fiction and we can't keep it in a bubble. Ultimately, after complaints and censorships, it was decided that the book demonstrated educative values. Even Chbosky states that his original purpose was to connect with many troubled and misguided youths as possible. He claims that the whole book is a blueprint for survival. It's for people who have been through terrible things and need help and support.

The novel has more or less the same over all coming-of-age theme as in J.D. Salinger's *The Catcher in the Rye*. Like the adolescent Holden, who is navigating through life, finding, observing and interpreting the world that surrounds him, Charlie too is the anonymous wallflower—the one who is not noticed but sees everything and tries to understand life from his own experiences. In both these worlds, life is not made of rainbows. As Holden struggles with the profanities of time, Charlie encounters drug, alcohol and rape—the only difference being that Holden is alone in the world, trying to figure out himself, Charlie finds friends who support him. However, both end up in a mental hospital and the recover from their mental illnesses with a hope of a better future.

The Perks of Being a Wallflower is thus, a brutally honest account of a teenager's high school experiences, in a way being both provocative and controversial at the same time. But it has obtained quite the cult following the years of it's accurate potrayal of the new experiences, obstacles and relationships. Charlie is definitely book smart, curious and incredibly passionate who really tries hard to see the best in people, even if it means getting a little too emotionally attached. He is forced into various degrees of experiences way beyond his apparent maturity level. Between domestic and psychological abuse also comes an account of a true love, a true friendship, and the exciting and terrifying aspects of growing up. Charlie is a true wallflower, expressing himself in the written words for million of readers to appreciate.

References

Chbosky, S. (1999). *The Perks of Being a Wallflower*. New York, NY: MTV Pocket Books.

Comeaux, P. (1999). "A person/a paper/a promise remembered". In S. Chbosky, *The Perks of Being a Wallflower* (70–73). New York, NY: MTV Pocket Books.

Salinger, J.D. (1951). *The Catcher in the Rye*. New York, NY: Little, Brown.

Wasserman, E. (2003). "The Epistolary in Young Adult Literature". *The ALAN Review*, 30(3), 48-51. Retrieved.

15

Robert Cormier: The Forebearer of Young Adult Fiction

Runa

Introduction

Robert Edmund Cormier was an American author, columnist and reporter, known for his deeply pessimistic, downbeat literature. *I Am the Cheese*, *After the First Death*, *We All Fall Down* and *The Chocolate War*, are some of his most popular works, all of which have won awards. *The Chocolate War* was challenged in multiple libraries. His books often are concerned with themes such as abuse, mental illness, violence, revenge, betrayal and conspiracy. In most of his novels, the protagonists do not win. Although he did not enjoy initial commercial success, he always received immense critical acclaim. Another interesting feature in his novels is that good may not necessarily win over evil. This tendency of his novels to stress on the 'negative' led to the rejection of his publications from educational institutions and library lists. However, the author and several critics have explained his works as simply a realistic depiction of human nature. Owing to stories' dark controversial nature, some of his works were initially banned. However, with time they have been accepted into mainstream publication houses and have also been translated into many languages. His works now appear frequently on the list of 'Best Books for Young Adults' of the American Library Association.

The Foundation and the Passage

The term "Young Adult" was coined by the Young Adult Library Services Association during the 1960s to represent the 12-18 age range. Novels of the time offered a mature contemporary realism directed at adolescents. More focus was given on popular culture and other serious themes in young adult paved the way for authors to write with more candors about teen issues in the 1970s. The first golden age is usually associated with the authors like Judy Blume, Lois Duncan and Robert Cormier. The young adult books of the 1970s remain true time capsules of the high school experience and the drama of being misunderstood. Books like Cormier's *The Chocolate War* brought a literary sense to books targeted at teens.

Following the stream of fiction written as *Fear Street* series, and adolescent high drama *Sweet Valley High*, the '90s witnessed an eclipse for young adult fiction. In 1992, there came a renaissance among teen readers and the second golden age began in 2000. The book world began marketing directly to teens for the first time at the turn of the millennium. Expansive young adult sections appeared in bookstores, targeting and welcoming teens to discover their very own genre. J.K. Rowling's *Harry Potter* series exploded the category and inspired a whole generation of fantasy series novelists. Following this were Stephanie Meyer's *Twilight* vampire saga and Suzanne Collins' futuristic *The Hunger Games*.

Young adult literature has its own historical legacy. In the United States, the antecedents of contemporary young adult literature can be traced back 130 years and include the *American Sunday School Union's Moral Lessons, Louisa May Alcott's Novels, Dime and Domestic Novels, Edward Stratemeyer's Syndicated Series, and the Junior Novel (NILSEN & DONELSON, 2001).* Winnowed from the generality of formulaic and simplistic texts, young adult literature has stood the test of time, gradually came of age, and actually exists today in its own right. This literary tradition is evident in scholarly criticism.

The Growth

Young adult fiction came to be recognized, chiefly in the west, as the genre encouraging fiction pertaining to youth, their predicaments and desires, chiefly hidden. Nineteenth century literature presents several early examples that appealed to young readers including: *Oliver Twist* (1838), *The Count of Monte Cristo* (1844), *Great Expectations* (1860), *Alice in Wonderland* (1865), *The Adventures of Tom Sawyer* (1876), *Adventures of Huckleberry Finn* (1884), *Kidnapped* (1886), *The Jungle Book* (1894), and *Moon Fleet* (1898). A few other novels published around the start of the 20th century include *Treasure Island* by Robert Louis Stevenson, *Heidi* by Johanna Spyri, and *Black Beauty* by Anna Sewell. J.R.R. Tolkien's *The Hobbit,* published in 1937, is read by many adolescents today at that level.

Unlike later fiction classified as YA, the 1950s novels by Hinton and Salinger were written with an adult audience in mind and were not initially marketed to adolescents. The modern classification of young-adult fiction originated during the 1950s and 1960s, especially after the publication of S.E. Hinton's *The Outsiders* (1967). The novel featured a truer, darker side of adolescent life that was not often represented in works of fiction of the time. Written during high school and published when Hinton was only 17, *The Outsiders* remains one of the best-selling young-adult novels of all time, and Hinton is often considered to be one of the founders of the genre.

As the decades moved on, the 1960s became the era "when the 'under 30' generation became a subject of popular concern, and that research on adolescence began to emerge. This catapulted discussions about adolescent experiences and the new idea of adolescent authors; 1967 sparked the production in growth of this now thriving genre. As publishers began to focus on the emerging adolescent market, booksellers and libraries began creating YA sections distinct from either child's literature or novels written for adults. The 1970s to the mid-1980s have been described as the golden age of young-adult fiction, when challenging novels began speaking directly to the interests of the identified adolescent market. In the 1990s, there was a visible thrust in the YA market when youngsters wanted to read more about themselves and the kind of issues they faced in their everyday life.

This led to the overwhelming response meted out by J.K. Rowling's *Harry Potter Series*. It was essentially about three adolescents trying to lead a normal life and cope with the banal struggles of coming of age and deal with their loss of innocence in an increasingly war-ridden 1990's Britain. The success of the Harry Potter series lead many to pinpoint Harry Potter and its author, J.K. Rowling, as the force responsible for the modern resurgence of YA literature seen in such successes as *The Hunger Games* trilogy by Suzanne Collins, and *The Twilight Saga* by Stephanie Meyer.

Robert Cormier: The Classic in *The Chocolate War*

"I can't remember a time, really, when I haven't been a writer.... Reading and writing were the two great escapes of my life and I suppose they still are."—Robert Cormier (web). What makes his works unique is his ability to make evil behavior understandable, though, of course, still evil. "I'm very much interested in intimidation," he told an interviewer from *School Library Journal*. "And the way people manipulate other people. And the obvious abuse of authority." All of these themes are evident in his young adult classic and best-known book, *The Chocolate War*. A 15-year-old fan of Cormier's told him, "You always write from inside the person" (Web).

Published at a medium receiving rate in 1970s, *The Chocolate War* was soon called to be one of the best young adult fictions of all time. Set at a fictional Catholic high school; the story depicts a secret student organization's manipulation of the student body, which descends into cruel and ugly mob mentality against a lone, non-conforming student. Because of the novel's language, the concept of a high school secret society using intimidation to enforce the cultural norms of the school and various characters' sexual ponderings, it has been embroiled in censorship controversies and appeared as third on the American Library Association's list of the "Top 100 Banned/Challenged Books in 2000–2009."

Jerry Renault, the hero of *The Chocolate War*, takes a beating on a football field. Not a literal one, just normal football practice abuse. He's a freshman at Trinity High School, and wants to make quarterback. His friend, The Goober, has already warned him to show no fear. The coach wants to see how much he can handle. After practice, Jerry muses about the recent death of his mother.

Archie (the mastermind) and Obie (one of his thugs) are in the bleachers, picking their newest victims. They decide that Roland Goubert, The Goober, will be given an "assignment" having to do with Brother Eugene's classroom. Jerry, Archie decides, get an assignment that has to do with chocolates. Obie protests, saying that Jerry's mom died only last spring; they should leave him alone. But, Archie isn't swayed. Soon, Archie learns that Brother Leon, the sadistic teacher, has ordered twice as many chocolates as last year, and he wants Archie and the Vigils to make sure they get sold as part of the school fundraiser. Archie is a bit reluctant, but agrees to help him make the sale a success. The Goober gets his assignment from The Vigils. He has to go to Room Nineteen, Brother Eugene's classroom, and unscrew all the screws in all the furniture, so that when you touch it, everything falls apart. Leon is tormenting a kid named Gregory Bailey and we're starting to see how twisted Leon really is. After a brief introduction to Emile Janza, another bully, we find The Goober in Room Nineteen, trying to do his assignment. When he's on the verge of giving up, some masked Vigils come in and help him finish the job.

Then, we get a glimpse into Jerry's home life. His dad is a nice guy, but Jerry thinks he's stuck in a boring routine. Jerry doesn't want to turn out like that; he wants something more, though he isn't sure what. Archie is standing by the door, very pleased with himself for thinking this prank up of distorting everything. When Brother Eugene starts crying, he's even more pleased. Then, after football practice, Jerry finds a note on his locker, summoning him to The Vigils' secret hideout, a supply closet behind the gym. The Goober is really bummed since the Room Nineteen prank. He feels awful that it made Brother Eugene cry. He's also afraid his involvement will be discovered and that he'll be punished.

Next day was the first day of the chocolate sale, and Brother Leon was using roll call to get kids to commit to selling. When he gets to Jerry, Jerry flat-out refuses the chocolates. The Goober can't believe it. Later, Archie is using some fake picture to blackmail Emile. Emile, who also wants to be a Vigil, tells Archie he'll do anything to get the picture back.

Now we're back to Brother Leon and the chocolate sale. We find out that Jerry has been refusing to sell the chocolates because The Vigils made him. That was his "assignment." The next day, however, Jerry is supposed to accept the chocolates just like everybody else. But, he doesn't. He says "No" again. He wasn't planning on refusing to sell the chocolates, and isn't sure why he says "No," though he knows it has something to do with standing up to Leon and The Vigils.

Obie convinces Archie that they need to force Jerry to sell the chocolates. By continuing to refuse the chocolates, Jerry is undermining The Vigils' power. Soon, the other students won't respect them. Plus, Archie promised Brother Leon that The Vigils would help with the sale. The Vigils don't want to be on Leon's bad side.

Next, we see Leon grumbling about the low chocolate sales. He totally blames Jerry, and wants to see something done about him. So, he gets Archie on the phone and tells him to make Jerry sell, and to do whatever it takes to get the chocolates sold. If not, Leon will destroy Archie and The Vigils. So, the terrorization of Jerry Renault begins. A giggling anonymous caller is ringing his phone off the hook. Somebody trashes his locker. Meanwhile, Archie and The Vigils are able to make selling chocolates seem cool, and Trinity is in a chocolate-selling frenzy. Lots of students are mad at Jerry for not doing his part to make the sale a success. Things take a turn for the worse when Emile Janza and at least ten other guys brutally attack Jerry in the pathway between the football field and the school. Jerry wants to tell his dad, but is afraid his dad will get hurt, so he doesn't.

Finally, all the chocolates have been sold—except for the fifty boxes Jerry was supposed to sell. Archie begins planning some kind of raffle of these chocolates. He calls Jerry and offers him a chance to get revenge on Emile Janza. Jerry accepts, and he and Emile both show up to the athletic field at night. They are led to the platform and told the rules of the game. Basically, Carter will draw a raffle ticket and read what the owner has written. Students have written in the name of the person they want to get hit, and how they want that person to get hit.

Jerry and Emile both get in a few punches, but then everything goes out of control. Emile's taking it too far, and though Jerry manages to fight back some, he's no match. Plus, the students are all screaming for his death. The Goober shows up near the end of the spectacle and calls for the fight to be stopped, but nobody hears him. The fight ends when the lights on the field go out. The students run off, and Archie heads to the utility room to see what happened. Brother Jacques is inside with his hand on the switch. He starts to lecture Archie, but soon Brother Leon comes to Archie's defense. Meanwhile, The Goober is with Archie and they are waiting for an ambulance. Jerry wishes he could tell his friend not to defy authority, because it's too dangerous. But he can't talk.

The novel ends with Archie and Obie walking home together in the dark.

Popularity among Youth

In 1974, Cormier published *The Chocolate War,* the novel that is still a bestseller. Instantly acclaimed, it was also the object of censorship attempts because of its uncompromising realism. In a front-page review in a special children's issue of *The New York Times Book Review,* it was described as "masterfully structured and rich in theme," and it went on to win countless awards and honors, was taught in schools and colleges throughout the world, and was translated into more than a dozen languages.

Cormier's novels have frequently come under attack by censorship groups because they are uncompromising in their depictions of the problems young people face each day in a turbulent world. Teachers and librarians have been quick to point out that his novels are eminently teachable, valuable, and moral. His novels are taught in hundreds of schools and in adolescent literature courses in colleges and universities. Though many of his books are described as written for young adults, in fact people of all ages read and enjoy Cormier's work. His themes of the ordinariness of evil and what happens when good people stand by and do nothing are treated seriously, and he never provides the easy comfort of a happy ending. Cormier's gripping stories explore some of the darker corners of the human psyche, but always with a moral focus and a probing intelligence that compel readers to examine their own feelings and ethical beliefs. Books like Cormier's *The Chocolate War* brought a literary sense to books targeted at teens.

Cormier explained in an interview that he was "interested in creating real people, dramatic situations that will keep the reader turning pages" (Web). He went on to say that although some adults dislike the book because of the topics discussed, "the kids can absorb my kind of book because they know this kind of thing happens in life" (Abingdon).

The *New York Times Book Review* declared, "Mr. Cormier is almost unique in his powerful integration of the personal, political and moral" and *The Australian* wrote that young readers "recognized his vision as authentic and admired his willingness to tell things as they are". However, the book has been banned from many schools and it is one of the most challenged books, of 2006, for its sexual content, strong language, and violence.

Following a growing sense of alarm and emergency created around censorship and book banning, the mood of 1990s news reports reflected a sense of permanence in the censorship debate. *New York Times* articles entitled "The next front in the book wars" and "Groups Square off over issue of barring books at schools" suggest that the issue of censorship had become a battle, with two sides in firm opposition. The number of books banned per year continued to increase throughout the 1990s, but instead of addressing the subject with the level of shock evident in the 1980s, journalists seemed to accept it as a fixture of political debate. Issues of censorship had saturated the media so deeply in the 1980s, that by the 1990s censorship had become ordinary, average news. Also, emerging issues involving the internet and filtering software took the forefront, as technology advanced toward the end of the century.

Conclusion

Young adult novelists don't shy away from tackling the deepest and darkest issues that teens face, from identity struggles and sexual abuse to drug/alcohol use and suicide. Authors like John Green write about the best and worst of adolescence fearlessly and honestly, building a trust within readers. At the current stage of the twenty-first century, young adult literature looks very different than it did fifty years ago. Indeed, fifty years ago, we were just getting started with the likes of Salinger's *The Catcher in the Rye* (1951), with Hinton's *The Outsiders* (1967), Zindel's *The Pigman* (1968), and Cormier's *The Chocolate War* (1974). We have come a long way since then, these humble, yet groundbreaking beginnings have yielded a bountiful harvest of literary works. Today, we face a plethora of young adult books that represent every conceivable genre and literary style. To be sure, we are on the precipice of reinventing ourselves because our young adult books are constantly in search of the new and revealing so that more and more young people will find their way to the delectable hallways of good and engaging reads.

References

Abingdon, G.B. *Contemporary Adolescent Literature and Culture*. Ashgate, 2012.

Brown, W. David. How *YA Fiction Came Of Age*. The Atlantic, Aug, 2011.

Cullingford, Cedric. *Children's Literature and its Effects: The Formative Years* (1). London, GB: Continuum, 2000.

Garcia, Antero. *Critical Foundations in Young Adult Literature: Challenging Genres*. Rotterdam, NLD: Sense Publishers, 2013.

Inflibnet.ac.in

New York Times.Com, retrieved on 25.03.17

Szymanski, Mallory. *Adolescence, Literature And Censorship: Unpacking The Controversy Surrounding Judy Blume*, NEO, Interdisciplinary Online Journal For America, Vol. 3 No. 1 (Spring/Summer 2007) Issue.

Strickland, Ashley. *A Brief History of YA Literature*. CNN.Com, April, 2015.

16

Judy Blume: An Undaunted Voice in Young Adult Fiction

Sapna Kumari

Introduction

Young adult fiction has gained a remarkable supremacy in the contemporary world of reading and writing. Not only cashing in on the young adult as the target audience but also including fantasy and supernatural has further accelerated the process. Over the years, with the advent of S.E. Hinton and J.D. Salinger, young adult fiction took the contemporary market to storm and impacted a vast population of young adult readers. The themes and characters are directly related with the young adult characters of real life that have their own issues and predicaments. The psychological, social, physical aspect of the adolescence has been well accentuated by the ingrained, insightful study in the field.

A large section, if not whole, is also interested in the young, wishful thinking of the adolescent minds who strive to break the ice and reach beyond their own world. There are some portraying the ups and lows of a youngster's life with all its predicament and youthful tantrums. Sixteen- to 29-year-olds are the largest groups checking out books from their local libraries: Wizards, vampires and dystopian future worlds didn't always dominate the genre, which hit its last peak of popularity in the 1970s with the success of controversial novels by the likes of Judy Blume. In the years between, young adult has managed to capture the singular passions of the teen audience over a spectrum of subgenres. Setting forth from the writings of J.D. Salinger and S.E. Hinton, the likes of Judy Blume and Robert Cormier have been responsible for the growth of YA fiction in what is known as *the glorious period in the history of the young adult literature.* The first golden age is associated with the authors who the parents of today's teens recognize: Judy Blume, Lois Duncan and Robert Cormier. The young adult books of the 1970s remain true source of delight for the high school experience and the drama of being misunderstood.

Young Adult Literature: A Brief History

The Very Beginning

The roots of young adult go back to when "teenagers" were given their own distinction as a social demographic. *Seventeenth Summer* released by Maureen Daly in 1942, is considered to be the first book written and published explicitly for teenagers, according to Cart, an author and the former president of the Young Adult Library Services Association. It was a novel largely for girls about first love. In its footsteps followed other romances, and sport novels for boys (Strickland).

The term "young adult" was coined by the Young Adult Library Services Association during the 1960s to represent the 12-18 age range. Novels of the time, like S.E. Hinton's "The Outsiders," offered a mature contemporary realism directed at adolescents. The focus on culture and serious themes in young adult paved the way for authors to write with more candors about teen issues in the 1970s, Cart said.

The 1980s welcomed in more genre fiction, like horror from Christopher Pike and the beginning of R.L. Stine's "Fear Street" series, and adolescent high drama "Sweet Valley High," while the '90s were an eclipse for young adult. With fewer teenagers around to soak up young adult literature due to low birth rates in the mid-1970s, books for teens and middle-age school children bloomed. But a baby boom in 1992 resulted in a renaissance among teen readers and the second golden age beginning in 2000.

The next few decades witnessed the expansive popularity of the works like "Harry Potter", Stephanie Meyer's "Twilight" and Suzanne Collins' futuristic "The Hunger Games." "Just like adolescence is between childhood and adulthood, paranormal, or other, is between human and supernatural," said Jennifer Lynn Barnes, a young adult author, Ph.D. and cognitive science scholar. "Teens are caught between two worlds, childhood and adulthood, and in YA, they can navigate those two worlds and sometimes dualities of other worlds" (Strickland).

Now, reveling in the continued success of fantasy subgenres and series, young adult fiction is enjoying a sustained boom rather than an afterglow.

The Transition

One early writer to recognize young adults as a distinct group was Sarah Trimmer, who, in 1802, described "young adulthood" as lasting from ages 14 to 21. In her children's literature periodical, The Guardian of Education, Trimmer introduced the terms "Books for Children" (for those under fourteen) and "Books for Young Persons" (for those between fourteen and twenty-one), establishing terms of reference for young adult literature that remain in use today (Wikipedia). Nineteenth century literature presents several early examples that appealed to young readers including: *The Swiss Family Robinson* (1812), *Waverley* (1814), *Great Expectations* (1860), *Alice in Wonderland* (1865), *The Adventures of Tom Sawyer* (1876). *Black Beauty* by Anna Sewell. J.R.R. Tolkien's *The Hobbit*, published in 1937, and Betty Smith's *A Tree Grows in Brooklyn*, published in 1943, although not specifically written for a younger people, are widely known all over the market.

In the 1950s, shortly before the advent of modern young-adult publishing surrounding the teen romance market, two influential novels drew the attention of adolescent readers: *The Catcher in the Rye* (1951) and *Lord of the Flies* (1954). Unlike later fiction classified as YA, these novels were written with an adult audience in mind and were not initially marketed to adolescents.

The modern classification of young-adult fiction originated during the 1950s and 1960s, especially after the publication of S.E. Hinton's *The Outsiders* (1967). The novel featured a truer, darker side of adolescent life that was not often represented in works of fiction of the time. Written during high school and published when Hinton was only 17, *The Outsiders* remains one of the best-selling young-adult novels of all time, and Hinton is often considered to be one of the founders of the genre.

With the turn of the decade, 1960s saw the subject of under 30 generation being chosen as popular among the young adult writers. Post 1967 witnessed the sparkling growth in this genre. Publishers too began to differentiate YA market from that of children's literature. The 1970s to the mid-1980s have been described as the golden age of young-adult fiction. In the 1990s, there was a substantial growth in the readership of young adult fiction. The average age of young adult readers expanded from youngsters between teen and early twenties.

J.K. Rowling's *Harry Potter Series*, an enthralling story of three adolescents trying to lead a normal life and cope with the banal struggles of coming of age and deal with their loss of innocence in an increasingly war-ridden 1990's Wizarding Britain. The success of the Harry Potter series lead many to pinpoint Harry Potter and its author, J.K. Rowling, as the force responsible for the modern resurgence of YA literature seen in such successes as *The Hunger Games* trilogy by Suzanne Collins, and *The Twilight Saga* by Stephanie Meyer.

Judy Blume: The Lady in Lead

For many, the mention of Judy Blume's name conjures up a specific adolescent memory or resonates with an experience in young adulthood. Blume is the author of more than twenty-three books, most of which are geared toward a youthful range of audiences from toddlers to teens. Since the publication of *Are You There, God? It's Me, Margaret* in 1970, Blume has stood as both an observer and a voice for adolescent girls and boys. Despite vast praise and popularity, Blume has received harsh criticism for addressing subject matters such as sex, masturbation, menstruation, death, puberty and religion in her youth novels. The American Library Association named Blume's novel *Forever*, published in 1975, the second "most challenged" book of 2005 due to its "sexual content and offensive language". Clear distinction emerges between those who love and admire Blume's work and those who are disgusted and offended by it.

Are You There God? It's me; Margaret begins with Margaret's silent conversation with God. From the onset, Blume invites the reader to enter into Margaret's innermost thoughts. Margaret, about to enter the sixth grade, moves with her family to a new town where she must enter a different school and establish new friends. She meets three other girls her age and quickly befriends them. The plotline includes anecdotes about making friends, crushing on boys and going to school, but the focus of the novel occurs in two parallel themes: religion and puberty. While some have challenged Blume's representation of religion to be inappropriate, the subject of Margaret's (and her friends') puberty caused the majority of the controversy. Menstruation lies at the center of Margaret's world and her thoughts are monopolized by anxiety about when her period will come, how it will happen, and what it will feel like. Her new friends interrogate her on the first day of school about her menstruation. For Margaret's peers, menstruation marks a rite of passage from little girl to grown-up woman. Breast development (and a lack thereof) also occupies much of the girls' attention. Margaret prays to God regularly, asking Him to help her breasts grow and to quickly deliver a period. In one frantic prayer, Margaret tells God: "Gretchen, my friend, got her period. I'm so jealous, God....Nancy's sure she's going to get it soon, too. And if I'm last, I don't know what I'll do. Oh, please God. I just want to be normal" (Web).

Portrayal of Youth and Its Predicaments in Blume's Works

Margaret and her friends have unanswered questions and confusion about the physical changes they are experiencing. Yet Blume's frank discussion of these issues has received countless challenges and bans. Puberty is a common human experience, one that is not often publicly addressed but that happens to everyone. Literature that involves such a mundane subject matter is certainly not threatening and inappropriate. Few other stages in life are as universal as puberty. Of course, each experience is unique, but as Margaret and her friends exemplify, puberty is shrouded in secrecy, making it mysterious and ominous for them. The pressure on them to somehow 'will' their body into puberty consumes much of Margaret's thoughts and conversations with her friends. Blume places these issues at the forefront of *Are You There God? It's Me, Margaret.* And invites young readers to relate to the characters she creates. Margaret obsesses about experiencing puberty normally and readers are able to engage in that struggle alongside her. The novel functions as a safe, honest form of communication to adolescents, letting them know that puberty *is* confusing and it *is* different for everyone, but that they are not alone.

In *Deenie,* the main character experiments with a different kind of struggle. An otherwise average 13-year-old suburban girl, Deenie is diagnosed with scoliosis. When she fails to make the cheerleading squad, her gym teacher alerts Deenie's parents that her posture might need some correction. Deenie sees several doctors until the final diagnosis is made: her spine is curved in an S-shape and she will have to wear a brace from her neck to her waist for the next four years. She feels "like a freak" and does not want anyone to know she is wearing it. This news devastates Deenie and her mom. Deenie fears that her crush, Buddy Brader, won't like her anymore; her mother's dream of Deenie becoming a model must be put on hold. The plot line of the story centers around Deenie's coming to terms with her 'illness' and at the same time growing more accepting of her peers. She befriends a girl in class with a disgusting rash all over her whom Deenie eventually recognizes as a human being, not a disease. While Blume makes a poignant (and stinging) point about disability and the fears children have of them, what makes Deenie controversial is the few scenes in which Deenie discusses masturbation.

While it is clear Deenie doesn't entirely understand what she is doing, she still feels embarrassed. When the gym teacher offers to answer any anonymous questions students might have, including those about sex, Deenie submits one question regarding her predicaments of late to which the teacher replies patiently. Daily existence for Deenie is difficult. She must walk around wearing an obvious brace and oversized clothes that are both immediate declarations (in the world of a 13-year-old) that she is not normal. She isn't comfortable about the subject and wishes someone would give her more information about it.

While few adolescents suffer from scoliosis, many have questions and curiosity about their body. Deenie is unable to find solid and reliable answers to her inquiries about masturbation from her gym teacher or her parents. As a result, she is inclined to believe the false information supplied by her peers. This situation resembles the lack of dialogue about these sensitive issues occurring between adults and youth, rendering young people uninformed and embarrassed about their bodies. Challenging this book and removing it from library shelves only perpetuates their ignorance about their body by silencing what is for some, their only source of information about some unheard voices.

Censorship vis-à-vis Readership of Blume

Despite the wealth of negative responses to Blume's novels, her books have sold 75 million copies worldwide and they have been translated into twenty different languages. She has won numerous awards, including the prestigious National Book Award in 2004. Clearly, Blume's work is recognized as valuable and lasting. But it is not only the slew of awards that validates Blume against her harshest critics; rather, her solid, loyal, and vocal fan base defends her with love and admiration. To many, she is not just an author, but a role model, mentor and friend. A 34-year old fan commented, upon meeting Judy Blume: "For so many torturous years, she was the only person who UNDERSTOOD. She helped us know what was normal, okay, exciting" (Web). Others echo this type of fondness. Ellen Barry wrote of an interview with young women who, when asked about their feelings about Judy Blume, replied with "We must—we must—we must increase our bust!," a memorable quote from *Are You There God? It's Me Margaret* (Web). While it is often difficult to assess readers' responses to literature, many women have published their thoughts about Judy Blume. Many mention of the integral role that her books played in their own adolescent experiences.

Another valuable representation of Judy Blume's appreciative and adoring fan base is *Letters to Judy: What Your Kids Wish They Could Tell You* (1986). It is a compilation of letters from readers of all ages (although mostly those under age 18), thanking her for addressing topics such as sex, death, menstruation and divorce. Readers have also shared stories about how her books have helped them through adolescence and many ask her to continue writing about topics that address the difficulties of growing up. Some letters are from parents, expressing the ways in which Blume's books have helped open conversation with their children about difficult topics. Many complicated issues are evident in such letters, such as lack of communication with parents, anxiety over menstruation and adjusting to changing body shape and size. But Lorna concludes with one overriding question: am I normal? Other children express similar uncertainty in their letters—the same uncertainty that Deenie and Margaret grapple with in Blume's novels.

Children write to Judy Blume, asking for her advice, not because these subjects are taboo, but because these girls and boys are struggling to construct a space for self-identification while attempting to position themselves among their peers. Meanwhile, their bodies are acting strange, feeling different and looking awkward. Adolescence is a challenging time in a young person's life, but teachers and parents make it more difficult by failing to provide information and guidance to make the transition easier. Blume's novels promise insight into the minds of other young teenagers so that readers can almost hear Margaret's thoughts as they read about her stuffing her bra for the first time. Blume's characters may be fictional, but she writes them with a true adolescent voice as the narrator which gives them a fresh honesty that allows for frank discussion of sex, masturbation, periods, etc. Blume comments on Lorna's letter: "Kids want reassurance that they're normal. Every week they write asking if I think they're okay. They ask me to explain what their parents haven't" (web).

These letters to Judy provide evidence that not only are Blume's novels entertaining, but they function as a mode of education, especially about the things that young people can't find adequate answers to elsewhere. Why, then, do parents strongly oppose them? What is so dangerous about children finding a way to assess their 'normality'? Why are novels published in the 1970s both widely popular and feverishly challenged in the twenty-first century? Perhaps the change in cultural climate over the past 35 years has inspired the reactions, both in favor of and against Judy Blume. Newspapers in the early 1970s, such as the *New York Times* and *The Christian Science Monitor* approached the subject of book banning as something that has been around since the early days of printed books. Yet several articles alluded to an attack on free speech looming in the near future. Journalists treated censorship as merely a threat from those who think "small and [carry] a big matchstick," but at the same time, winked at the possibility that change in social behavior and moral values may result in an increase of censorship in the future. By 1979 this premonition became reality. The *New York Times* published an article entitled "Wave of Censors Hits Schools" that listed J.D. Salinger, Anne Frank and Ernest Hemingway as challenged authors.

The tone in newspaper articles about book banning moved from concerned, in the 1970s to alarm in the 1980s. In a 1981 *New York Times* article, Colin Campbell argues: "A censorial spirit is at work in the United States, and for the past year or so, it has focused more and more on books." The number of challenges made to the American Library Association's Office of Intellectual Freedom jumped dramatically; in the early 1970s, approximately 100 challenges were made each year, in the late 1970s that number increased to 300 per year and in 1981, nearly 1000 challenges were reported. The "right to read" was under siege. Most often, vulgarity or sexuality was cited as the reason for challenging a book, but other controversial issues included unorthodox family structure, speculation about Christianity, unflattering depictions of authority, critiques of corporate business and radical political ideals. Finally, in the early 1980s as the "junior novel" was increasingly considered valuable literature among academics, Judy Blume's work began to appear on challenged lists.

Conclusion

According to Jerome Smiley of *The English Journal*, Blume's *Blubber* was one of over 70 books banned between May 1983 and May 1984. Despite the onslaught of negativity surrounding controversial books, Blume's readership remained strong. A 1982 survey of 3399 students revealed that one of the best books in 4th-6th graders read on their own time was *Are You There God? It's Me, Margaret.* Writers like Judy are well deservedly responsible to bring back teen sentiments on pages. Her books have been quite a mark in the world of young adult fiction. These have opened new vistas of explorations pertaining to young adult generation.

References

Kaplan, S. Jeffrey. *Young Adult Literature in the 21st Century:* The Alan Review, winter 2005.

Blakemore, Erin. *A Brief History of YA Fiction*: Weekly Digest, JSTOR Daily, April, 2015.

Szymanski, Mallory. *Adolescence, Literature And Censorship: Unpacking The Controversy Surrounding Judy Blume*, NEO, Interdisciplinary Online Journal For America, Vol. 3 No. 1 (Spring/Summer 2007) Issue.

Strickland, Ashley. *A Brief History Of YA Literature*: CNN. Com, April, 2015.

Brown, W. David. *How YA Fiction Came Of Age*: The Atlantic, Aug, 2011.

The Outsiders By S. E. Hinton, YA Literature, Wiki By English Education Students, Grand Valley State University.

New York Times.Com, retrieved on 21.04.17.

Amazon.Com, retrieved on 25.04.17.

Inflibnet.ac.in

Cullingford, Cedric. *Children's Literature and its Effects: The Formative Years* (1). London, GB: Continuum, 2000. Print.

Garcia, Antero. *Critical Foundations in Young Adult Literature: Challenging Genres.* Rotterdam, NLD: Sense Publishers, 2013. Print.

Abingdon, G.B. *Contemporary Adolescent Literature and Culture*: Ashgate, 2012. Print.